Fergus H

The Pink Shop

Fergus Hume

The Pink Shop

1st Edition | ISBN: 978-3-75235-294-8

Place of Publication: Frankfurt am Main, Germany

Year of Publication: 2020

Outlook Verlag GmbH, Germany.

THE PINK SHOP

BY

FERGUS HUME

CHAPTER I.

IN THE EVENING

Madame Coralie was a magician. Emulating the dark-browed Medea, she restored the aged to their pristine youth; but her methods were more painless and less thorough than those of the lady from Colchis. That enchantress chopped up the senile who sought her aid, and boiled their fragments in a cauldron, so that they reappeared juvenile to the marrow of their bones; whereas her modern representative dealt only with externals, and painted rather than rebuilt the ruined house of life. Moreover, Medea exercised her arts on men, while Madame Coralie attended exclusively to women.

Numberless elderly dames, both in Society and out of it, owed their surprising looks of youth and beauty to the mistress of the Turkish Shop. It was situated in a mean little lane, leading from the High Street, Kensington, to nowhere in particular; and was, to the faded belles of Mayfair, a veritable fountain of youth, hidden in a shady corner. Ladies entered the shop old, and came out young; they left their broughams ugly, and returned beautiful.

The shop was a pink-painted building which faced the blank walls of other houses on the opposite side of the crooked lane, so that it could not be overlooked by any Peeping Tom. No spy could remark who went into the beauty factory or who came out of it, which was highly convenient, since Madame Coralie's clients conducted their visits with great secrecy for obvious reasons. The remaining dwellings in the lane were inhabited by poor people, who found their time sufficiently occupied in earning a bare livelihood, and who, consequently, paid no attention to the concerns of this particular neighbourhood. The lane formed a short cut between the High Street and the back portions of Kensington Palace, but few people passed through it, preferring to go round by the Gardens. A more central or a more retiring spot for the peculiar business of the shop could scarcely have been found; and this modest seclusion had much to do with Madame Coralie's success. Her customers usually came in broughams, motor or horse, and, as a rule, at nightfall, when few people were about. If the restorative treatment required time—which it frequently did—the comfortable bedrooms on the first floor could be occupied, and generally were, at a high rate of payment. Madame Coralie's clients declared unanimously that she was a true daughter of the horse-leech; but, however loudly they objected to her charges, they rarely refused to pay them. If they did, the miracle of rejuvenation did not transpire.

Those Society ladies who wished to retain or regain their good looks—and they formed a large majority—were well acquainted with that fantastic little shop, although their husbands and lovers and brothers and fathers did not dream of its existence. The police knew, but the police said nothing—partly because Madame Coralie skilfully kept on the right side of the law, and partly for the excellent reason that many of her clients were the wives and daughters, sisters, cousins, and aunts of the men who governed. Madame Coralie was blatantly respectable, and if she *did* supplement her acknowledged business by telling fortunes, and lending money, and arranging assignations and smothering scandals, she always acted so discreetly that no one in authority could say a word. Vice in this instance aped Virtue by assuming a modest demeanour.

Although coloured a bright pink, the shop really presented a demure appearance, as if unwilling to thrust itself into notice. Clients sometimes suggested that it should be painted as grey as a warship, since that unobtrusive hue was more in keeping with its necessary secrecy; but Madame Coralie held—and not unreasonably—that the flamboyant front was an excellent clue to the whereabouts of her business premises. Any lady told by a friend to go to the pink shop in Walpole Lane had no difficulty in finding her destination. The house, with its glaring tint, looked like a single peony in a colourless winter field, and just hinted sufficient publicity to lure customers into its perfumed seclusion. To womankind it was as a candle to many moths, and they all flocked round it with eagerness. And to do Madame Coralie justice, none of the moths were ever burnt, or even singed—she knew her business too well to risk any catastrophe which might attract the attention of Scotland Yard.

The ground floor of the building, decorated in a picturesque Saracenic fashion, and draped with oddly-patterned Eastern hangings, looked very much like an ordinary drawing-room, though somewhat more artistic and striking. Its polished floor was strewn with Persian praying-mats, while both ceiling and walls were painted in vivid colours with arabesque fancies, interspersed with poetic sentences from the poems of Sadi, Hafiz, and Omar Khayyam, written in flowery Turkish script. Broad divans of pink silk filled in various alcoves, masked by pierced horse-shoe arches of thin white-painted wood. In the centre bubbled a tiny fountain from a basin of snowy marble, and round this were Turkish stools of black wood, inlaid with mother-of-pearl, convenient to small tables adorned with ivory. The broad, low windows looking out on to the lane were hidden by fluted curtains of pink silk, interwoven with silver thread, and the light filtering through these being somewhat dim, even at noon, artificial illumination was supplied by many Moorish lamps fed with perfumed oil.

The whole shop reeked with scent, so that the atmosphere was heavy, sensuous and stupefying. Stepping through the street door—plain without, and elaborately carved within—Madame Coralie's customers at once left foggy, prosaic England for the allurements of the Near East; and in this secret chamber they found those rich suggestions of the Orient which awakened the latent longing for luxury common to all women.

And the costumes of Madame Coralie and her four assistants were in complete keeping with these surroundings—so characteristic of a Pasha's harem. They wore Turkish trousers, Turkish slippers and jackets, and voluminous Turkish veils; but the mistress alone assumed the yashmak—that well-known Eastern covering for the face, which reveals only the eyes, and accentuates the brilliancy of the same. No one had ever seen Madame Coralie without this concealment, and not even when alone with her quartette of young girls did she lay it aside. Consequently, it is impossible to say what her looks were like. Only two hard, piercing black eyes were visible, and, staring in an unwinking manner above the yashmak, they looked as sinister as those of an octopus. At least, one of Madame's overcharged customers said as much when the bill was presented, and it is probable that she was correct in her description. The fat little woman with the shapeless figure and deft fingers, and the cajoling tongue, belied by the hard eyes, was a veritable octopus, so far as money was concerned. She gathered in everything and gave out nothing. Even her assistants were not paid; for she lodged and boarded them, and taught them her doubtful trade, in lieu of giving wages.

These same assistants—four pretty, fresh and charming girls—were peculiar, to say the least of it. They bore Eastern names, to match their garb and the shop; but only the eldest of them—fancifully called Badoura—was in full possession of the five senses appertaining to humanity. Zobeide was adder-deaf, Peri Banou could not speak, and Parizade's beautiful blue eyes were sightless. Why Madame Coralie should have chosen these defective beings to attend on her customers was a mystery to all. But there was method in the old woman's apparent madness; for each of the trio, lacking a single sense, had more or less developed the remaining ones to unusual perfection. The blind

4

Parizade possessed a marvellously deft touch, and her olfactory nerves were so keen as to cause her positive pain. Dumb Peri Banou had eyes like those of a lynx, and could spy out wrinkles and flaws and spots and grey hairs in a way which no other woman could have done; while Zobeide's deafness was more than compensated by her instinct for colouring complexions, and her faultless judgment in blending and preparing the various herbs, drugs and spices which combined to form those wares Madame Coralie's customers so eagerly purchased.

Badoura overlooked the three girls when Madame was absent, and being in full possession of her senses was extremely clever, diplomatic and managing. She attended mainly to the shop, while Parizade massaged wrinkled faces and kneaded figures into shape. Of the other two girls—Zobeide tinted wan cheeks, burnished drab hair, and pencilled delicate eyebrows, leaving Peri Banou to diagnose fresh cases, to point out defects, make suggestions, and put the final touches to renovated beauty. These four girls, under the able superintendence of Madame, could give a bulky matron the shape of Hebe, and could change the yellow of an unpleasant complexion to the rosy hues of dawn. The weary, worn women who passed through their hands said good-bye to them—with many thanks—as sprightly, blooming girls, with at least ten or twenty years taken from their ages. No wonder Madame Coralie was adored as Medea, and was looked upon by Society dames as their best and dearest friend, with the emphasis on the second adjective.

Madame Coralie boasted that no woman, not even the plainest, need despair while the wonder-shop—as some called it—was in existence; but it must be confessed that she found it sometimes difficult to work the expected miracle. Nature had done her worst with some customers, and no artificial aids could improve them, while others had left the renovative process too late, and there remained only unpromising material out of which to reconstruct the youthful past. Lady Branwin, for instance—really, it was impossible to do anything with Lady Branwin. When she came one June evening at five o'clock to the Turkish Shop, its owner told her so in the rude, bullying manner of a despot, who knows that her victim cannot object. Madame Coralie only assumed her cajoling voice and manner when her customers were insolent in a well-bred way—to the meek, she spoke like the skipper of a tramp with a Dago crew.

"I can't do anything for you," said Madame Coralie, bluntly; "you never had a good figure, or even the makings of one. All the massage and stays and dieting in the world can never improve it into anything decent."

"My complexion isn't so very bad," faltered Lady Branwin, not daring to rebel against this priestess of the toilette mysteries.

"Your what? Leather, my dear; thick, yellow leather, through which the blood can never show. No wash will make any impression on it, so why waste my time and your money?"

Lady Branwin, inwardly furious but outwardly submissive, dropped panting on to the soft divan of the particular alcove wherein this agreeable conversation was taking place. She somewhat resembled the autocrat of Mayfair, being stout and black-eyed, and short in stature. Her face had once been pretty and piquant, but being small and delicate was now sketched, as it were, on superabundant adipose. Her hair was really white with age, but from the use of many dyes had become parti-coloured, and her complexion was sinfully muddy. The sole beauty she possessed were two magnificent Spanish eyes, as large as of Madame Coralie, but scarcely so hard in expression. She was richly arrayed in a dove-coloured silk dress and a loose mantle of brown velvet trimmed with moonlight beads, together with a "Merry Widow" hat, appallingly un-becoming to her tiny features. Also she glittered with many brooches, bracelets, chains, and jewelled buttons, and even dangled a pair of lengthy earrings, after the barbaric fashion of the Albert period. Indeed, Lady Branwin did not look unlike a barbarian, say, an Esquimau, or an Indian squaw, with her yellow face, her squat figure, and her multiplicity of jewellery, although in this last respect she more resembled an Oriental. She breathed hard, and the tears came into her eyes as Madame Coralie continued her very personal remarks. "A sack," said the restorer of youth, "mere sack— a ruin of what you were sixty years ago."

This was too much, and the worm turned. "I am only fifty—you know I am."

"You look like a hundred, and nothing I can do for you will make you look less," was the relentless answer. "You eat and drink and sleep too much, and never take exercise, and your eyes show that you take morphia."

"I don't—it's not true. How dare you say so—how cruel to—"

"Don't waste your breath on me, my dear," advised Madame, coolly. "I am only a shop-keeper, who is honest enough to tell the truth. It's against my own interest, I admit; but why should I give expensive treatment to a woman who can do me no credit?"

"I can pay for the treatment—there is no reason why I shouldn't have it."

"Oh! you can pay, can you? How can I be sure of that?" sneered the other.

"There is no question of being sure," replied Lady Branwin, with dignity, "for my husband, Sir Joseph, is wealthy, as you know. You have only to name your price to have it."

This made an impression on Madame Coralie, who was nothing if not greedy. "My price has gone up since you called last."

"I don't care what the price is."

"Your husband may," snapped Madame Coralie, venomously. "However, that is his affair. I should like to know what you expect me to do?" and she ran her eyes superciliously over her stout customer.

"I want my complexion attended to, and my size reduced, and my—"

"That will do to begin with," interrupted the other, rudely. "That will do to go on with. You will have to stay for a few nights. To-night I am free, and you can have the empty bedroom at the back, on the ground floor. Then I can see what is to be done with you. But I'm afraid," added Madame, with a shrug, "that you are too far gone."

"I'll stay to-night with pleasure—you will do what I want, won't you?" and she looked very directly at the shop-woman.

In her turn Madame Coralie also fastened a penetrating gaze on her customer, and the two pair of black eyes met steadily. "I may, or may not," said the mistress of the Turkish Shop, frowning; "but this is not the place to talk over matters. Let me show you to your bedroom."

"Wait a minute," said Lady Branwin, rising heavily and waddling towards the door. "I must speak to my daughter," and she stepped into the lane.

Here a large and smart motor-car was waiting, which contained a remarkably pretty girl, who certainly had no need to seek Madame Coralie's advice in any way. She was reading a letter, but put it away with a blush when her mother appeared. "Well, mamma," she asked inquiringly, "will Madame Coralie give you the treatment?"

"Yes, she will; and she will charge, as she always does, in an extortionate manner," lamented Lady Branwin. "Give me that red bag, child; it's under the seat. You can drive home now, as I am staying for an hour or so. I may even stay to-night, after Madame Coralie has examined me. You had better call here, on your way to the theatre to-night, and then I shall know for certain if I am to stay."

"But you arranged to go to the theatre also, mamma."

"I can't go, Audrey. Madame Coralie may change her mind, and you know she is the only person who can make me look decent. Ask your father to go."

Audrey tapped her foot petulantly. "You know papa hates going to the theatre, and will grumble all the time."

"Then get Mrs. Mellop to take you," advised her mother, waddling back into the shop; "and don't forget to call, so that I may tell you if I am to remain for the night here. Madame may arrange for me to stay next week; but now I'm in

7

I shan't go out, lest she should refuse to give me the treatment."

When Lady Branwin vanished Audrey shook her pretty head, greatly annoyed, as she did not care very much for Mrs. Mellop. But there was nothing else for her to do, unless Madame Coralie, after examination, refused to permit Lady Branwin to remain for the night. But that could be settled when calling in on her way to the theatre, and then Mrs. Mellop would be with her. There was evidently no escape from Mrs. Mellop, although Audrey would greatly have preferred her mother's company. With a shrug she told the chauffeur to return to the house on Camden Hill, and leant back to adjust the rug over her knees; as she did so, the admiring looks of a young man caught her eye.

He was slim and undersized, puny-limbed and effeminate in a fair-haired, anæmic way, which argued poverty of blood; but being over-dressed, and wearing his straw hat at a rakish tilt, he seemed virile enough to admire a pretty woman when he saw one. In his opinion Audrey deserved his attention, and he bestowed a fascinating leer on her, of which she naturally did not take the slightest notice. The car hummed slowly down the lane, and the young man followed quickly to watch it turn into the High Street; but, for all his pains, he did not catch a second glimpse of its charming occupant.

Meanwhile Madame Coralie conducted Lady Branwin to a bedroom on the ground floor, which looked out on to a lonely court, surrounded by a high brick wall. The shop was left entirely to Zobeide and Peri Banou, and as the first was deaf and the second dumb it would not seem easy for them to converse. But they managed to do so without difficulty, as Peri Banou spoke with her fingers, and, not suffering from Zobeide's defect, could hear her replies without difficulty. She asked a question about Lady Branwin. "She's the wife of Sir Joseph Branwin, the millionaire, who made his money by building seaside towns," answered Zobeide, in the flat tones of the deaf. "As you know, she often comes here to have her looks improved, but until to-day Madame has always refused to help her."

Peri Banou asked another question, and Zobeide nodded. "Oh, yes, she can pay well, but it will cost her a lot before she can be made to look respectable. I say, did you see Madame's husband outside just now?"

Peri Banou laughed, and, smiling very prettily, explained with her fingers that the husband in question had been trying to flirt with the young lady in the motor-car, but without result.

"Lady Branwin's daughter," said Zobeide, stealing to the window and peeping through the pink curtains; "she's a pretty girl and no mistake. But Madame is frightfully jealous, and if she catches her Eddy flirting she'll make it hot for him. He depends entirely on her for his bread-and-butter, you know. Wicked man—he's followed the car. Oh"—she drew back—"here's that tiresome Mrs. Warder, who is never satisfied." And in a few minutes both the girls were attending to a faded, lean woman, who insisted upon having ten years taken from her age, and explained her wants in a querulous voice.

As the hours passed the shop filled with women of all ages and all looks and all positions. There was a babel of voices, and the assistants flew hither and thither like brightly-coloured butterflies. Madame, leaving Lady Branwin to repose in the bedroom, reappeared, and, adopting her cajoling voice, dominated the rattle of tongues, as one who speaks with authority. It was hot enough outside, being a warm June evening, but within, the atmosphere was truly stifling with the glare of the lamps and perfumes of the wares, to say nothing of the fragrant scents used by the customers. One by one they were attended to, and one by one took reluctant leave of that fascinating shop. The four girls began to look weary and fagged, and Badoura with Parizade went upstairs to the room wherein the cosmetics were prepared. Madame Coralie heaved a sigh of relief when the door closed on the last worrying customer— and they all worried—and directed Zobeide and Peri Banou to tidy up the shop.

"It's long past seven," said Madame, with a yawn. "I must return to Lady Branwin, who is to stay for the night."

When she retired the girls made the shop as neat as a new pin, and the time passed very speedily as it always does with the busy. Peri Banou lay down to rest on a divan, but Zobeide, who had to prepare some particular paste required for Lady Branwin's complexion, went up to the still-room. Here she found the effeminate young man who had leered so rakishly at Audrey, and smiled graciously. Eddy Vail—Madame Coralie in private life was Mrs. Vail —knew the finger alphabet and asked her questions.

"Where is my wife?" he demanded anxiously.

Zobeide, noting his eager looks, decided that he wanted money, and laughed. "I think she is with Lady Branwin in the lower back bedroom."

"What, at this time! Why, it's five minutes to eight." And he glanced at the clock over the still-room mantelpiece, again speaking with his fingers.

"I thought it was much later myself," said Zobeide. "Wait for her. I daresay she won't be long. Where are Badoura and Parizade?"

"Behind the curtain," said Vail, with his fingers, and pointing to a figured drapery hanging from the ceiling to the floor, and which ran along a brass rod. "Can't you hear them chattering and laughing?"

Zobeide shot an angry glance at him, as she hated to have any allusion made to her deafness.

She would have said something disagreeable, but that Madame, adjusting her yashmak, entered the room. She looked, so far as could be judged from her eyes, irritated and startled. "I wish Lady Branwin was at the bottom of the sea," she said crossly. "Zobeide, attend to your work. And what do you mean, Eddy, coming up to trouble my girls? You have no right in this room, and I won't have it."

"You never objected before," grumbled Eddy, crossly.

"Then I object now. Go away; I'm busy. Lady Branwin is in the house, and— and others." She hesitated and snapped savagely: "I wish you would go away."

"I want a fiver."

"Then you shan't get it. Come to-morrow, and I'll see what I can do. By the way, I want you to go to Brighton for me."

"I don't mind, if you pay."

"Do I ever object to pay when you go on my business?" asked his wife, crossly, for the heat seemed to have worn her nerves thin.

"What's the business?" asked Eddy, taking out a cigarette.

"I'll tell you to-morrow. Go away now."

"And you'll give me the fiverto-morrow?"

"I'll give you ten pounds."

"Oh, I say, that deserves a kiss. Do remove that beastly yashmak and let me kiss you!"

Madame Coralie pushed him back violently. "Certainly not. I have no time for frivolity. Go away."

The young man looked astonished. "You always liked being kissed before," he remarked sulkily. "Are you going back to Lady Branwin?"

"No. She has had some supper, and will now sleep. I must attend to the paste for her complexion. Zobeide? Go away, Eddy. It's getting late."

"Five minutes after eight," said the young man, and sauntered out of the door. "I'll turn up to-morrow before midday. Good-bye."

Madame Coralie nodded wearily, and stared at the clock on the mantelpiece in a vague way. "Five minutes past eight," she murmured; "well, I thought—"

Her speech was interrupted by a ring at the front door of the shop. Badoura appeared from between the curtains. "Shall I go, Madame?"

"No. It is Miss Branwin. I'll go down myself," and with a tired sigh the stout woman rolled out of the room.

Eddy, apparently, had left the house by the side door at the end of the lower passage, for she saw nothing of him. Shortly she was on the pavement speaking to Audrey, who, clothed in a simple white dress, was waiting with Mrs. Mellop in the car.

"Will mamma stop for the night, Madame?" asked Audrey.

"Yes," replied the woman, adjusting her yashmak carefully. "Lady Branwin will stop for the night."

CHAPTER II.

IN THE MORNING

Audrey was one of the prettiest girls in the world, and beyond question the very prettiest in London. At least, Ralph Shawe said as much, and, although the statement was prejudiced by love, it undoubtedly was true in the main. For what other damsel, as the young man often pointed out, possessed such striking charms as Audrey displayed? Her bronzed and curling hair, her sparkling brown eyes, her transparent complexion, delicately hued as the dawn—these were desirable attributes in the eyes of a lover. Then her small figure—she was really diminutive—had the dainty grace of a gazelle. All Madame Coralie's art could not have created such a buoyant figure, nor could her taste have suggested any improvement in the various frocks which clothed it on various occasions. And those slim hands and feet, that radiant smile, and the general air of youthful gaiety were the envy of the women and the admiration of the men. These declarations sound somewhat too emphatic; but they must be taken as a précis of Ralph Shawe's thoughts. And, being a true lover, what could he do but think in superlatives?

How such a fairy came to be the sole daughter of a prosperous, commonplace pair such as Sir Joseph and his wife certainly were puzzled many people. Only the large quantity of money which they possessed excused their existence in the eyes of most people, although Shawe found another apology for them in the undoubted fact—strange as it may appear—that they were the parents of Audrey.

Certainly Sir Joseph was clever, or he would scarcely have started life with the proverbial penny, to end as the owner of over a million. But Audrey did not even inherit his type of brain, much less his massive looks. His capabilities were of the cunning, business kind, which turn others' needs to their owners' advantage, whereas the talents of Audrey were more artistic and intellectual. She knew nothing of business, but she painted in water-colour with great taste, played the piano with wonderful sympathy and brilliancy, and sang like the sirens of old. Also she could dance like the daughter of Herodias, and if she did not win a head as her reward, she assuredly gained a heart—that of Ralph Shawe, of the Middle Temple, barrister-at-law. Audrey, however, had not that one strong original talent which makes for fame in its particular direction; but she possessed a bundle of small accomplishments, which went to make up a singularly charming personality. She was an angel, said Shawe, and, speaking broadly, he was correct in saying so, for Audrey was as angelical as mere flesh and blood well could be.

The lovers were sauntering in Kensington Gardens when he said this—not for the first time—and the hour was so early that few people were about. Audrey had risen at six o'clock to meet Ralph at seven in the morning near the Round Pond, and save for the handful of working men and office-workmen, who were taking short cuts to their various employments, they had the whole delightful paradise to themselves. The sky was of a turquoise hue, not yet over-warmed by the sun, and both trees and sward looked as though they had been newly washed in the dews of night. At that early hour everything seemed paler and more delicate than in the fierce glare of noonday, and "the silent workings of the dawn"—to use Keats's wonderful expression—were still in progress. A cool, dewy zephyr was breathing across the green expanse, and the leaves of many trees talked joyously. London lay all round, stirring alertly under the faint dun cloud of smoke, but the fragrant Eden of the Gardens preserved its almost primeval calm. And these two walked therein, like a modern Adam and Eve, with a sense that the surrounding loveliness exactly expressed their unspoken feelings.

"I wish we could walk here all day," said Shawe, trying to express the inexpressible, and grudging the swift passing of the golden moments.

"We should only be two in a crowd," replied Audrey, with the more prosaic instinct of women. "Endless people come to the Gardens during the day. If they were sensible they would be here now. I can't understand why the silly things remain in bed when the weather is so perfect."

"Perhaps not one of them has an Audrey to meet."

Miss Branwin laughed gaily. "I daresay every young man has an Audrey of his own, just as every girl has a Ralph."

"Then why aren't they walking here along with us?"

"Ah, they know we wish to be alone, and so have the good sense to stop in bed. And then"—she broke off laughing—"what nonsense we talk!"

"Delicious nonsense, I think. Let us go on talking, as we'll have enough commonsense during the day. Don't you think"—Ralph slipped an eager arm round her slender waist—"that you might—"

She drew back from his approaching lips with a blush, and dexterously twisted away to a safe distance. "Certainly not. Those workmen would see us."

"And envy me," replied Ralph, sentimentally, glancing round meanwhile for some secluded spot. "Don't you think that we might sit under this elm? It's not so open to—to—er—to observation, you know. May I smoke?"

"What, before breakfast?" questioned Audrey, sitting down on the grass.

"I have had my breakfast—that is, so much as I could eat, with you in my thoughts, darling. And you?"

"I had a cup of tea and some thin bread-and-butter. But I shall have my real breakfast when I return home."

"And you will think of me?"

"If," said Audrey, with mischievous gravity, "if it is possible to do two things at one time I shall think of you."

"Darling!" And this time he really kissed her.

Of course, it was all very silly, but extremely delightful, all the same; for love's commonsense is the nonsense of everyday life. A cynic would have considered the conversation of Audrey and Ralph to be drivel; and no doubt it was, to anyone but their very own selves. But only the birds could hear the billing and cooing which went on, until his wooing and her coquetting ended in a long silence, wherein they held each other's hand and, looking eye to eye, sighed at intervals. Yet Audrey was a sensible girl, and Ralph was a rising barrister, winning golden opinions in the Law Courts. If his clients could have seen him now, acting Hercules in the toils of Omphale, he would never have secured another brief.

Shawe was slim and dark-complexioned, with a clear-cut, classical face, eminently suited, with its steady grey eyes and firm lips, to his profession. He

13

was handsome in a severe way, and rarely smiled, perhaps because he saw too persistently and too closely the seamy side of life with which the law has to deal. Only a glance from Audrey could soften his granite looks, and her mere presence changed him into a more companionable being. He loved her more than he did his profession—and that is saying a great deal, for he was ambitious, and had visions of the Woolsack. Many said that he might attain even to that high altitude, as he was admitted on all hands to be brilliantly clever. But just now, while playing in Cupid's garden, he looked and acted like a young man of the ordinary type, because love, which is common to all, had ousted for the moment that genius which is given to few. So he sighed and she sighed, and she looked and he looked; their hands thrilled when in contact, and the birds overhead sang the songs of their hearts, which, being limited by speech, they could not utter. In this manner did they dwell in Arcady and recall one hour of the Golden Age, when gods wooed mortal maids.

"But it's all very well," said Audrey, withdrawing her hand, and breathing a final sigh of silent delight, "time is pressing, and I have to call at Madame Coralie's before I go home."

"Who is Madame Coralie?" asked Shawe, also sighing, as he awakened to the fact that the work-a-day world had need of him.

Audrey laughed. "No mere man can understand who Madame Coralie is, or what she is. But if you will walk with me to Walpole Lane I can show you her shop—not that the shop will explain."

"What kind of goods does she sell?" asked the young barrister, lazily, and admiring the profile of his beloved.

"She sells figures and complexions and false hair and lip-salve, and—"

"Stop! Stop! You surely don't want any of those beastly things?"

"Not yet," said Audrey, significantly; "but I may some day. It is mamma who wants them just now. She has no figure, poor dear, and her complexion is like a frog's skin. I am going to call and ask how she passed the night, and I take you because we have no secrets from one another."

"Is Lady Branwin's presence at this shop a secret?"

"Of course. Mamma wants to be made young and beautiful, so she goes secretly to Madame Coralie. A woman doesn't advertise her need of restoration."

"But I don't quite understand what sort of shop this Madame Coralie keeps?" said Ralph, looking puzzled and contracting his dark brows.

"It's a beauty-factory," explained Audrey, hugging her knees; "women like mamma go there to regain whatever looks they may have had. I shall go also some day, when I am old and scraggy."

"Never, if you are my wife, dear. I want to see you grow old gracefully."

"I don't want to grow old at all; no woman ever does, you stupid thing. As to becoming your wife, I never may be. You know that."

"No, I don't, sweetest." Ralph possessed himself of her frock hem and kissed it fervently. "I know that your father doesn't think I am a good match for you, and that your mother wishes you to marry a title. All the same, I intend to have my own way and make you Mrs. Shawe for a time."

"For a time!" cried Audrey, indignantly. "What do you mean, Ralph?"

"Until you are Lady Shawe, dearest, or perhaps Lady Bleakleigh. That is the Somerset village where I was born," explained Ralph. "My father is the squire. When I get my title—and I shall some day, by sheer dint of brain-power—I shall take that title; then you will be—"

But Audrey was not listening. "Bleakleigh—Bleakleigh," she muttered; "where have I heard that name?"

"From your father," said Shawe, promptly. "He told me one evening, in a moment of expansion after dinner, that he came from Bleakleigh, starting as a farm labourer to end as Sir Joseph Branwin, the millionaire."

"He won't end at that," said Audrey, gravely; "papa is too ambitious. Like yourself, he intends to gain a Peerage, and may some day be Lord Bleakleigh, before you can secure the title."

"Well, it doesn't matter, so long as I secure you."

"You won't, if my parents are to be considered."

"Then why consider them?" asked Ralph, coolly. "I know that they both want you to marry a Duke or an Earl, so as to forward their plans for social advancement; but I don't see why you should be sacrificed in this way."

"Oh, I shan't be sacrificed, I promise you," said Audrey, nodding her small head vigorously; "and when it comes to fighting, I think that mamma will be on my side. She is very fond of me."

"Of course. Aren't both of your parents fond of you?"

"Mamma is, but I don't think papa loves me much. He looks upon me as one of the pawns in the game of life, to be moved that he may win. You must have seen that, from the way in which he has forbidden you the house."

"I think he treated me very badly," said Ralph, flushing. "I went to him and stated frankly that I loved you, explaining my prospects, which are of the best. He behaved like a—well, I can't say—"

"I can," interrupted the girl, rising, with a shrug—"like a pig."

"My dear!" Shawe rose also, and looked somewhat shocked.

"Oh, what is the use of mincing matters?" said Audrey, wearily. "You know, and I know, and everyone else knows, that my father is a rude, blatant, uncouth labourer, just as he was when he left Bleakleigh years ago. He treats my mother shamefully, and shows in every way that he has no love for me. 'Honour thy father' doesn't apply to me, I assure you. I am most unhappy at home."

"I wish we could marry at once," said Ralph, biting his fingers, "and then we could see little or nothing of him; but I am not yet in a position to marry, unfortunately."

"Never mind, darling"—she took his arm, and they strolled across the grass towards the gravelled path—"until you are ready to marry me I shall remain true to you. I shan't marry anyone with a title, unless you become Lord Bleakleigh, of course; and by that time I shall be a client of Madame Coralie's, since you won't be Lord Chancellor for years and years."

"I wish you wouldn't talk of going to this beauty-factory, Audrey," said the young man, irritably; "you know that I prefer you as God made you."

"*Now*, dearest; but when I am old—"

"I shall love you all the same."

"I hope so," said Audrey, with a little sigh; "but men love good looks in a woman, and when those go love grows cold."

"With mere animal men, but not with one like myself. I love with my heart more than with my eye. Don't class me with your father."

"I wouldn't marry you if I did," she retorted. "It's bad enough to have Sir Joseph Branwin as a father without taking one of his nature as a husband. If you only knew how he has insulted poor mamma about her looks! That is why she has gone to Madame Coralie. But I don't think that anything will do much good, even if poor mamma became as beautiful as Venus. Papa seems to have taken a dislike to her. It makes me very unhappy," ended the girl, with a mournful shake of the head.

Ralph frowned, and considered. He hated to think that Audrey's youthful spirits should be damped by the disagreement between her parents—a disagreement which rose solely from Sir Joseph's animal nature. With all his brain power he was a mere hog of the fields, and good looks in women alone attracted him towards the sex. Shawe knew of Sir Joseph's attentions to various actresses and Society beauties, which had been spoken about openly enough at the clubs; and it was quite likely that, now his purse gave him the power to lure women into liking, if not into love, he was growing weary of his uncomely old wife. There was something very pathetic in the shapeless, homely Lady Branwin seeking to recover her husband's affections by making herself attractive artificially. But he privately agreed with Audrey that it was too late, and even if Lady Branwin became, unnaturally, as beautiful as Venus, he felt certain that Sir Joseph would continue to dislike her. His distaste for his old wife was more than skin deep; of that Ralph felt sure.

"Is Lady Branwin at the shop now?" asked Ralph, when the two passed through the side gate of the Gardens at the back of the Palace, and speaking anything rather than his thoughts, for obvious reasons.

"Yes. She stayed there last night, so that Madame Coralie could decide if she would undertake to give her the necessary treatment. If she does, mamma will have to remain for a week or more. I am calling to ask what is to be done, as papa is in a bad temper because my mother stopped away. He insists that she shall return home."

"I wonder Lady Branwin doesn't get a separation," muttered the barrister, again reflecting on Sir Joseph's attentions to other women.

"If she dared to take legal proceedings papa would turn her into the street without a penny," said Audrey, calmly. "I am under no illusion as to his nature, my dear. But let us get on. I wish to be home as soon as possible to give papa his breakfast. If I am not there, since mamma is still absent, he will make himself so disagreeable."

"He invariably does," said Ralph, grimly; for a single interview with the millionaire had given him an astonishing insight into the man's brutal nature. "Where is this shop, Audrey?"

"Down this lane. Yonder it is, painted pink."

"What a glaring advertisement," remarked Shawe, as they walked quickly down the crooked by-way. "If Madame Coralie paints her customers as she has done her shop, they must all look like blowsy dairymaids. She seems to be doing a good trade this morning."

"There is a crowd," admitted Audrey, with an anxious glance; "but it's odd a crowd should be round the shop at this hour. Madame's clients usually come at night, and very privately."

"I don't think these are customers," said Shawe, as they reached the large assemblage of people which blocked the lane.

The individuals who composed the mob certainly were not the Society customers of Madame Coralie, as they comprised poor men and women of the lowest classes, with here and there a better-dressed person. Policemen were directing the throng and keeping order, but they could not prevent tongues clacking, and there was quite a babel of voices.

"What is the matter?" Audrey asked a red-faced female in rusty black.

"Murder!" said the woman, with relish. "One of them fine ladies who comes here to get painted has been done for."

Audrey grew white and started. "Do you know the name?"

"Ho yes, miss. I heard a policeman say as she was called Lady Branwin."

"Ralph, Ralph!" whispered the girl, and clutched her lover to keep herself from falling. "My mother! Murdered! Oh, Ralph!"

CHAPTER III

THE LOST BAG

Notwithstanding her delicate looks, Audrey possessed a strong spirit, fully capable of controlling emotions, even when markedly powerful. The tragic and unexpected news of the murder shattered her nerves for the moment; but after the first shock of surprise she pushed her way hastily through the crowd, fully bent upon discovering exactly what had happened. Ralph, not yet thoroughly acquainted with her self-control under trying circumstances, followed immediately behind, urging her in whispers to go home and wait developments. To his importunities she turned a deaf ear, and addressed herself anxiously to the officer who guarded the door of the Turkish Shop. He naturally refused to reply to her questions.

"But I am Lady Branwin's daughter," said Audrey, softly, so that the crowd might not hear, "and they say that Lady Branwin is dead."

"Very sorry, miss," said the constable, not answering directly, "but my orders are to admit no one."

Audrey's eyes began to glitter with ill-concealed anger, and Ralph hastily intervened.

"Who is in charge of this case, officer?"

"Inspector Lanton, sir."

"Then pass my card into him, and—"

"Are you a relative of the deceased, sir?"

"No. But I am engaged to Miss Branwin here, and she—"

"I'll send in the card," interrupted the policeman, quickly; then raised his voice to rebuke the crowd. "Keep back there; keep back!"

Audrey remained silent, holding her feelings well under, while Ralph rapidly scribbled her name on his card. The constable knocked at the door and gave the message to the policeman who opened it. Then the door was closed again, and the lovers remained on the step anxiously waiting to see what would come of their application. The mob of people whispered and pointed, and looked askance at the young couple, evidently wondering why they were there. The position was highly unpleasant, and Audrey felt a great sense of relief when she was permitted to enter with her lover. In a moment they passed through the jealously-guarded door, and it was closed again the minute they were inside.

"Wait here, please," said the constable who received them. "Inspector Lanton is upstairs with Madame Coralie, and will be down shortly."

Audrey laid a detaining hand on his sleeve as he moved away. "Can you tell me if Lady Branwin—"

"I am not allowed to answer any questions, miss," he replied, and went away in a stolid manner, as though the business in hand were an everyday occurrence.

"Won't you sit down, darling?" whispered Ralph, tenderly. "You must keep up your strength, as there is much to be done."

"My poor mother!" Audrey sank down on to a stool with a gasp. "Who could have killed her? How was she killed? When did the murder take place? Oh, it's too awful! Perhaps"—she looked pleadingly up into her lover's face —"perhaps it is not true."

"It *is* true, Miss Branwin," said a soft voice before Ralph could reply; and out of a near alcove came a pretty girl with red eyes and a tear-stained face. "It's quite true and very terrible."

"Who are you?" asked Audrey, lifting her white face. "How do you come to know my name?"

"I am Badoura, the forewoman of Madame Coralie," was the reply, "and I saw you yesterday when you came here with your mother. Poor Lady Branwin! It is awful to think that she should have been strangled in—"

"Strangled!" interrupted Audrey, with another gasp. "Who strangled her?"

"No one knows," said Badoura, shuddering. "Madame found her dead in her bed when she went at seven this morning to see how she had passed the night. I heard her say that Lady Branwin had been strangled, and then she sent for the police at once. It's really dreadful," added the girl, mournfully, "as everything is upset, and we don't know what is going to happen. See here!" and she swept aside the pink silk curtain which was draped over the Moorish arch of the alcove whence she had emerged.

Here Audrey beheld the other assistants huddled together on the divan, with tear-stained faces and terror-stricken looks. The catastrophe had disorganised the whole establishment, and the girls feared lest the scandal, which certainly would arise from the fact of the murder, might result in the closing of the shop. This was a very probable contingency indeed, and none of them could face with equanimity the dismal prospect of losing her employment. They had been driven like sheep into the alcove by the police, and waited developments with strained nerves. As yet not one of the three had been examined.

Badoura, having full possession of her senses, was the most composed, and seemed glad to find someone to talk to, less upset than her three friends, "It will ruin Madame's business," she wailed.

"Please tell us exactly what happened," said Ralph, who was anxious to get at the facts of the case.

"There's nothing to tell, sir. Lady Branwin came with this young lady yesterday about five, and retired to a back bedroom on the ground floor almost immediately with Madame, who wished to see what could be done by way of treatment. Lady Branwin had not even made up her mind to stop; but after Madame had given her opinion she decided to remain for the night, and Madame told you, Miss Branwin, that such was the case, when—"

"When I called here on my way to the theatre," finished Audrey, whose face was colourless but wonderfully composed. "I remember. When did Madame Coralie last see my mother?"

"Shortly before eight o'clock, miss. She left her quite comfortable for the night after she had taken a light supper. We all went to bed about nine, as we were all so tired with a busy day. Then at seven this morning Madame came to me while I was tidying up the shop, and told me that Lady Branwin was dead. She could scarcely speak." Badoura paused for a moment, then added, as an after-thought: "The window was open."

"The window?" repeated Ralph, fastening his eyes on her face searchingly.

"The window of the back bedroom on the ground floor," explained the girl, readily. "It looks out on to a closed court, which has a high wall round it."

"Then you think that the assassin entered and left by the window?"

"I didn't say that, for I do not know," replied Badoura, quickly. "All Madame said was that the bedroom window was open, although she had closed it on the previous night. But even if the assassin did get into the room in that way, I don't see how he could leave the court. The door in the wall of the court is locked, and the key is lost."

"He could climb over the wall, perhaps?" suggested Audrey, thoughtfully.

"It's a difficult, smooth wall to climb, miss."

"What is on the other side of the wall?" asked Shawe, sharply.

"A narrow alley, which runs into the High Street."

"Then if the assassin could get over the wall, he could easily escape?"

"Oh, yes, sir; but the wall is difficult to climb."

"Is there no other entrance into the court?"

"Only from the house. There is a door which is kept locked, as no one ever goes into the court at the back. Besides, no one was in the house last night but myself, the three girls, Madame, Lady Branwin and a lady customer."

"What is her name?"

"I can't tell you," said Badoura, hesitating. "Only Madame knows; as many ladies don't care to give their names, save to Madame, when under treatment."

"Tell me," said Ralph, waiving this point for the time being, "you call the assassin 'he.' What reason have you to believe that a man strangled Lady Branwin?"

Badoura looked surprised. "I only think so, sir, as, of course, I know nothing. But surely, sir, only a man would have the strength to strangle?"

Audrey shook her head. "A strong woman could do that also. Especially as my mother was stout and rather apoplectic. Very little pressure on her throat would have killed her, I am certain. And then—"

Here Audrey's conjectures were cut short by the entrance of a tall, soldierly-looking man in uniform. His eyes were grey and steady, and he looked sharply at the young couple, who rose to meet him. It was Lanton.

"Miss Branwin and Mr. Ralph Shawe," said the inspector, glancing at the barrister's card, which he held in his hand. "How is it that you are here?"

"Let me explain," said Audrey, stopping her lover from speaking. "I met Mr. Shawe in Kensington Gardens this morning early, as we are engaged, and called with him to see how my mother was this morning. We learnt—" Her face worked with emotion, and she sat down again.

"I understand—I understand," said Lanton, comprehending her feelings. "It is very sad, Miss Branwin, and must have been a great shock to you."

"Is my mother really dead?"

"Yes," answered the inspector, promptly. "The doctor who examined the body declares that she was strangled at eight o'clock last night—that is, a few minutes before or after. If you would like to see the body—"

"No, no," interposed Ralph, hurriedly. "Miss Branwin is not strong enough to —"

Audrey rose to her feet, and braced herself with an effort. "Yes, I am," she declared. "It is necessary for me to see my poor mother's remains. Take me to the room, Mr. Inspector."

"You are a brave young lady," muttered the officer, and led the way out of the shop without further comment.

The trio—for Shawe naturally went with Audrey—walked along a narrow corridor, which ran the whole length of the building. It divided the shop, which likewise stretched from wall to wall of the house, from four bedrooms, the windows of which looked out on to the closed court mentioned by Badoura. At the end of the passage, to the right—looking from the shop—was a door which led into a right-of-way opening on to Walpole Lane. But this right-of-way did not afford any access to the court, its upper-end being blocked by a high brick wall with broken glass on top. The only two ways of gaining admittance to the court were by the house-door, and the door in the wall of the court itself. These, as Badoura had said, and as Inspector Lanton had ascertained from Madame Coralie, were always kept locked. The court was narrow and paved with flagstones, and had a disused air, which was very natural since no one ever entered it.

Lanton conducted the couple into one of the bedrooms, and here they found Madame Coralie in her quaint Turkish dress, and wearing the filmy black yashmak. She was seated near the door, apparently guarding the dead from

22

the prying curiosity of anyone in the house. The room was of no great size, but was luxuriously furnished in green and silver. There was only one window, draped with curtains, which looked out on to the court, and the lower sash of this was wide open. In a far corner, with its head against the inner wall, stood the bed, and on this, under a sheet, the dead woman was stiffly stretched out. Owing to the absence of sunlight and the presence of the dead, there was a chill feeling in the room, and Audrey shivered.

"Can you go through with it?" asked Ralph, anxiously.

"Yes, I must," she replied, in a low tone; and walking towards the bed she lifted the sheet.

Madame Coralie had risen, and with tightly-clasped hands watched the girl's every action. Her black eyes peering above the yashmak were less hard, and the red rims round them showed that she had been weeping. She had every reason to, for what had happened might ruin her trade.

"Is it Lady Branwin?" asked Lanton, softly, since Audrey did not speak.

"Yes," she replied, with a sigh, and apparently could scarcely stand. On seeing this, Ralph slipped his arm round her waist. "I won't give way," she added firmly, and withdrew from his support. "Yes, Mr. Inspector, this is my mother's body. I see from the black marks on her neck that she has been strangled. Who murdered her, and why?"

Madame Coralie replied. "Ah, my dear young lady," she said, in a choking voice, "that is what we wish to find out. It will ruin my business."

"I don't see that," said Lanton, quietly; "you have always conducted your business respectably."

"It's the first time that I have ever had the police in my house," murmured Madame Coralie, in despair. "But a murder!—oh, what lady will ever come and pass the night here for treatment, when she may be murdered? I wish I knew the villain who killed poor Lady Branwin"—Madame Coralie shook her fist in the air—"I should have him hanged."

"We'll hunt him down yet," said Lanton, confidentially.

"Do you think that the assassin is a man?" asked Ralph, putting the same question to the inspector as he had done to Badoura.

Lanton looked taken aback. "In the absence of all proof, I believe the assassin to be a man—unless Lady Branwin had a woman enemy."

"Mamma had no enemies at all," said Audrey, in a firm voice. "Madame, where were you when my mother was murdered?"

"Upstairs in the still-room," said the woman, quietly. "At about eight o'clock the murder took place, according to the doctor. I was with my girls—that is, Badoura, Parizade and Zobeide were in the still-room, and Peri Banou in the shop. My husband was also there. He went away, and then I came down to tell you at the door that Lady Branwin would stop for the night."

"She must have been dead then," muttered Audrey, shivering. "You heard no noise, or—"

"I heard nothing, neither did my husband or Badoura. I left Lady Branwin quite comfortable shortly before eight o'clock. The assassin must have opened the window and murdered her almost immediately after I left."

"But why was she murdered?" asked Shawe, insistently.

"I can't say, sir, no more than I can say how the assassin managed to enter the court. Why," added Madame Coralie, quickly, "so sure am I that the court cannot be entered that the windows of the bedrooms are never fastened. It would, therefore, not be difficult for the assassin to enter. I expect that he found Lady Branwin asleep, and—"

"So quickly after you left?" interrupted the inspector.

"I gave Lady Branwin a sleeping-draught," explained Madame Coralie, "as her nerves were bad and she could not rest. For the treatment which I intended to give her it was necessary that her nerves should be in better order."

Audrey nodded. "I remember," she said, gravely, "mamma was very much agitated when she came here, and very restless."

"Why?" asked Lanton, sharply.

"On account of her desire for this treatment, which she feared Madame Coralie would not give her. Mamma explained that to me. Then, of course, there were the diamonds—oh!"—Audrey started—"where are the diamonds?"

Inspector Lanton pricked up his ears, and looked at Madame Coralie. "The diamonds!" he repeated. "Where are the diamonds?"

Madame Coralie started back and wrung her hands. "Oh, here is another trouble—another trouble!" she wailed. "I never knew that Lady Branwin brought any diamonds. Are you sure—are you certain?"

"Quite sure," said Audrey, excitedly. "Mamma had two thousand pounds' worth of diamonds in a red morocco bag. She intended to take them to a jeweller and get them reset, but as she stopped here she took the bag out of the motor and carried it into this house with her."

"I saw the red bag," said Madame Coralie, much agitated, "but I swear that I did not know that it contained diamonds. Lady Branwin did not mention what the bag contained. I paid no attention to it."

"Is the bag in this room?" asked Lanton, looking round.

"It must be—it must be," said Madame Coralie, beginning to search. "She had such a bag with her. I remember that; but I did not notice what she did with it. Why should I, not knowing it contained diamonds?"

A thorough search was made, but without result. Audrey again described the bag, and mentioned that her mother had attached a small label to it, so that its owner should be known if it were lost. Inspector Lanton seized on the last word: "Did she expect it to be lost?"

"No; certainly not. She intended, I understood from her own lips, to take the diamonds to the jeweller; but, because she remained here, she took the bag in with her. It must be somewhere."

"In the hands of the assassin, probably," remarked Shawe, nodding.

Lanton looked at him. "Do you think that robbery is the motive for the murder?"

"Yes, I do, since the diamonds are missing. Else why should Lady Branwin, who had no enemies, be strangled? The assassin must have known that she had the jewels with her, and must have climbed the wall of the court to gain entrance by the window. Are there no footmarks?" "I have not searched the court," muttered Lanton, doubtfully; "but this mention of the diamonds puts a different complexion on the case." He paused for a moment, then scrambled through the window, and crossed the court. At the foot of the wall, near the closed door, he picked up a scrap of paper. "It's the label," he called out triumphantly. "Evidently the string became loose, and it fell off while the thief was making off with his plunder." He then turned to examine the door, and uttered a cry as he peered down to look through the key-hole. "This door has been opened," he declared loudly; "the key is in the lock on the outside."

"Ah!" said Ralph, with satisfaction, "now we are on the trail of the assassin."

"Catch him!" screamed Madame Coralie, fiercely. "Catch him and hang him!"

CHAPTER IV.

There were many interesting items of news in the newspapers when the Turkish Shop tragedy took place; for it was the middle of the London season, and social events succeeded one another rapidly. Nevertheless, the affair created a sensation, as Lady Branwin was the wife of a millionaire, and a well-known figure in Society. Especially did the female population of Mayfair and Belgravia comment on the murder, as, having taken place in their own particular pet shop, it concerned them nearly. It was dreadful to think that if any one of them passed the night under Madame Coralie's roof death might be the result. Many declared that they would never go near the place again. But this was when the news of the crime was fresh and startling. Later, these ladies saw reason to revise their opinion, since there was no one but Madame Coralie to perform miracles of rejuvenation.

The immediate result of the murder was to send Sir Joseph Branwin to bed. He was a burly, red-faced man, who ate and drank largely; so it was not surprising that the announcement of his wife's terrible death should cause him to have a fit. When he grasped the truth he dropped down straightway, and for quite two weeks he was unable to leave his bed or to attend to any necessary matters. He was neither at the inquest nor at the funeral, and his daughter, along with Ralph Shawe, had to look after everything. Sir Joseph was not grateful—he never was, being a singularly selfish man. It was quite a surprise to Audrey that he should have fallen ill when told the truth. "I daresay he was fonder of mamma than I thought," she said to Ralph, and blamed herself for having misjudged her father; "yet they always quarrelled, and did not seem to get on at all well together."

"The quarrelling may have been a matter of habit," said Shawe, doubtfully. "Married couples may be devoted to one another, and yet may be always bickering. And I think, Audrey, that you told me your parents' marriage was a love-match of a romantic nature."

"So mamma said," replied the girl, nodding gravely. "She and papa were boy and girl together at Bleakleigh. He promised to marry her when he made his fortune, and years afterwards he returned to keep his promise. Both papa and mamma were the children of labourers."

"So I should think," remarked Ralph, caustically, and remembering the excessively plebeian looks of the couple. "I can never understand how you come to be their daughter, Audrey. You are no more like them than a lily is like a cabbage-rose."

Audrey nodded her head absently as she was thinking of other things. "What will the verdict of the inquest be?" she demanded anxiously.

"In the absence of any proof likely to identify the assassin there can only be one verdict—wilful murder against some person or persons unknown."

"Oh! do you think, then, that there is more than one assassin?"

"No, dear. The inclusion of the plural is merely a matter of form. Undoubtedly poor Lady Branwin was murdered by one person only—the man who afterwards stole the jewels."

"You think it was a man, then?"

"In the absence of evidence I presume so. By the way, Audrey, how is it that your mother had a label attached to that red morocco bag? It is unusual."

"Oh, that was a peculiarity of mamma's nature. She attached labels to almost everything she took out of doors, as she always seemed to fancy that what she carried might be lost, and in this way—as she thought—provided against contingencies. Papa and I both used to laugh at her for the care with which she prepared those little pieces of parchment, and jokingly said that she must have been a baggage porter. Poor mamma!" Audrey sighed. "It is strange that her odd habit should be the means of tracing her murderer."

"It has not traced him, unfortunately," said Ralph, shaking his head; "but the finding of the label at the foot of the wall undoubtedly shows that he escaped in that way."

"It was strange that he should have left the key in the lock."

"Very strange," assented Shawe, emphatically; "and it shows how deliberate he was in his behaviour. He must have known that he had plenty of time to escape, and even then a smarter man would have taken the key with him. This is one of the mistakes the cleverest criminal makes."

"How did he get the key from Madame Coralie?"

"He did not. Madame declares that she never had a key to the door in the court wall, as it was never used, and certainly has never been opened during her tenancy. The key used is what is known as a skeleton key, such as burglars carry."

"Then this assassin was a burglar?"

"I think so; one of the criminal classes, at all events, as no amateur could have managed so cleverly. The leaving of the key, however, was a mistake."

"Can he be traced by it?"

"I doubt if he can. The door opens on to an alley paved with stone, and no footmarks can be found. From the time the man left the court by the door he was safe. No, dear, if there is any chance of his being taken, it will be by means of the diamonds—and even that is doubtful. All he has to do is to unset the stones and sell them separately. I am anxious to hear what further evidence may be collected by Lanton for the inquest."

But Shawe's anxiety was quite unnecessary, as very little evidence was forthcoming when the inquest was held. The inspector did what he could; but to trace the assassin was like looking for a needle in a bottle of hay. A great crowd collected outside the building wherein the inquest was held; but few people were admitted. Audrey came with her lover, as it was necessary that she should state how her mother had been in possession of the missing jewels, and Ralph came with her as a moral support. Sir Joseph, unfortunately, could not attend, owing to illness; but he sent his solicitor to watch the case on his behalf, and ordered that everything should be done to trace the assassin, even to offering a reward of one thousand pounds for the villain's apprehension. This offer, being well known before the inquest took place, brought many people to hear what they could of the evidence, in the hope of being able to lay the murderer by the heels and claim the money. But, as has before been stated, Lanton did not allow the general public to crowd the room wherein the proceedings took place.

Inspector Lanton himself was the first witness, and gave a succinct account of how he had been called in when the fact of the murder became known. He detailed all that he had learnt; produced a plan of the building wherein the crime had taken place; also the label, together with the key of the court door; and stated the names of the witnesses he proposed to call. Of these, the doctor who had examined the body of the unfortunate woman was the first to follow Lanton in giving evidence, and deposed that the deceased had been strangled —so far as he could judge from the condition of the body—at eight o'clock in the evening. He had made the examination at 7.30 the next morning, almost immediately the fact of the murder had been discovered. The doctor's evidence was short and dry, and provided no clue whereby to trace the assassin, as the creature had left behind him nothing by which he could be identified.

Madame Coralie came next, and appeared—perhaps for the purposes of advertisement—in her Turkish dress and wearing her yashmak. Before entering the court she had drawn Inspector Lanton aside to ask him not to request her to remove the yashmak, on the grounds that it would be detrimental to her business. Lanton then saw—for she drew aside the veil to reveal the truth—that Madame Coralie had a disfiguring birthmark on cheek and mouth and chin, which made her look anything but attractive. Naturally, as she pointed out, if her customers knew that she could not remove such a birthmark from her own face, she could scarcely—as they might think—do all she claimed towards beautifying them. Lanton pointed out that, as she had already made her reputation, the birthmark did not matter; but, as he quite saw the point and recognised the reason why the woman concealed the lower part of her face, he passed round word to the Coroner and the jury that it was needless for the yashmak to be removed. Madame Coralie therefore gave her evidence holding the silken covering over her mouth, and, as only her black eyes were visible, she presented a weird figure. Many of the illustrated papers had pictures of her in the odd dress, and many were the comments thereon. All of which, as Madame Coralie knew and probably counted upon, was good for business.

The woman stated that she received Lady Branwin on the night of the murder for the purpose of diagnosing her case, that she might be treated as to complexion and figure. Lady Branwin decided to remain for the night, and Madame Coralie herself told this to Miss Branwin when the girl called at the shop—according to instructions from her mother—on her way to the theatre. Lady Branwin was then in bed, and Madame did not see her again until the next morning at seven when she went to rouse her and discovered that she was dead.

"The window looking into the court was open," said the witness, "although I had closed it on the previous night. I did not lock it, of course, as no one ever entered the court, and none of the windows of the ground-floor bedrooms were locked."

"Then the window could easily have been opened from the outside?" asked the Coroner, making notes.

"Oh, yes. It was not even snicked," replied the witness. "There was no necessity, as no one could enter the court save from the house, or by the door in the court wall."

It was proved very conclusively that the court door had not been opened since Madame had taken the house. Also, the door leading into the court from the building had rarely been opened.

"No one wanted to go into the court," explained Madame again, and insisted upon this point. "I left Lady Branwin quite cheerful, in bed, at about ten minutes to eight o'clock, and came up, to the still-room about five minutes to eight. My assistant, Zobeide, was in the room, and so was my husband, Mr. Vail. Also I believe that two other girls of mine, Badoura and Parizade, were behind the curtain of the room attending to some hair and skin washes. My husband drew my attention to this fact."

"Are you sure it was five minutes to eight when you were in the room?" was the Coroner's question.

"I am positive," was the emphatic reply. "Eddy—my husband—mentioned as he went out that it was five minutes after eight, and I had been talking to him for ten minutes, more or less."

The result of this statement was that Edmund Vail was called, and he proved that what his wife had asserted was correct. He mentioned (by talking with his fingers) to Zobeide, who was deaf, that it was five minutes to eight o'clock immediately before his wife entered. He talked to her of business—private business—for some time, and left the house by the side door ten minutes later. Zobeide—who gave evidence through an interpreter of the deaf and dumb language—corroborated this evidence, and it was well established that Madame Coralie had been with the two witnesses from five minutes to eight until five minutes past eight. This being the case, since Lady Branwin was murdered at eight o'clock, Madame Coralie could not be guilty of the crime, yet before this evidence had been given several people had hinted at her complicity; but what was said by Vail and Zobeide, and indeed afterwards by Badoura and Parizade, provided her with an alibi beyond question.

Madame Coralie was afterwards recalled and questioned about the diamonds. She denied all knowledge of these, saying that Lady Branwin brought in a red morocco bag with a label attached, of which she took the greatest care. "She did not mention to me what was in the bag," said Madame, emphatically; "but when I tucked her in for the night she placed it under her pillow. I never thought of asking any questions."

The witness also stated that she had never possessed any key to the court wall door, and did not recognise the one produced to the jury. The house door leading into the court was locked, and the key had been left, with others, on a nail in the still-room. "No one could have got into the court by that door on that night," stated Madame Coralie. "As to the remaining door, out of which my husband went when he left me, it is at the end of the long passage on the ground floor, and leads into a right-of-way which can be approached from Walpole Lane. I locked this myself after I had seen Miss Branwin at the street door, and took the key to my room. No one could have entered the house after that, as both this side door and the street door were locked when I and my assistants retired to bed."

Audrey's evidence was confined to the fact that her mother had taken the two thousand pounds' worth of diamonds to get certain of them reset. She had intended to take them straight to the jeweller, but having arranged to consult with Madame Coralie, and subsequently to remain for the night, she had taken the bag out of the motorcar and into the house. The label produced was in her mother's handwriting, and Audrey stated Lady Branwin's fancy for labelling anything she took out of doors.

On the whole, as the Coroner remarked, the evidence was satisfactory. If it did not prove who had committed the murder, it certainly exonerated all who were in the house. It had been proved that Madame Coralie and her four assistants slept in two rooms which opened into one another, and also that Madame herself had been with other people at the very time when the crime —according to the medical evidence—had been committed. Undoubtedly, robbery was the motive for the committal of the crime, and probably the strangling had been unpremeditated. Lady Branwin—this was the Coroner's reading of what had happened—had gone to sleep with the diamonds under her pillow, as Madame Coralie had stated. It was only reasonable to believe that she had awakened to find the robber removing the jewels. Her natural outcry was prevented immediately by the strangulation, since the assassin—as the man had become—could silence her in no other way. Then the criminal had escaped by the window through which he had entered, and through the door of the court wall. The dropping of the label, which possibly had been loosely tied to the bag, was a positive clue to the way in which the man had got away, and the presence of the skeleton key in the door was further evidence. These things being taken into consideration, it was apparent that no blame could be attached to Madame Coralie or to her assistants, and there was not the slightest breath of suspicion against them in any way. "The jury," added the Coroner, "would be well advised to return an open verdict."

The result of this speech, and a recollection of the meagre evidence placed before them, was the verdict which Ralph Shawe had predicted. "Wilful murder against some person or persons unknown," was the statement of the foreman, and the inquest ended with the belief in many minds that the murder of Lady Branwin would have to be added to the already long list of undiscovered crimes. Chattering and arguing, and greatly disappointed that nothing more tangible had resulted from the proceedings, everyone went his or her way, and the reporters hastened to their several papers with details, more or less veracious, of all that had taken place. But one fact was certain— that the murder, so far, was a mystery.

Lady Branwin was duly buried at Kensal Green, amidst a large concourse of people, and many were the letters and telegrams of condolence which Sir Joseph received. For a week or so paragraphs appeared in the papers suggesting possible clues, and the offer of one thousand pounds reward prompted many people to keep the matter of the crime in their minds. Also some busybody wrote to the journals insisting that the Turkish Shop should be closed; but it was pointed out that Madame Coralie had always conducted her business respectably, and that neither she nor her assistants were to blame in any way for what had taken place. It was, therefore, scarcely fair that the woman should lose her means of livelihood for not preventing what was beyond her power to prevent. Finally, after a nine days' wonder, the matter of the crime was permitted to drop into oblivion, so far as the general public were concerned. Lady Branwin, as someone observed, was dead and buried, and the secret of her murder was buried with her. Within a month the wretched woman and her sensational death were forgotten, and the Turkish Shop continued to open its doors.

"But there is a falling-off," sighed Madame Coralie. "Some women won't come—just as if I could help that miserable Lady Branwin dying in the way she did. I wish she had died anywhere but in my house. But it's all over, and I am ruined."

However, Madame Coralie was not ruined, for business speedily picked up again; also it was not "all over," for in the dark at least one person was trying to trace the assassin. This was Ralph Shawe, and he attended to the matter because of Audrey's wish and for the sake of his own happiness.

"I shall never marry you," Audrey stated, when returning from the funeral, "until the truth about my mother's death is made public."

"It seems impossible to discover the truth," said Ralph, gloomily.

"Then we shall never become husband and wife," was Audrey's reply; and to this decision she firmly adhered.

CHAPTER V.

SIR JOSEPH'S INTENTIONS

In time Sir Joseph Branwin gradually recovered his usual rude health, although there was no doubt that the unexpected and tragic death of his wife had shaken his system severely. But his feeling for her decease was not one of regret. Doubtless he had once loved her in an animal way, which might have had its beginning in a purer affection, when the rustic lovers wandered as boy and girl through the Bleakleigh Woods in Somersetshire. But since the big man had become a prominent personage in the political, social and stockbroking worlds, the uncomely looks of the poor woman had rapidly become offensive to his more cultivated taste. He was annoyed by her unwieldy appearance, by her simple manners; and it irritated him that she was not sufficiently educated to shine in the circles to which his wealth procured him admission. The rich setting of success suited to a diamond was thrown away on a common stone. And Lady Branwin—as Sir Joseph wrathfully told himself on many occasions—was merely an ordinary pebble on the beach.

In his daughter Audrey the millionaire could have found the hostess he required for the gorgeous mansion on Camden Hill. She had been born in the purple of wealth; she had been admirably educated; and, besides being an exceptionally pretty girl, her manners were attractive. But Sir Joseph had never loved this daughter of the wife he disliked, even though he was her father. Audrey was far too frank and honest for him, and did not seem to appreciate her advantages as the only child and heiress of a wealthy man. Her preference was for the simple life, and she found the frivolous doings and trifling chatter of society excessively boring. Also she had set her affections on a young man who, as yet, occupied no position in the world. Branwin did not mind if Audrey married a pauper, so long as that pauper possessed a title; but that she should wish to become the wife of a commoner who had yet to make his way in the world was a heinous sin in the successful parvenu's eyes. Finally, Sir Joseph had always resented the sex of Audrey. He had ardently desired an heir, and it was one of his grievances against the unhappy Lady Branwin that she had not presented him with a son. Now that the stumbling-block of an objectionable wife had been removed Sir Joseph saw a chance of realising his ambition. Before he rose from his sick-bed he determined to marry again as speedily as possible, in the hope that a male child would be born to inherit his wealth and title. Then Audrey could marry her barrister, and he would wash his hands of her once and for all. Branwin would not have admitted his feelings to the world, but in his heart he was thankful that his wife was dead.

Advised by the doctor, the millionaire prepared forthwith to remove to Brighton for a few weeks' fresh air; but when Audrey offered dutifully to accompany him, he refused brusquely. The father and daughter were at breakfast when she made the offer which was so rudely declined, and Sir Joseph, who prided himself on never letting the grass grow under his feet—so he put it—hinted to the girl that some day he would provide her with a stepmother. This point in the conversation he reached by easy stages, and began by advising her to cultivate Mrs. Mellop during his absence.

"Now your poor mother is out of the way," growled Sir Joseph, using the adjective as a grudging concession to the dead, "you can go about with Mrs. Mellop. She's a fool, but amusing and clever in her own way. As she's a widow with a limited income, you can offer her money if you like. She'll jump at the chance of doing the season for nothing. Then you can go to the theatres, garden-parties, and all the rest of the frivolities you like."

"I don't like such things," replied the girl, wearily. "I have been to so many, and they are nearly always the same—just like a stale circus. Besides, how can I go out when poor mother is scarcely cold in her grave?"

"I wish you wouldn't harp on that, Audrey," snapped Branwin, irritably, and rose from his chair. "You're always talking about your mother."

"Isn't it natural, papa? I loved her."

"Oh, it goes without speaking that you loved her; but she had a great many faults, my dear."

"Bury them with her, then," said Audrey, turning white with anger.

Sir Joseph, who still retained many habits of his youth, lighted his pipe in the breakfast-room, and turned with a bullying air. "I intend to," said he, harshly, "along with all memory of her. I shall make a funeral of the whole thing. She never understood her position or my position, and was—"

Audrey rose quickly, with a look of pain. "Papa," she said slowly, "I know that you did not love my mother. But she is dead, and died in a very painful way. My memory of her is concerned wholly with her kind heart and her many kind actions. Surely your recollections must be similar. You must have loved her, since you went back to Bleakleigh to marry her, after you had made your money."

"I was a romantic young fool, my girl, and, seeing that I had already got the start in life, I should have left Bleakleigh and your mother alone. But I said I'd come back and marry her, and I did, more fool I. Ah!"—Sir Joseph drew a deep breath—"if I did want to make a fool of myself I should have married Flora instead of Dora."

"Who is Flora?" asked Audrey. "I know that my mother's name was Dora, and—"

"Flora is, or was, your mother's sister, for I don't know if she's alive or dead. She was the clever one, and nearly as pretty as your mother, who was always a fool. But I was caught by the prettier face, and so married Dora—to my cost. Well"—Sir Joseph waved his arm, as though dismissing the subject —"she is dead and gone, so let us talk no more about her."

"I think it will be as well, papa, since you find nothing but bad to say about her," remarked Audrey, wincing at her father's brusque speech.

"I don't say anything bad," retorted Branwin, sharply. "Your mother was a good woman, and kind-hearted, and all that sort of thing. But she was a fool, and I should never have married her."

"Perhaps if you had married my Aunt Flora it would have been better!" said Audrey, sarcastically.

"It would. You are right there, my girl. Flora had brains and a will of her own, and would have been a help to a man, instead of a hindrance."

"You never mentioned my aunt to me before."

"There was no need. I wished to forget all that lot and all that time of poverty and struggle. But your mother must have—"

"She never did," interrupted the girl, quickly. "Until you mentioned the name just now, I never knew that I had an aunt. If you think so much of her, why not seek her out and marry her? The Deceased Wife's Sister Bill is law now, and you can make her the second Lady Branwin."

Sir Joseph winced at the scorn in the young voice. "No!" said he. "I have had enough of the Arkwright family. I married one sister; I don't intend to marry the other, let alone the fact that I don't know where she is. She may be married—she may be dead. I don't care. For me, Flora is as dead as Dora, and when I marry again—" He hesitated.

Audrey clasped her hands together tightly, and her face was whiter than pearls. "I spoke in joke," she said, in a low voice. "Surely, papa, you will not marry again?"

"Why should I not?" cried Branwin, irritably. "I am not so very old. I want someone to sit at the head of my table and to receive my guests."

"I can do that, papa."

"You!" said the millionaire, contemptuously. "Oh, yes, so long as it suits your own purpose. But when you feel inclined you will marry that young fool."

"Ralph is not a fool, papa." Audrey drew herself up. "Everyone says that he is extremely clever, and has a great future before him."

"Well, it couldn't very well be behind him," said Sir Joseph, sneeringly. "It's all rubbish, Audrey; you must marry a title."

"I shall marry Ralph, and no one else," said Audrey, fiercely.

"We'll see about that," roared the millionaire, indignant at being thus defied.

"Don't you know that I can turn you out of this house without a single penny? And I will, too, if you dare to disobey me."

Audrey clenched her hands to keep herself from speaking, and turned away to look out of the window. What her father said was perfectly true. She was an absolute pauper, dependent on his whim and fancy. Never having been taught how to earn her own living, she could see nothing but starvation ahead if Sir Joseph chose to carry out his threat. And that he would do so she felt very certain, as she knew from experience how brutal was his nature when aroused to action by opposition. In the meantime, and until she had consulted with Ralph, it was wiser not to fan the flame of his wrath to fiercer heat. Silence on this occasion was veritably golden.

"Listen to me," said Branwin, somewhat mollified by his daughter's silence, which he mistook for victory. "For a few months at least we must mourn in the conventional way for your mother. During that time you shall be the mistress of my house, with Mrs. Mellop to help you, since you are more or less inexperienced."

"I don't want Mrs. Mellop in the house," cried Audrey, glowing with anger.

"It is not what you want, but what I wish," said her father, tartly. "Mrs. Mellop must come here on a visit to look after you, and see that you act properly as mistress. Meanwhile I shall look out for a husband for you amongst some of these pauper noblemen, who will be glad enough to sell a title for your dowry. Not a word," he cried, raising his voice, when he saw that she was about to speak. "And I may tell you straightly, Audrey, that I wish you to marry at the end of our necessary period of mourning, as I do not think you will get on with your stepmother."

"My—my—my stepmother!" stammered the girl, aghast.

"Yes," said the man, curtly; and the two stared at one another until Sir Joseph, unable to bear the reproach in his daughter's eyes, broke into a furious rage. He felt that he could only meet that look and defend his position by giving way to an outburst of temper. "Why do you stand there without a word, and look as though I had told you I was about to commit a crime? Why shouldn't I marry and be happy? I was never happy with your mother, and you are ready enough to leave me for that barrister sweep. Yes, I'm going to give you a stepmother—in name only, that is, for you will be out of this house, and married to the man I choose for you, before my wife enters."

"I shall assuredly be out of the house before the second Lady Branwin appears," said Audrey, very white but very courageous. "I owe that much to my mother's memory."

"Leave your mother's name out of it."

"But," went on the girl, just as though she had not been interrupted, "I go out to marry Ralph, and not a husband of your choosing."

"You'll do what you're told, or starve," said her father, gruffly. "Let us have no more of this nonsense." He looked at his watch. "The motor is at the door, and I have to catch the Brighton train. I made up my mind to have an explanation before I left. That you should receive my expressed wishes in this way, when I am still weak from illness, shows how much you really care for me. But you understand."

"I understand that you intend to marry a second time, and that I am to be the mistress of this house until your wife enters it."

"Quite so; and you understand also that you are to ask Mrs. Mellop to come and stay here during my absence. Good! That's all. Good-bye," and without offering to kiss her, the man walked to the door.

"Papa," cried Audrey, before he could reach it, and struck with a sudden thought, "are you going to marry Mrs. Mellop?"

"No," retorted Sir Joseph, pulling open the door with a swing, "I am going to marry Miss Rosy Pearl"; and, flinging the name at her with a snarl, he marched out sullenly. The way in which Audrey had received his news was displeasing to a man who always had his own way.

The girl sank into a chair, for her limbs now refused to support her, although pride had hitherto held her up. With a blank, bewildered stare she looked round the dainty, bright breakfast-room, the white walls of which were painted gracefully with cupids and wreaths of flowers bound with knots of airy blue ribbon. Sorrow seemed out of place in so frivolous an apartment; yet its mere beauty enhanced the grief felt by the girl. The loss of her mother had been terrible to her, for although mother and daughter, educationally speaking, were leagues asunder, yet they had been greatly attached, and Audrey loved the uncouth, stupid woman at whom so many people laughed. And Audrey alone had been kind to poor Lady Branwin, who was scorned even by her own husband. No one regretted the simple creature's death but her daughter, who was unlike her in every way. As for Sir Joseph, Audrey saw that he was quite glad to be relieved of his ill-fated wife's presence.

Now he intended to marry again, and after the first feeling of natural resentment Audrey could not condemn him. Had her father only broken the news more kindly; had he only behaved less like a bully and more like a parent, and had he delayed to announce his determination for a few months, the girl would have received the intelligence differently. But the information coming with such indecent haste, coupled with his fiat that she was not to think of marrying Ralph Shawe, had brought the worst elements in Audrey's nature to the front. Her affections were deep and her temper was strong, so she felt anxious to resent the insult conveyed by the entire interview. But reflection calmed her early determination to leave the house before her domestic tyrant could return from Brighton. She had nowhere to go to, and she had no money, so it was necessary to wait for at least a time before deciding what to do. But she arose with a shudder, and felt that the luxury around was repellent to her. In fact, her feeling was that she dwelt in the house of a stranger, so hostile and self-centred did her father now appear to be. And yet, even at the best, they had never been parent and child.

"I shall see Ralph and tell him, and be guided by what he says," Audrey murmured to herself. "But—who is Rosy Pearl?"

She had never heard the name, and yet in some way it sounded familiar. As she walked out of the breakfast-room reflecting on her father's abrupt announcement, and wondering what the future Lady Branwin was like, a servant respectfully informed her that Mrs. Mellop had arrived and was in the drawing-room. Audrey frowned, as she felt that, after such a trying interview, it would be somewhat difficult to put up with the widow's frivolous chatter. However, while she remained under her father's roof, she felt bound to obey his orders, and remembered that Mrs. Mellop was to be invited to stay during Sir Joseph's absence at Brighton. She therefore composed her face, and rubbed her cheeks to bring a little colour into them. When she opened the drawing-room door Mrs. Mellop rushed at her, cooing like a dove.

"You dear child, you sweet child, my heart aches for you," said the widow, who was all chiffons and scent, and gush and restlessness. "This dreadful death, the illness of your poor father"—she put a tiny lace handkerchief to her eyes—"it's too awful for words."

"Thank you," said Audrey, coldly, and then irrelevantly asked a question which haunted her mind, and was on the top of her tongue. "Mrs. Mellop, you usually know everyone. Who is Rosy Pearl?"

Mrs. Mellop stared aghast. "My dear child," she said, in a shocked tone, "you should know nothing about such a creature."

"A creature! What creature?" asked Audrey, colouring vividly.

"She is a music-hall artist," said Mrs. Mellop, solemnly—"a painted butterfly."

CHAPTER VI.

AUDREY'S KNIGHT-ERRANT

"A painted butterfly!" Audrey's lip curled at the phrase. It exactly described the kind of woman her father's animal nature would be drawn to. In her mind's eye she saw the pathetic figure of her mother trying to recover her faded prettiness with Madame Coralie's assistance, so as to win back a love that required to be stimulated by mere beauty of form and face. And a music-hall artist!

"Is she respectable?" asked Audrey, suddenly.

"Oh, quite," said Mrs. Mellop, laughing artificially. "But I wonder why you ask?"

"Oh, I merely heard her name," answered Audrey, quietly. "Why do you laugh?"

Mrs. Mellop tried to stop tittering. "Oh, my dear, I can see it all," she said gaily; "your face betrays you. To think that he should run after her!"

"He? Who?" asked Audrey, drawing up her slight figure, and wincing at the thought that this gossiping woman was about to pronounce her father's name.

"Why, Mr. Shawe, of course."

"Mr. Shawe!" The girl grew violently red. "He doesn't run after Miss Pearl."

"Oh, I know he loves you, dear," said the widow, in a tantalising way. "Anyone can see that when he's in the room, and everyone knows that he is as good as engaged to you, although your father won't hear of your marrying the poor man. But"—she made a gesture of contempt—"he's a man after all."

"Have you any ground to say that Mr. Shawe runs after—"

"Only your face, dear, and your strong desire to know about Miss Pearl."

"If that is all," said Audrey, with quiet scorn, "you can exonerate Ralph from being an admirer of Miss Pearl. I know that he is true to me."

"And you call him Ralph," said her visitor, glibly; "my dear, what will your father say? He wants you to marry Lord Anvers."

"What! That puny little racing man? He has never said anything to me about it, Mrs. Mellop, and if he does I shall certainly refuse to entertain the idea. And since you have hinted that all the world knows my business," she went on, looking the widow straight in the face, "you can inform everyone, on my authority, that I intend to marry Mr. Shawe, and that we are engaged."

"With your father's consent, dear?"

"Never mind." Audrey was glad to see that Mrs. Mellop's attention had been taken off the name of Rosy Pearl, as she did not want, for obvious reasons, to talk about the lady. "My father and I understand one another."

"Oh, I dare say, dear; but do your father and Mr. Shawe understand one another? I'm sure I hope so, as it means so much money toMr. Shawe."

"Ralph marries me for myself, and not for my money," said the girl, hotly.

"No doubt, dear; but he's got an eye to the main chance, like the rest of us."

Audrey again looked straightly at the pretty, artificial, frivolous face. "I think not," she said coolly; "Ralph is not like other men."

"Ah!"—Mrs. Mellop became serious—"we all think men are angels until we marry them, dear. And this Rosy Pearl attracts—"

"She doesn't attract Ralph," interrupted Miss Branwin, resolutely, and saw the necessity of drawing another red herring across the trail. "I told you that I merely asked about her because the name had struck my fancy. And now I have to give you a message from my father."

"Yes, dear?" said Mrs. Mellop, anxiously; for now that Sir Joseph was a widower she had a sudden vision of possible matrimony.

"He has gone to Brighton for a week or so, since the doctor has ordered him the sea air. He told me to ask you to chaperon me while he was absent, as he does not like the idea of my being alone. But I am afraid you will find it rather dull here. I am in mourning, you know."

The widow gasped with delight. That Sir Joseph should select her from amongst all his friends to stay at Camden Hill as a temporary companion to his only daughter surely showed that he took a deep interest in her; and such interest could only mean that marriage— "Oh," cried Mrs. Mellop, shutting her eyes to conjure up more clearly the golden vision, "how sweet of you! I like a quiet time, as my poor husband did not leave me very well off, and it is so expensive to go about in London; besides, your darling mother was a good friend to me, and my heart is wrung."

Audrey knew perfectly well that Lady Branwin had been a very good friend indeed to Mrs. Mellop, who was something of a parasite, and knew also that the lady's heart was not wrung in the least. She had used the phrase because it sounded well, and because she wished to ingratiate herself with the heiress. Not that Mrs. Mellop was a bad-hearted woman. She was simply frivolous and incapable of feeling any deep emotion. In her own silly way she had been attached to the late Lady Branwin, because she had found her a useful friend. In the same way she was prepared to lavish her shallow affections on Audrey.

Mrs. Mellop duly arrived with many boxes, and was given a charming suite of apartments, luxuriously furnished with all that civilisation could provide in the way of comfort. Certainly the life was somewhat quiet, as Audrey rarely left the grounds, and even when in the house preferred to be alone with her books and music. But the surroundings were costly, the food was excellent, and there were innumerable servants ready to obey the widow's beck and call. Mrs. Mellop, during her three weeks' stay, felt that she was already the wife of the millionaire, and took advantage of the opportunity to go out daily in one of the luxurious motor-cars to shop extensively and run up many bills, on the assumption that Sir Joseph would certainly pay them when he proposed. And the shopkeepers, who hitherto had been rather shy of the pretty little widow, trusted her readily when they knew that she was chaperoning Miss Branwin, and saw that she used Sir Joseph's up-to-date vehicles. Also, she might have dropped a hint or two that she had come to stay at the Camden Hill house. But, at all events, during that halcyon time Mrs. Mellop assuredly gathered together a wardrobe and a quantity of jewellery which stood her in good service afterwards when the gates of this millionaire Eden closed behind her. But as yet she never believed that they would close; or, if they did, that she would be within as the second Lady Branwin.

Meanwhile, since the chaperon was discreet, and Sir Joseph was at the seaside, Audrey saw a great deal of Ralph. Because of her mourning for her mother she could not meet him as usual in Kensington Gardens; but he came to afternoon tea, and sometimes to dinner. Mrs. Mellop, only too anxious to get Audrey married, so that she could prosecute her matrimonial plans when the millionaire returned, was rarely present at these meetings, or if she was speedily got out of the way on the plea of fatigue, or that she had to write letters. Audrey might have had no chaperon, so far as Mrs. Mellop was concerned, and it was evident that the little widow had taken the hint given by the girl at that first candid interview. But Mrs. Mellop wrote Sir Joseph gushing letters about his sweet child, without mentioning the almost constant presence of the young barrister.

Audrey and Ralph did not talk like lovers now. The girl was consumed by a fierce desire to hunt down the assassin of her mother, and talked of little else but the chance of tracing the murderer. Ralph assured her that he had kept in touch with Inspector Lanton and with the police generally, to say nothing of his frequent visits to the detectives at Scotland Yard. "But nothing can be found out," said the barrister, sadly.

"Something must be found out," cried Audrey at the last of these interviews; "and if the police fail we must succeed."

"But your father—"

Audrey made a gesture of contempt. "My father thinks that he has done his duty by offering this thousand pounds' reward. He will not lift a finger to find the assassin of my poor mother. He is glad she is dead."

"Oh! surely not," remarked Ralph, rather shocked by this blunt speech.

"Surely yes," said the girl, bitterly. "I did not tell you before, Ralph, because I was ashamed to tell you, but my father is going to marry again."

Shawe was startled. "Mrs. Mellop?" he asked, after a bewildered pause.

"No. Although his mere invitation to Mrs. Mellop that she should be my chaperon has caused her to entertain ideas of marriage. Do you know Rosy Pearl?"

"The music-hall dancer? Yes."

"Well, she is to be the future Lady Branwin."

"Oh! Audrey," cried Shawe, greatly astonished, "you must be mistaken."

"I had the information from my father's own lips," insisted Audrey. "What do you know of this woman?"

"Very little. She is a handsome woman in the style of Juno, and is a wonderful dancer. I heard that Sir Joseph had been paying attentions to her, but I did not dream that he contemplated marriage with her."

"He does, then. Mrs. Mellop calls her a painted butterfly."

"She's a very substantial butterfly," said Shawe, with the ghost of a smile; for Audrey was too much in earnest to tolerate lightness of any sort. "And I believe she is rather a respectable woman."

"Such a woman as should stand in the place of my dead mother?" asked Audrey, looking searchingly at his face.

"No," rejoined Ralph, promptly. "And yet I can't say that I have heard a word against Rosy Pearl. I simply mean that you would not like one who had been a dancer to be your stepmother."

"I certainly should not," said Audrey, decisively; "and yet if I object, my

42

father—as he hinted—is quite capable of turning me out of doors. He will do that in any case, unless I marry Lord Anvers."

"What!" Shawe flushed. "That little reptile, who—"

"I know a great deal about him," said Audrey, cutting him short, "and I do not wish to hear any more. I shall leave this house rather than marry him, and rather than see this Pearl woman occupying my mother's place."

"Come to me, darling," said Ralph, holding out his arms. "Let us get married at once and defy your father."

"I should lose my money then, dear."

"Oh, what does that matter? I want you and not your money."

"Dear"—she placed her hands on his shoulders and looked deeply into his keen grey eyes, now filled with the love-light—"I am too fond of you to allow you to ruin yourself for my sake."

"Ruin myself"—his arms slipped round her waist, and he placed his cheek against hers—"how could you do that, you silly darling?"

"Very easily," she replied, in a tired voice; for all she had gone through was wearing her out. "You have just enough money to get along with, as a bachelor. But what is enough for one is not enough for two, in spite of the proverb. If I married you in haste we should both repent at leisure. Not only would we be poor, but my father, being thwarted, would do his best to hinder you."

"He could not do that," declared Shawe, who believed that he was capable of defying the world, much less Sir Joseph.

"Oh, yes, he could, and he would. He would use his money and his influence to prevent any solicitor giving you a brief. He would turn people against you, and would give you a bad name. I know my father's hard nature, and his pertinacious way of following up things. My poor mother told me how he had ruined and disgraced several people who had crossed his path."

Ralph pushed her slightly away from him, and taking her hands looked into her eyes. "And do you think that I am ready to give you up because your father would act in this way?" he demanded. "I am not afraid of Sir Joseph, or of any man. Two people can play at every game, and if your father tries to crush me, he will find that I am not a man to be cast out of his path. If he has money, I have brains, and I am quite willing to pit my intellect against his wealth. Hang Sir Joseph, and a dozen like him; I beg your pardon, dear, for, after all, he is your father."

"A father in name only," said Audrey, admiring her lover's indignation, which was righteous and masterful in her eyes. "You know what I think of him, Ralph. I wish I had a better opinion of his nature, but my experience and my mother's experience—what she has told me—show that my father is a hard man with a strong will. He does not care what anyone suffers so long as he gets his way. The mere fact that he has already decided to marry again—and marry a music-hall artist—shows how callous he is. It's like Hamlet's mother," ended Audrey, bitterly, "with the funeral baked meats not yet cold, as in the play."

Ralph took a turn up and down the room, with a frowning brow and looking deeply perplexed. "What's to be done, then?" he demanded, stopping before the girl. "Things can't go on in this way. You won't marry me—"

"For your own sake I won't marry you at present," interpolated the girl.

"Audrey, you say that your father intends to marry Rosy Pearl as soon as he possibly can without shocking public opinion. When he does, you can't stay in the house, as you declare, and also you say that you will not marry Lord Anvers. Your father, so you tell me, is bound to turn you out if you refuse to obey him, so it seems to me that the evil day is only postponed for a few months."

"I daresay, Ralph. But much may happen in a few months. For one thing, we —you and I—may find out who killed my mother. And even if you had money and could offer me a home, I should refuse to marry you until that truth comes to light."

"But it's impossible, and, after all, can do little good."

"It's not impossible, and can at least punish the assassin. No one but myself cares for my poor mother's memory, and I must avenge her death. Come, dear"—she placed her arms round his neck—"you will be my knight-errant?"

"Yes," said Ralph, promptly, and kissed her. "But where shall I begin?"

"Begin?" replied Audrey, seriously. "Begin at Madame Coralie's—at the Pink Shop."

"At the Pink Shop?" repeated her lover. "Good! I shall start to-morrow."

CHAPTER VII.

Influenced by Audrey's love, and touched by her devotion to her mother's memory, Shawe had committed himself beyond withdrawal to the *rôle* of knight-errant. Like those of old he was going out, if not to redress a cruel wrong, at least to revenge it. He quite understood why the girl wished to punish the assassin of her mother; but he could not see how the fulfilment of the task she had set him would bring about their marriage. Sir Joseph cared so little for his late wife that he was quite willing to bury the bitter fact of her existence in oblivion. To reawaken recollections of the objectionable Lady Branwin by bringing her murderer to justice, and thus revive the whole terrible episode for the benefit of the public, would not be pleasing to the millionaire.

Moreover, if Shawe did accomplish his aim, Branwin would only pay to him the already promised reward. He would be ready enough to give the money, since he had ample means at his disposal, but he certainly would remain firm on the question of the marriage. Of course, Ralph knew well enough that Audrey would not fail him and would remain true. But since she refused to marry him because she fancied she would hinder his career, and since Sir Joseph certainly would disinherit her if she so persisted, and thus she would not bring him any money to aid that career, it seemed that there was but a faint hope she would become Mrs. Shawe. Still, he had promised, and it only remained for him to keep his promise, with the hope that events would so turn out that the desire of his heart might be fulfilled. With this idea in his mind Shawe returned to his chambers in the Temple and set about making a start. But it was like looking for a needle in a haystack.

In the first place, Shawe did not see how he could enter Madame Coralie's shop and ask questions from the woman and her assistants; yet, if he wished to learn anything, it was absolutely necessary to do so. Madame Coralie herself would certainly refuse to answer any questions, since Shawe was not an accredited agent of the police. Moreover, for obvious reasons connected with business, she wished the murder to be relegated to the list of undiscovered crimes. The trail assuredly started at the Pink Shop, as Audrey had stated; but if he could not find anyone likely to give him a clue to the beginning of things, Ralph disconsolately considered—and very sensibly— that there would be little chance of success. It was at this point of his meditations that he thought of Perry Toat.

It was a good idea, as she was the very person he required for this especial purpose. Peronella Toat—called Perry for business purposes—was a woman-detective with whom he had come into contact over a divorce case. It was mainly owing to her shadowing of the guilty couple that the petitioner had obtained his freedom, and the judge had complimented Miss Toat on the way in which she had managed the business. Moreover, as she was a woman, she would easily be able to penetrate into a shop entirely devoted to the needs of women, and once within those sacred walls might be able to learn what was necessary in the way of clues.

"I shall write to her at once," Shawe said to himself, and drew writing materials towards him. "She's a clever little woman, and I daresay can cajole or force Madame Coralie into answering what questions are necessary to be put; but I'm hanged if I can see where, or how, she's going to start."

His letter brought Miss Toat next day to his chambers at ten o'clock, before he started for the Courts. She was an undersized, colourless little woman, with a white face and drab-hued hair. Her mouth was firm, with thin, pale lips, and her eyes were of a sharp grey, almost steely in their glitter. Quietly arrayed in a tailor-made costume, she looked very businesslike, and her crisp, decisive manner showed that she knew the value of time. In silence she listened to Shawe's exposition of the case. "It's a difficult mystery to unravel," she said, when he had finished.

"Where's the mystery?" asked Ralph, somewhat surprised. "The murder was no doubt committed for the sake of the diamonds. The motive is clear."

"How did the assassin know that Lady Branwin had jewels with her?" asked Perry Toat, fixing her pale eyes on his face "How did he know the position of the room in which she slept, and how did he gain admission into the court?"

"I can answer that last question," said Shawe, easily. "He gained admission into the court by means of a skeleton key, which is now in the possession of the police. Inspector Lanton has it, I believe."

Miss Toat drummed on the table with her thin fingers, which were not unlike the claws of a bird of prey. "If the assassin used such a key," she remarked, "he must have examined the lock and have bought a key to fit. That would take some time, Mr. Shawe."

"Well?" asked the barrister, puzzled.

"Well," she repeated, raising her sandy eyebrows, "can't you see that the procuring of the key would take some time? Yet Lady Branwin slept at the Pink Shop on the spur of the moment, as it were, and merely had the diamonds with her by chance; since—according to her daughter—she was taking them to be reset by a jeweller. If I am right," added Miss Toat, with emphasis—"and I think that I am right in my surmise—the assassin must have had some idea beforehand that Lady Branwin would sleep in the room wherein she was murdered, and would have the diamonds with her."

"But if, as you say, she slept there on the spur of the moment—"

"Exactly. Therein lies the difficulty—the mystery to which I alluded. The arrangement of Lady Branwin to stay was decided in five minutes, let us say; yet the key to the door of the court must have taken a longer time to procure. And it is strange also," mused Perry Toat, "that the assassin should have known the plan of the shop. How did he learn that when within the court he would be able to gain entrance into the bedrooms, let alone the fact that he could not be sure any visitors were sleeping in them?"

"Then you infer," said Shawe, promptly, "that the assassin must be someone attached to the Pink Shop?"

"Why not—on the grounds that I have stated?"

"Because the evidence went to show that everyone connected with the business accounted for their time. Madame Coralie, her husband, Zobeide, Badoura, and Parizade, to give them their fantastical names, were in the room devoted to preparing the wares on or about the very time the murder was being committed, according to the medical evidence. Peri Banou was in the shop, and is the only person who was on the same floor as that of the bedroom wherein the crime took place. Do you accuse her?"

"I don't accuse anyone as yet. I shall go to the shop and ask questions."

Shawe shook his head sceptically. "If things are as you hint, no one will answer any questions."

"Oh, I think so," said Miss Toat, quietly. "I know how to ask questions."

"Madame Coralie may not allow you to enter the shop."

"Give me a five-pound note," said the detective lady, irrelevantly; and after Ralph had placed one in her hand, she continued: "With this I shall buy a few things to make me beautiful for ever"—there was a faint smile on her grey face as she spoke—"between whiles I shall keep my eyes open, and find out what I wish to know."

"If you do, you're a wonder," said the barrister, quickly, for he was very doubtful of the success of her enterprise.

"You can say that," said Miss Toat, in an unemotional tone, "when I indicate the assassin of Lady Branwin. Good-day."

"But when am I to see you again?" asked Ralph, following her to the door.

Perry Toat looked back with a demure face. "When I have something to report."

"You'll do your best?" Shawe urged her.

"I always do my best for my clients," she said, in a tone of faint rebuke.

"But in this case there is much money also."

"Oh, I shan't charge you much, Mr. Shawe."

"I am not alluding to that. I shall pay you well. But if you lay hands on the assassin you shall have the thousand pounds' reward offered by—"

Peronella Toat interrupted with a flushed face. "One thousand pounds!" she said, drawing a deep breath. "Yes, I forgot that. I must earn it. If I do, I can gain my heart's desire."

"What is that?"

She smiled demurely. "A husband," was her reply, and she vanished.

Ralph went back to his room with a look of wonder. It seemed impossible that this shadow of a woman should ever be able to gain a husband, even if she had a bribe of one thousand pounds to offer her bridegroom.

For more than a week Miss Toat remained absent, and during that period she haunted Walpole Lane. She sought out Madame Coralie, and declared that she wanted her complexion improved. The owner of the Pink Shop thought that there was much room for improvement, and did wonders for the five-pound note. This was a less charge than she usually made, but since the murder, business had been bad with Madame Coralie, and she was willing enough to capture small fish, as the big ones, for the moment, would not be enticed into her net. After Miss Toat's complexion had been renovated that wily person decided to undergo a course of treatment for hair and figure, which necessitated two or three nights' stay in the shop. It was for this reason that she wrote to Shawe and asked him to forward twenty pounds. He did so rather ruefully, for he was not well off, and the search for the assassin promised to be expensive. However, it was for Audrey's sake, so Ralph parted with very good grace with his hard-earned money.

Having thus obtained funds in plenty, the detective took up her abode in the very bedroom wherein Lady Branwin had been murdered. She knew that it was the fatal chamber, as she had seen the plan of the shop, which the daily papers had published when the murder was the sensation of the day. Madame Coralie was rather vexed when Miss Toat mentioned this artlessly to her, on being installed in the room.

"That murder will ruin my business," said the Medea of Walpole Lane, gloomily.

"Oh, I don't think so," said her client, sweetly. "I don't mind in the least sleeping in the room where a crime has been committed."

"You are a very sensible woman, Miss Toat," said Madame Coralie, energetically. "All my friends seem to have deserted me since the death of Lady Branwin."

"They will come back, Madame." Miss Toat nodded vigorously. "The event will soon pass out of their minds. By the way, has anything been heard likely to show who is guilty?"

"No," said Madame Coralie, savagely. "I wish I could find out. I'd kill the man for ruining my business."

"He will be killed in any case, and by the law," said Miss Toat, in a silky voice. "Let us hope that he will be caught."

"Amen to that. But I don't think he ever will."

Plainly, little evidence was to be got out of Madame Coralie, and probably she knew nothing of the truth. If she did, she would assuredly have denounced the culprit to the police, if only out of revenge. Miss Toat saw that she would get no clue in that direction, and submitted herself to the treatment for hair and figure with very good grace. But the proprietress of the Pink Shop would have been ill-pleased had she seen the little woman slipping about the premises in the dead of night like an eel. Being tiny and light-footed—especially since she wore list slippers—Miss Toat, when all the inmates of the place were buried in slumber, would take a dark lantern and steal round the rooms. She examined the shop itself, the passage running at the back and terminating in the door which opened on to the right-of-way, leading into Walpole Lane, and noticed that the house-door into the empty court was flush with those of the four bedrooms. To be precise—and Miss Toat in her investigation was very precise—a quartette of doors led to their several apartments, and the fifth door admitted anyone who was curious into the court. Miss Toat *was* curious, and as she found the key on a nail in the still-room—as had been mentioned in the evidence at the inquest—she opened the door and explored the court from end to end.

When her hair had been burnished to a soft golden hue, and her figure had been made less angular, she took an effusive leave of the magician, and went round to make inquiries about her of this person and that. During her stay in the shop, and by dexterous questioning, both by word of mouth and by means of the deaf-and-dumb language, Perry had found out a great deal which Madame Coralie would have rather she had not known. Armed with this knowledge, she went from pillar to post, and added to her stock of information, finally presenting herself by appointment at Shawe's chambers to report progress.

The barrister scarcely knew her; for, instead of looking like a drab nonentity, she appeared quite pretty in an artificial manner. He really thought that thus transmogrified she would be able to gain the husband she had hinted at, and complimented her on her changed appearance.

"It's all in the way of business," said Perry Toat, disdainfully, "and as soon as I conclude my task I shall revert to my former state."

"But why?" demanded Shawe, wondering if her vanity would allow this sacrifice.

But it appeared that Miss Toat had no vanity at all. "Madame Coralie's adornments are too conspicuous for one of my calling," she explained, "and I attract attention in quarters where I wish to be unknown. Better to be the ugly duckling, Mr. Shawe, for then I can be more successful in my profession."

This remark recalled Ralph to the business in hand. "I sincerely hope that you have been successful in this instance?" he said eagerly.

The woman, with her artificial air of youth and her garish mask of aggressive beauty, looked thoughtfully at the young man. "I have learnt a great deal which may be of use to you," she said slowly; "but I cannot say—so far as my opinion goes—that I have been successful."

"Oh!" Ralph dropped back into the chair whence he had risen, and seemed extremely disappointed. "Then you have failed?"

"I don't say that."

"In that case you must have succeeded."

"I don't say that either," remarked Miss Toat, drily.

"You must have done one or the other," cried Shawe, exasperated.

"No. I have learnt nothing very definite; but there are certain facts." She drummed on the table—her usual gesture when puzzled. "It is a very difficult case, Mr. Shawe."

"I know that, and for such a reason I placed it in your hands," he retorted.

Miss Toat nodded. "I am gratified by your opinion of my skill," she said politely. "All the same, you can't expect me to work miracles."

"Is a miracle required in this case?"

"I think so." She produced a mass of notes from her bag, and laid them down before the barrister. "There you will find all that I have been able to learn," she said to her employer. "They contain information about Madame Coralie—information which reveals much she would give her ears not to have known. Read these notes."

Ralph turned over the loose papers. "I would rather hear what you have discovered by word of mouth," he said fretfully; for this beating round the bush annoyed him. "In a word, Miss Toat, do you suspect anyone?"

"Yes, I do"—the detective leant forward with bright eyes—"but only theoretically. I suspect"—she paused for effect—"I suspect Madame Coralie herself as having strangled Lady Branwin."

CHAPTER VIII.

A MYSTERIOUS COMMUNICATION

Ralph stared at the woman, then threw himself back in his chair with a short laugh. He was greatly disappointed in the reply.

"It is ridiculous to believe or even hint that Madame Coralie should be guilty," he remarked sharply. "She proved a very clear alibi. No less than four people—her husband and her three assistants—proved that she was in the still-room when the crime was taking place below."

"Yes," assented Miss Toat, leaning her chin on her hand and her elbow on the table, "that is what puzzles me. The alibi is very clear, and yet—of course, you understand that I am merely theorising."

"Yes! Yes! Yes!"—Shawe made an irritable gesture, for the strain on his nerves was great—"but the idea is ridiculous. If you had accused that dumb girl, who was in the shop on the ground floor when the crime was committed, it would have been more feasible. The bedroom is on the ground floor also."

"I see no reason to accuse Peri Banou," said Miss Toat, quietly.

"And you see a reason to accuse Madame Coralie?"

"Yes. My theory is—"

"Oh, never mind your theory, Miss Toat. Come to facts."

The detective was not at all put out by his short temper, as she saw that his nerves were worn thin, and sympathised with him. With a quick movement she drew the loose notes to her own side of the table. "Very good," she said in a brisk, businesslike tone. "Let us come to facts, if you please. Do you know why Madame Coralie wears a yashmak?"

"Inspector Lanton hinted something about it to me when at the inquest. It is to add to the attractions of the Turkish shop—to make it more mysterious, as it were."

"Ah!"—Miss Toat raised her pencilled eyebrows—"then the inspector did not tell you the exact truth. I expect Madame Coralie asked him to keep it quiet for obvious reasons."

"Obvious they may be," said Ralph, impatiently, "but I can't see them."

"Why, they are plain enough. The wearing of the yashmak is partly by way of a good advertisement, as it suggests mystery, and partly—this is the real reason, I expect—it is worn from necessity."

"From necessity?" Shawe stared hard at his visitor.

"Madame Coralie has a disfiguring birthmark on her right cheek, which, extending over mouth and chin, spoils her good looks. And she must have had some beauty when younger. Strange, is it not, Mr. Shawe, that she who can restore another woman's looks can do nothing with her own?"

"How do you know that she is marked in this way?"

"I saw it when she was asleep."

"But how did you enter her bedroom?" asked Ralph, much astonished.

The detective laughed. "When everyone was asleep I stole about the house investigating in list slippers and with a bull's-eye lantern. Madame Coralie lays aside her yashmak when in bed, so I easily saw that which she wishes to keep concealed."

"But why should she so very much want to conceal it?"

Miss Toat looked at him greatly amazed. "Have you not been listening to what I have been saying, Mr. Shawe? Why, if Madame's customers knew that she could not remove a birthmark from her face, it would be a case of 'Physician, heal thyself' with them. They would lose confidence, and—"

"Yes, yes!" Ralph assented impatiently, and waved his hand. "I understand now; very naturally they would doubt her capability, in spite of her reputation. But what has this birthmark to do with the murder?"

"Nothing," said Perry Toat, promptly; "yet I was glad enough to see it for all that, in connection with a case. But never mind," she broke off abruptly, "we can talk of that later. I tell you about the disfigurement because it is just as well that you should learn everything about a woman so closely connected with the death of Lady Branwin. Also, it will be a useful mark to know in case she tries to get rid of more diamonds."

"What!" Shawe jumped up with an exclamation. "Do you mean to say that she has pawned the diamonds? In that case she must be guilty."

"It would look like it; but I am only theorising, remember."

"Oh, hang your theories! I think—" He stopped short, conscious that he had been rude to the little woman. "I beg your pardon," he went on ceremoniously, "but my nerves are out of order. Don't be vexed with me. I apologise."

Miss Toat nodded in a friendly way. "I quite understand," she said smoothly. "People unaccustomed to be mixed up with criminal matters usually do let their nerves get out of order, although I can't say that they usually apologise. There you have the advantage of the greater part of my clients. But to come to business. It is now some six or seven weeks since the murder. I discovered, by various inquiries, which I made here, there, and everywhere, that two months ago Madame Coralie was in deep water—financially. Now she is more prosperous." Miss Toat paused. "You can draw your own inference."

"You mean to say that she committed the murder in order to steal the diamonds, and has sold or pawned them to realise the spoil?"

Miss Toat nodded again. "That is my theory." The barrister put his hands into his pockets and began to pace the room, as was his custom when perplexed. "I don't see what evidence you have to support your theory," he remarked, after a pause.

"Well, as we agreed at our first interview, Lady Branwin only arranged in five minutes to sleep at the Pink Shop, and it was merely by chance that she had the diamonds with her. That the murder was committed for the sake of the jewels is positive, since they are missing. Yet any outside person could not have known that the unfortunate woman was possessed of those jewels at that particular time. Madame Coralie knew—"

"Pardon me," interrupted Shawe. "In my own hearing she declared that she did not know what Lady Branwin had in the red bag."

Miss Toat shrugged her shoulders. "Naturally, for her own sake, she would say that, Mr. Shawe. But the fact remains that owing to the rapidity and unexpectedness of Lady Branwin's decision to sleep at the shop no outsider could have arranged beforehand to commit the crime for the sake of the jewels."

"But the key in the outside door of the court was—"

"That might all have been arranged as a false clue to throw the police off the scent."

"I doubt it," said Shawe, decisively, "and remember that your theory is entirely destroyed by the very strong alibi of Madame Coralie. The woman could not have been in two places at once."

"Well," said Perry Toat, cautiously, "I stated that I suspected Madame Coralie had strangled Lady Branwin, but I did not say that she had actually committed the deed herself."

"Oh! Then you think she employed someone else to commit the murder?"

"Yes, and for her own sake was careful to provide the alibi we know of. Lady Branwin came at five o'clock to the shop, and was murdered, according to the medical evidence, about eight. Madame Coralie had, therefore, ample time to tell her accomplice that Lady Branwin possessed the diamonds. Also, as Lady Branwin talked frequently of coming for treatment, and Madame always refused her, the evening when she agreed to give the treatment might have been arranged. Madame could also explain to her accomplice about the door in the outer wall of the court, and have arranged for the window of the bedroom to be open. Then—well, the rest is easy."

"But the woman declared that the window was shut."

"Of course, for her own sake, in the same way that she declared her ignorance of the diamonds being in the red bag. I said lately," went on Miss Toat, in an apologetic manner, "that the key in the outer door of the court might have been arranged as a false clue. I am right in one way, as the key was, I fancy, left in the door to avert suspicion from Madame Coralie. But her accomplice must have entered and escaped in that way, and afterwards, when Lady Branwin was dead and buried and the inquest was over, she must have met her accomplice to share the spoil. Hence she is now in possession of money which, according to many people, she sadly needed."

"Have you traced the diamonds?" asked Ralph, abruptly.

"No; and it will not be an easy task to trace them, especially if they have been unset and sold as separate stones. But I am shortly going round the pawnshops and to various fences—you know what a fence is, a person who receives stolen goods, I suppose, Mr. Shawe?—and if Madame sold them or pawned them herself the mark may help to identify her."

"I think not," said Shawe, grimly, "as she would probably wear a veil."

"Certainly not a yashmak," said Miss Toat, quietly. "However, I can but make inquiries, as I say. Moreover, I shall go back to the shop again and ask further questions. But I think—so far as I can judge—that my theory is a correct one."

Ralph again walked the floor. "Who do you think is the accomplice?"

"I can't say," said the detective, promptly. "At first I thought that Madame's husband might be the one; but he was with her and the three assistants in the still-room, and can prove as strong an alibi as his wife."

"What sort of person is this husband, and what is his name?"

"Edward Vail is his name, and he is what you would call a wastrel," replied Perry Toat, quickly; "one of those dandified idiots who walk the streets and dress loudly in order to attract the eyes of women. He is good-looking in an effeminate way, and has never done a stroke of work in his life."

"Strange that so clever a woman as Madame Coralie should marry such a character."

"It is the clever women who generally make fools of themselves in this particular way," said Miss Toat, enigmatically. "However, I don't think Eddy Vail—he is usually called Eddy, which to my mind stamps his character—I don't think he is the accomplice, owing to the alibi, unless—" The little woman paused suggestively.

"Unless what?"

"Unless the three assistants have been bribed or threatened into providing the alibi. For her own sake, of course, Madame would say she was in the still-room; but Zobeide, Badoura and Parizade may have been bullied or cajoled into supporting a false statement."

"It is possible," said Shawe, musingly; "and if Madame or her husband is guilty, it is easy to see how they could have learnt beforehand about the diamonds. How can you get at the truth?"

"By working on Badoura's jealousy. She is in love with Eddy, and as she is a pretty girl, the unscrupulous scamp has encouraged her, in spite of the fact that he is a married man. I intend to go back to the shop and to get her to state what she knows."

"If she knows anything."

"Quite so; but if she does, her jealousy of Eddy Vail will make her speak. I don't know exactly how to unloosen her tongue, but I shall try to."

"But it seems ridiculous that Eddy Vail should be in love with a dumb or blind girl."

"I didn't say that he was in love with her," said Miss Toat, drily, "but that she was in love with him, which is quite a different way of looking at the matter. Moreover, Badoura, as the forewoman, is in possession of all her senses, Mr. Shawe. Zobeide is deaf, Parizade is blind, and Peri Banou is dumb. Badoura is all right, and is simply a pretty, commonplace girl who has been attracted by Eddy Vail's good looks."

"Well," said the barrister, after a long pause, "I hope you will be successful, although I am bound to say that you have no evidence that I can see to support your wild theories."

"They may not be so very wild after all. Wait until I can make Badoura speak. Yes," added Miss Toat, with an after-thought, "and Peri Banou also."

"The dumb girl, who was in the shop when the crime was committed. Humph! I suppose she may know something."

"She may. I am going to ask her. Meanwhile I must have more money—say, another twenty pounds."

Ralph looked rueful. "I can get it for you to-morrow," he said doubtfully, "for to tell you the truth, Miss Toat, I am not very well off just now. Can't you do without it?"

"No, Mr. Shawe," she replied plainly. "I would if I could. But it is necessary that I should go back to the Pink Shop and spend money, as that is the only way in which I can come into contact with Badoura and Peri Banou in order to question them. Of course, if you wish me to give up the case—"

"No, no—certainly not!" he exclaimed hastily. "I shall send you the twenty pounds to your office to-morrow before twelve o'clock. The solution of this mystery means a lot to me, and I am willing to spend my last farthing on it."

"I don't think you will have to do that," said Miss Toat, getting ready to go. "I expect to get some tangible clue from those two girls;" and with this piece of comfort she departed, leaving Ralph rather disconsolate.

While the case was being examined into, Shawe had seen very little of Audrey. Sir Joseph had returned unexpectedly from Brighton, for he had grown weary of the seaside and wished to get back to business. Mrs. Mellop still remained at the house on Camden Hill, as the millionaire, finding her an amusing woman to have at his dinner-table, asked her to chaperon his daughter for a longer period. The widow augured from this that Branwin was really in love with her, and did all she could to fascinate him still further. She was glad that he had come back to be under her spell.

But Ralph was far from pleased by this unexpected return, as he could not visit the house so freely as formerly. Twice or thrice he did call, but Sir Joseph was so grim and glacial in his welcome that the young man thought it was best to remain away. Also, Mrs. Mellop, taking her cue from the millionaire, behaved disagreeably, and kept a closer watch on Audrey. Ralph was very unhappy, and could only see his sweetheart at odd times and in odd ways. The course of true love was not running smoothly by any means.

Shawe, however, busied himself with searching into the case with the assistance of Perry Toat. That wily person came to him again and again, and related various details which she had learnt from Badoura, Parizade and Peri Banou, which more or less helped on the matter. But so busy was the barrister in fixing the pieces of the puzzle together—for by this time he had learnt some tangible scraps of evidence from Perry Toat's investigations—that he quite neglected Audrey. He was not, therefore, surprised to receive a note from her asking him to come to the Round Pond in Kensington Gardens the next morning at seven o'clock. At that hour neither Sir Joseph nor Mrs. Mellop was likely to be up, and Audrey would be free from their watchful eyes. Ralph promptly decided to go, but sent no answer to the note, since it might fall into the hands of his enemies—for so he regarded the millionaire and the widow who wished to marry the millionaire.

Early as he was at the rendezvous Audrey was still earlier, and came towards him hurriedly, a pathetic figure in her black dress. She kissed him hastily, then at once announced the reason why she had sent for him.

"I have received an anonymous letter," said Audrey, unexpectedly.

"An anonymous letter," repeated Ralph, curiously. "What about?"

"You can read it for yourself." She produced it from her pocket. "It advises me to refrain from investigating the murder of my mother. If I do, it declares that I shall suffer the greatest grief of my life."

Shawe was evidently startled. "Show me the letter," he said abruptly.

CHAPTER IX.

THE QUESTION OF THE CLOCK

Audrey handed over a dingy envelope, bearing the London postmark, and addressed to her at the Camden Hill house. Out of this Shawe took an equally dingy piece of paper—a single sheet of very cheap stationery. On it a few lines in vile caligraphy were scrawled. He read them at once, while Audrey sat down on a near chair and watched him silently.

"DEAR MISS"—ran the anonymous letter,—"This is to warn you from invistigiting your poor ma's deth, as I know you are doing. Keip off the gras and don't be silly, or you will sueffer the gratest grief of your life. This is from one who sines as you see—A FREND."

"What do you think of it?" asked the girl, when her lover silently replaced the paper in its envelope and sat down beside her.

"I think there may be something in it," said Shawe, slowly. "I wonder—"

"You wonder what?"

"If it would not be as well to take the advice of this," and he tapped the envelope as he handed it back to her.

"No!" cried Audrey, her worn face flushing.

"A thousand times no. I shall learn the truth at all costs."

"But if it leads to more sorrow, dear?"

"I don't care what it leads to. To know the worst—whatever the worst may be —is better than this terrible suspense." She looked at the dingy communication dubiously. "I wonder who wrote this?"

"An uneducated person, apparently."

"I don't believe it," declared the girl, quickly. "All that bad spelling and bad writing is intended to mislead."

Shawe shook his head. "How can you be sure of that?"

"I am sure of nothing. I am only assuming that such is the case. But, at all events, the person who wrote this letter knows that the matter of the death is being looked into."

"I don't see who can possibly know, save you and myself and Perry Toat."

"Who is Perry Toat?"

"The detective whom I am employing to search."

"What has he found out?"

"She, dear. Miss Toat's name is Peronella Toat, and she calls herself Perry on her card for business reasons. She has found out nothing very tangible, and confines herself to theorising a lot." Ralph paused, and shook his head once more. "I fancy she is growing tired of the case." And he related Perry Toat's discoveries—such as they were—and also detailed her theories. When he ended Audrey was almost as despairing as he appeared to be.

"There doesn't seem to be a single ray of light," lamented the girl, putting the envelope into her pocket. "Madame Coralie, her assistants, and her husband seem to be all innocent; unless," she added, with a quick look, "there is something in this idea of a prepared alibi."

"Well, Miss Toat has learnt nothing likely to show that her surmise is right in that way, Audrey. Badoura apparently knows nothing, or, infatuated with Eddy Vail, refuses to say what she may know. As to Peri Banou, who is dumb, no information can be got from her, although she was in the shop when the crime was committed. She says that she was asleep on a divan, and Zobeide certainly admits that she left her there when she went up to the still-room."

"Badoura, Peri Banou, Zobeide," said Miss Branwin, ticking off the quaint and musical names on her fingers. "You have mentioned only three of the assistants. What about the fourth?"

"Parizade? Oh! being blind, of course she can see nothing at all. She was behind the curtain in the still-room preparing some wash when Madame Coralie came to speak to her husband. That was about eight o'clock, just before Madame came down to tell you that your mother would remain for the night."

"It was about half-past eight that Madame came to the door."

"Oh! my dear girl, you must be mistaken. Madame herself and her husband both say it was five or ten minutes after eight o'clock when she came to you."

Audrey shook her head vehemently. "Mrs. Mellop will tell you that we did not leave the house until a quarter past eight."

"The Pink Shop? That, of course, would make it right."

"No, our own house. There was a first piece at the theatre which Mrs. Mellop and I did not care about seeing. We only left in time to get to the theatre by nine, when the chief drama of the evening began. It was nearly half-past eight when we reached the Pink Shop, as it took us ten minutes, more or less, to get to Walpole Lane."

"There must be some mistake," said Shawe, rather puzzled by this clear and positive explanation. "Why, Badoura says that Eddy Vail drew her attention to the clock in the still-room, and then it was five minutes to eight. Almost immediately afterwards Madame came up from seeing your mother tucked in for the night, and very shortly went to the shop door to speak to you."

"Then the clock in the still-room must be wrong," said Audrey. "Tell Miss Toat what I say, and she may be able to learn if it is so."

"Well, and supposing you prove that the still-room clock is wrong?"

"Can't you see? In that case Madame Coralie could not have come up from seeing my mother safely to bed, for she must have come up to the still-room at about fifteen or twenty minutes past the hour. And the medical evidence says that my poor mother was murdered at eight o'clock."

"It does seem strange," said Shawe, reflectively. "Humph! I wonder if Perry Toat is right after all, and if this alibi—a very convincing one, I must say—is a faked affair. Audrey"—he turned earnestly towards the girl—"say nothing of this to anyone."

"Will you tell Miss Toat?"

"Yes, I shall certainly do that. But, after all, both you and the still-room clock may be right. It only means that Madame waited twenty minutes or so talking to her husband instead of coming down at once."

"But if she came at once—"

"Then the matter will have to be looked into. I shall ask Miss Toat to question Badoura and Eddy Vail, who noticed the time. They may be able to say how long Madame Coralie remained in the still-room. But, my dear, it is all a mere theory—"

"And one that may prove to be true. Really, Ralph"—Audrey spoke with a flush on her face—"you don't seem anxious to learn the truth."

"I am in one way, and not in another. I remember that anonymous letter."

"I don't care what the letter says. The person who wrote it is evidently concerned in the death of my poor mother, and is afraid lest he or she should be caught."

"There may be some truth in that," admitted Shawe. "However, you had better leave the matter in my hands. I shall tell Perry Toat what you say about the difference in time, always supposing that Madame Coralie did not linger in the still-room. When I hear of anything definite likely to supply a clue I shall let you know."

"You have let me know very little hitherto," said Audrey, bitterly.

"My darling"—he took her hands and looked into her eyes—"surely you are not dissatisfied with me?"

"I am in a way," she admitted, blushing guiltily. "I am so anxious to learn the truth and revenge my mother. If you won't search, I shall search myself."

Shawe could do nothing in the face of this determination but agree. He scribbled Perry Toat's address on his card and gave it to the girl. Audrey slipped it into the dingy envelope which held the anonymous letter, with the intention of calling on the detective whenever she could.

"If you go on with the matter I shall help you to the best of my ability," he said earnestly, as she turned away. "Don't think that I do not desire your wish to be gratified. I only want you to be happy."

"I won't be happy until I learn who murdered my dear mother," said the girl, obstinately; then she took his arm, and they walked across to the gate near the Palace. "But I am glad that you will help me. All I ask is that you will let me assist you."

"You shall go to Perry Tat yourself and take an immediate hand in the game we are playing," said the barrister, decidedly, "as I see that in no other way will you be satisfied. And now let me see you home."

"Don't come too far with me, dear. My father may have risen by this time, and if he meets you there will be trouble."

"I don't mind that," said Shawe, throwing back his well-shaped head. "I am not afraid of Sir Joseph. By the way, talking about the possibility of that clock being wrong, was your father with you in the car?"

"No. He went out at six o'clock for one of his prowls."

"What do you mean by one of his prowls?" asked Shawe, surprised.

"Well, papa, for all our talking, is really kind when he chooses. He is sorry for poor people—for the really ragged, unwashed poor, that is—and sometimes he goes out quietly and wanders round the streets, giving money to beggars and helping those who need help."

"You throw quite a light on your father's character," said Ralph, grimly. "I should have thought that Sir Joseph was the last person in the world to help anyone or to act the secret philanthropist."

"Mrs. Mellop told me that he did so. She saw him once or twice in a tweed suit in the evening helping people—giving money, that is. And papa must go out for some such purpose, for he usually puts on evening dress for dinner."

"And changes it afterwards?"

"No; on the nights he goes out he doesn't change his clothes, and very often doesn't come to dinner. On that night Mrs. Mellop and I had the meal to ourselves, and went alone to the theatre. Papa had gone out at six in his usual clothes for a prowl. Perhaps," ended Audrey, wistfully, "I have misjudged my father, and he may not be so hard as I think. I never knew that he helped the poor until Mrs. Mellop told me; and she only saw him by chance when her taxi-cab broke down one evening on the Embankment."

"Well, I am glad to hear that Sir Joseph has some redeeming qualities," said Shawe, somewhat cynically; for the whole story sounded improbable, seeing what he knew of the man.

Neither of the young people noticed at the time that they were near the gates of Branwin's mansion, and were therefore astonished when Sir Joseph himself stepped out. He was dressed in a rough tweed suit, and looked more bulky and aggressive than ever. With a scowl he fairly snatched his daughter from the barrister's arm. "I expected something of this sort, Audrey, when you went out so early," he said, in his domineering tones. "I was just coming to Kensington Gardens. Mrs. Mellop kindly told me how you met this rascal in —"

"I am no rascal, sir," said Shawe, spiritedly.

"Yes, you are. You know that I don't wish my daughter to marry you, and yet you arrange secret meetings in the Gardens."

"I am to blame, if anyone," said Audrey, hotly, "for I arranged the meeting."

"A pretty confession for a young lady," said her father, grimly; "but I shall take care that you arrange no more. As for you, sir"—he turned on Ralph—"I forbid you to think of Miss Branwin. She is to marry Lord Anvers."

"I shall not," cried Audrey, growing white, but perfectly determined.

"You shall. I have spoken to Lord Anvers, and he is willing to make you his wife. You understand, Mr. Shawe?"

"I understand that I intend to marry Audrey," said the barrister, coolly, "so it matters little what arrangements you have made with Anvers, who is indeed the rascal you called me."

"Go inside, Audrey," said Branwin, and pushed his daughter within the gates hurriedly. "Mr. Shawe, good-day!" and he also stalked in, without commenting on the young man's speech.

Ralph thus Was left outside, like the Peri at the Gates of Paradise.

CHAPTER X.

A SURPRISE

Between her father and Mrs. Mellop Audrey had a most unpleasant time for the next two weeks. Sir Joseph was more bent than ever upon her marriage with Lord Anvers, and asked him to dinner, so that he might prosecute his suit. The proposed suitor was a pale-faced, sandy-haired, insignificant little man, with a pair of wicked-looking black eyes. At the first sight people never took Anvers to be the strong man he really was, as they were deceived by his uninteresting looks. But his eyes, and subsequently his acts, soon showed him in his true light as a capable little scoundrel, who extracted all he could from anyone and anything in order to benefit himself. Just now Anvers, being desperately hard up, decided that it was necessary for him to marry Audrey and Audrey's dowry. He wanted the money more than the maid, but, seeing that she was pretty, he was not unwilling to take the two together, even though this meant the loss of his freedom.

Audrey took a violent dislike to him. Even before he had been suggested to her as a possible husband she had never liked him, as there was an atmosphere of impurity about him which repelled her. But that he should seek to be her husband made her more active in her dislike, and when he pressed his suit she told him plainly that she would never marry him. Lord Anvers, not being troubled with delicacy, simply laughed.

"Oh, but you must marry me," he said brutally to the quivering girl; "your father wishes it."

"My father can wish it, but he won't get it," retorted Miss Branwin, all her outraged soul flashing with sapphire lights in her eyes. "I don't love you, and I never shall love you."

"Oh, I know there's another man," said Anvers, coolly. "Your father told me to be prepared for the objection, that your affections were engaged."

"My affections have nothing to do with the matter, Lord Anvers. If there wasn't another man in the world, I wouldn't marry you."

"Why not?"

"Oh! we won't go into particulars," she said sharply. "I have heard—"

"A lot of lies, I assure you. I'm not a bad chap, as chaps go, and, upon my soul, I'll try and make you happy."

"I want a better husband than one who is not bad as chaps go," said Audrey, coldly. "I want a man I can respect—a Galahad."

"Never heard of him," confessed Anvers, candidly, "unless it's another name for a fellow called Shawe."

"Perhaps it is," replied Miss Branwin, holding herself very straight, "and you can tell my father that I shall marry no one else but Mr. Shawe."

"Oh, come, give me a chance," pleaded the aristocratic black sheep.

"I have given you a chance to propose to me and I refuse you."

Anvers looked bewildered. He was unaccustomed to this very plain speaking on the part of a spinster. "You don't let a chap down easy; and I shan't lose heart, anyhow. Your 'No' means 'Yes.' A woman sometimes doesn't accept a chap straight away."

"This woman will never accept you, Lord Anvers. So if you are a gentleman you will refrain from troubling me."

"'Fraid I can't, Miss Branwin. I love you."

"You love my money," she retorted scornfully, and exasperated by this obstinacy. "You know it is only the money."

"Oh, money's a good thing," said the truthful Anvers, easily; "but, really, upon my word, you know, you're so pretty that I'd marry you without a penny."

Audrey burst out laughing. "Such candour on your part deserves candour on mine," she said quietly. "I say 'No' to your proposal, and I mean it."

For the time being Anvers saw that he was beaten, so took his leave. "But I shall come back again," he warned his lady-love. "I'll bring you up to the scratch somehow, see if I don't." And he reported the conversation to Sir Joseph, with the remark that he would never stop proposing until Audrey accepted his soiled title and his brutal self.

Of course, Branwin scolded the girl. She made no protest during the storm of words, and let Sir Joseph talk himself into exhaustion. When the millionaire could say no more she faced him calmly. "I shall never marry Lord Anvers, papa, and I shall marry Ralph whenever I can."

"Oh, you will, and when—when, confound you?" roared Branwin.

"When he learns who killed my mother," said Audrey, and passed out of the room without noticing the sudden greyness which replaced the purple hues of her father's large face.

What with anxiety to learn who had murdered her mother, and with the insistent troubles around her, Audrey felt angry with everyone and everything. Even Ralph seemed to be against her since he had waxed lukewarm in prosecuting his search for the assassin. Audrey had not seen him since he had advised her to heed the warning of the anonymous letter, and she had received no communication likely to show that he was looking into the matter of the murder. Under these circumstances, she resolved to take up the *rôle* of an amateur detective herself. Since there was no one else who loved the dead sufficiently to avenge the crime, Audrey at least made up her mind to hunt down the murderer.

She began one afternoon by driving to Perry Toat's office, for Ralph had written down its whereabouts. Sir Joseph, sullen and angry with his daughter, had gone to his club, and Mrs. Mellop in her bedroom was fretting over the destruction of her hopes. Therefore, there was no one to spy on the girl, and, having dressed herself plainly, she took a taxi-cab in Kensington High Street and drove to the Strand. Perry Toat's office was in Buckingham Street, and the detective herself was disengaged. She admitted Audrey into her private sanctum the moment she read the name on the card.

"I thought you would come, Miss Branwin," said Perry Toat, cordially, "as Mr. Shawe told me that you were different from most girls. Few would wish to undertake the search you propose to make."

"Few girls, if any, have had a mother murdered in so barbarous a fashion," was Audrey's reply, and she eyed with some disapproval the garish complexion and burnished hair and general renovation of Miss Toat.

The detective smiled, guessing the thought of her visitor. "This and this"—she touched her hair and skin—"are a concession to business demands. I had to submit to this sort of thing in order to gain permission to remain for searching purposes at the Pink Shop."

"Oh!" Audrey understood. "And did you find out anything?"

"I told Mr. Shawe all I had discovered, and what theories I formed on the discoveries," said Miss Toat, glancing at her watch. "He explained to me that he had reported everything to you over a week ago."

"Yes," admitted Miss Branwin, "but he did not give me any hope that anything would come of what you have learnt."

"I fear not. The clues are so slight, Miss Branwin. By the way"—Perry Toat looked again at her watch—"I can only give you ten minutes or so, as I am expecting another client—Colonel Ilse. Ah! poor man, he comes to me to be helped in finding his stolen daughter."

"His stolen daughter?" echoed Audrey.

"Yes. His wife died in child-birth some twenty years ago, and the child was stolen by an hospital nurse who attended her. There was some grudge, I believe. But why should I bother you with the troubles of other people when you have so many of your own?" said Miss Toat, in a lively way. "Come, time is short. What do you wish me to tell you?"

"What is your opinion of the case as it now stands?" asked Audrey, abruptly.

"It's a difficult and mysterious case," said the detective, slowly, "and it is my opinion that Madame Coralie can tell the truth."

"Do you think that she is guilty?"

"No. That is, if she is guilty, it is because she employed someone else to murder your mother. I don't believe she strangled Lady Branwin herself."

"Why not?"

"Because Madame Coralie proved an alibi."

"Ah!" Audrey nodded. "Then Mr. Shawe did not tell you about my idea as to the clock in the still-room being wrong?"

Miss Toat looked at her quickly. "No. What is your idea?"

Audrey related what she knew of the discrepancy between the statement of Madame Coralie, her husband, and Badoura, and her own. "It was nearly half-past eight when Madame came to see me at the door," said Audrey, positively.

Miss Toat looked steadily at the girl. "Strange," she said, in a musing tone. "Now, I wonder why Mr. Shawe did not tell me this?"

"It is important, is it not?" asked Audrey, eagerly.

"Very important. If we can prove what you say, it will show that it was possible for Madame Coralie to have been with Lady Branwin at eight."

"Then she must be guilty," said Audrey, triumphantly.

"No. I suspect Eddy Vail, her husband. He, as well as his wife, was in dire need of money, and he may have committed the deed, although his wife may have suggested its commission. If I could only trace the diamonds"—and Miss Toat, thinking hard, began to trace figures on her blotting-paper.

"I have seen that man Vail," said Miss Branwin, after a pause. "Mr. Shawe described him to me, and I recognised the description at once. He was hanging about Walpole Lane when my mother came back for the red bag which contained the diamonds."

"Oh!"—Miss Toat looked up—"that's a strong point. Did your mother happen to mention, when in the lane, that the diamonds were in the bag?"

"No," said Audrey, after some thought; "she simply asked for the bag. But I am sure that Madame Coralie must have known about the diamonds, as my poor mother would be sure to tell her."

"Have you ever seen Madame Coralie?" asked Miss Toat, sharply.

"Only in the half-darkness, when she came to the door at half-past eight to tell me that my mother would remain for the night."

"Then," said Perry Toat, rising, "go to the Pink Shop and see her now. You are so straightforward and earnest that you may succeed where I fail. Ask all the questions you can think of, and see what Madame Coralie looks like."

"Hear what she says, you mean."

"No, I do not. Hear what she says, of course; but you may be sure that if she has anything to hide she will be most guarded in her answers. But look into her face, and watch the change of colour, and—oh!" Miss Toat stopped in dismay. "I forgot, Madame Coralie wears a yashmak constantly."

"In that case I shall get her to remove it," said Audrey, quickly. "I see what you mean, and I shall manage in some way to see her face. If she is guilty I shall know somehow."

"I wish I could come with you myself," said Miss Toat, hastily following Audrey to the door, which opened into a small outer office; "but I fear that Colonel Ilse—ah! here he is."

Miss Branwin saw before her a slender and very straight man, with a grey moustache and grey hair, with a tanned face and a general military look. He had kind blue eyes, and when he saw so pretty a girl emerge from the dingy office of Perry Toat these same eyes lighted up with admiration. With a bow to the detective he stood on one side to let the girl pass. Audrey gave a swift glance at his clearly-cut face as she went out. There seemed to be something familiar about Colonel Ilse's countenance; but she could not say precisely what it was. Besides, her mind was too much taken up with the late conversation with Miss Toat to concern itself with so trifling a matter. The detective accompanied her to the outer door.

"See me to-morrow at three o'clock," she said, in a low voice, "and tell me if you have succeeded in getting Madame Coralie to remove her yashmak."

67

Miss Branwin readily promised this, as she felt that she needed Miss Toat's professional assistance in the quest which she was now undertaking. She felt eager to reach the Pink Shop and to question Madame Coralie, and her heart beat quickly as she climbed into a 'bus which would take her to Kensington. Sir Joseph would have been furious had he seen his daughter travelling on so humble a vehicle; but Audrey enjoyed the novelty of the sensation. Indeed, she was beginning to find out, for the first time since her mother's death, that life was worth living. And, although she did not know it, she was suffering from a severe attack of detective fever.

The progress of the 'bus seemed slow to the impatient girl; but in due time she came to Kensington High Street. Here she alighted, and turned into Walpole Lane without delay. Shortly she found herself before the mysterious door of the Pink Shop, and entered with a beating heart and a general sense that there was a crisis at hand.

"Is Madame Coralie to be seen?" she asked Badoura, who came forward in her quaint Turkish dress to receive her.

"I will inquire, miss," said Badoura, looking at her closely. "Oh! it is Miss Branwin, is it not?"

"Yes, and I wish particularly to see Madame Coralie."

"Will you please wait here, miss?" said Badoura, and, leaving Audrey near the door of the empty shop—it was too early for the usual customers—she walked towards an alcove on the left.

Audrey saw the girl pass through the pink silk curtains into the alcove, and heard a faint murmur of voices. Deeming that all was fair in the dangerous and anxious search which she was undertaking she drew near, and distinctly heard Madame Coralie gasp with dismay.

"Tell Miss Branwin that I cannot see her," said Madame Coralie, sharply.

Audrey at once stepped forward and swept aside the pink curtain. "But you must, Madame," she said quietly.

The woman waved Badoura to leave the alcove, and beckoned Miss Branwin to enter, making some remark in muffled tones as she did so. Suddenly, as she rose quickly to her feet, a tack caught the yashmak, and it was ripped off. Audrey saw Madame Coralie's side face, and gave a cry of surprise and terror.

"Mother!" she cried, then sank her voice with fear. "Mother! Oh, mother!"

CHAPTER XI.

A STORY OF THE PAST

So there had been no need for Audrey to plot for the removal of Madame Coralie's yashmak. With the trifling aid of a tack, which had caught the veil when the woman rose suddenly from the divan, the truth immediately became known to the horrified and astonished girl. But was it the truth? At the first glance Audrey recognised the side face turned towards her as that of her mother. But when Madame Coralie looked round fairly, and the light, filtering through the curtains of the shop window, fell on her full countenance, then Audrey became doubtful. The wine-dark birthmark which disfigured mouth and chin and cheek had been absent from Lady Branwin's face.

"But—but you are my mother!" gasped the girl, still struck by the marvellous resemblance to the supposed dead.

"I am not your mother," replied the other, coldly, and evading the outstretched arms of her visitor. "But since you have seen my face, I had better confess the truth. I am your aunt, Flora."

"Oh!" Audrey recollected what her father had said about the two sisters of Bleakleigh. "Flora Arkwright?"

"Yes. I see your mother told you about me."

"No, she did not."

Madame Coralie raised her hand imperatively. "This alcove is too public a place in which to discuss family matters. We must go upstairs. Indeed, I fancy your exclamation of 'Mother!' must have aroused Badoura's suspicions."

Apparently this was true, for when Madame Coralie drew her visitor through the pink silk curtains into the deserted shop, Badoura was standing before them with an astonished look on her face. Her employer at once sent her off on a false scent.

"Miss Branwin has called to see me about her mother's death," said Madame Coralie, quietly. "She is slightly hysterical, and you have, no doubt, heard what she cried out. I trust"—the speaker looked anxiously round the shop —"that no one else heard?"

"I am alone here," replied Badoura, evidently accepting this explanation as a reasonable one. "Can I get Miss Branwin a glass of water?"

"No, my dear," said the owner of the shop, who had replaced her yashmak. "I am taking up Miss Branwin to the still-room for a little quiet conversation. See that we are not disturbed."

"Peri Banou, Zobeide and Parizade are there, Madame."

"I shall send them down. Give them something to do here. Come, Miss Branwin, if you don't mind climbing the stairs."

Although Audrey felt considerably annoyed at being described as hysterical, she nevertheless saw the necessity of some such explanation to satisfy the curiosity of the forewoman. Therefore she wisely said nothing, and followed Madame into the narrow back passage and up the stairs. On arriving in the still-room, the elder woman dismissed her assistants, and having looked behind the curtain to see that no one was hidden there likely to overhear the conversation, she closed the door. Audrey watched her as she sat down with her back to the window, and tried to steady her nerves, which naturally had sustained a shock.

"Now, Miss Branwin," said Madame Coralie, in a quiet voice, "we can talk. But first, so that you may be certain of my identity, I shall lay this aside," and she flung the long veil of the yashmak over her shoulder.

The girl examined that face carefully. Madame Coralie was certainly extremely like Lady Branwin. She had the same muddy complexion and large black eyes, and the same stout, shapeless figure. But the aggressive birthmark made all the difference, and after a single glimpse of it, much less this cautious and lengthy survey, there could be no question that the woman before her was not Lady Branwin.

"But my mistake was natural," said Audrey, with a sigh.

"Very natural," answered Madame Coralie, who had evidently followed her train of thought—no very difficult thing to do—"especially as you first saw my side face. The mark does not show when I look thus." She adapted her position to her words, and the resemblance became even more apparent. "Dora and I were twins," ended Madame, with a nod.

"My father did not tell me that."

"Oh! so your father told you about me, my dear. I thought he had long ago forgotten the existence of poor Flora Arkwright."

"Far from forgetting you," Audrey assured her aunt, "he said that he wished he had married you instead of mother."

The information did not seem to please Madame Coralie, for her thin lips tightened, and she gave vent to a short laugh. Then Audrey noted, as a further difference between the sisters, that the woman before her spoke in a hoarse and loud, domineering voice. Lady Branwin, on the other hand, had always talked softly, and possessed a musical utterance, which was one of the few poor charms she owned.

"So Joseph remembers me in that way, does he, my dear?" said Madame Coralie, clasping her hands. "Ha! if I hadn't been a fool I should have married him."

"Why didn't you?" asked Audrey, bluntly.

"I have stated the reason," said Madame Coralie, drily. "I was a fool. But I am bound to say in my own defence that I never believed Joseph would become so wealthy. He never struck me as particularly clever."

"Yet he must be, to have so much money."

"There I disagree with you, my dear—I can call you my dear in private, as you are my niece—but Joseph was always hard and grasping, and ever had an eye to the main chance. Well, he is rich, and has now got rid of his wife, so he can marry into the Peerage if he likes. I expect Dora is glad she is dead, now that she is on the other side of the grave. Joseph killed her."

"Killed her?" Audrey, with a sudden fear, turned deadly white.

"Oh, I don't mean to say that he strangled her," said Madame Coralie, hastily, "for he is too careful of his skin to risk hanging; but his neglect killed her. She was always a good and faithful wife to him, and he broke her heart."

"Papa was rather unkind," said Audrey, nervously, but relieved by this explanation.

Madame again laughed shortly. "Unkind—rather unkind!" she repeated. "Why, he treated her like a brute. She told me all about it. Fancy the poor soul coming to me to be made young again, in the hope that she could regain Joseph's affections. I told her that she was a fool; but she *would* waste her money. And perhaps she wanted to help me also," added Madame Coralie, in a softer tone. "Dora was always fond of me."

"She knew that you kept this shop?"

"Yes. In fact, she helped me to set up the shop some years ago. I made her promise that she would never tell Joseph of my existence, and she kept her word. Yet Joseph remembered me. Strange."

"Papa said that you had the brains."

Madame Coralie looked round the room disdainfully. "And to what have my brains brought me? I am simply a renovator of faded women, and had to borrow money from Dora to set up the establishment. Flora Arkwright is lost in Madame Coralie."

"Mrs. Edward Vail, you mean," said Audrey, quietly.

"Oh!"—the woman shrugged her heavy shoulders—"I married Eddy so as to have a companion. He's a handsome fool, and goes about making love to younger women, while he lives on my money. However, he is always good-tempered, and suits me well enough. But in Bleakleigh I believed that my destiny would have been a better one. Dreams, my dear dreams."

"You were born at Bleakleigh?"

Madame Coralie nodded and folded her stout arms. Then, rocking to and fro, she related her story and the story of her sister. It was strange to Audrey, this history of her mother's early life. Lady Branwin had always been too much afraid of her husband to tell about her early struggles.

"Dora and I were the daughters of a labourer," said Madame Coralie. "She was very pretty, and I—well, my dear, who could be pretty with this?" and she touched the birthmark. "Although it was lighter when I was a girl, I have tried so hard to remove it that I expect I made it worse. If my customers saw it they would never believe that I could remove blemishes from their silly faces. For that reason I always wear the yashmak. My keeping what is called a Turkish shop gives me a chance of doing so."

"I quite understand," said Audrey, gently. "But tell me about my mother."

Madame Coralie looked at her swiftly. "You were fond of her?"

"Of course. Was she not my mother? Besides, she was all that was good and kind to me. And," added Audrey, clenching her fist so tightly that her glove split, "if no one else will revenge her by finding out who killed her, I shall do so."

"I fear you have undertaken a search which will never be ended," said her aunt, in a pitying tone; "but the feeling does you credit. I shall assist you by all the means in my power, my dear; for not only was poor Dora my sister, but her death has harmed my business."

"We can talk of what we will do later," said Audrey, quickly. "Meanwhile, go on with your story."

"A very dull story, I fear, my dear," said Madame Coralie, with a sigh. "Joseph, like Dora and myself, was the child of a labourer. We lived next door to one another. Then Joseph fell in love with Dora, because she was pretty, and went away to make his fortune. The papers will tell you how he did, so there is no need for me to talk about that. But I will say that Joseph behaved well to Dora, for he returned to marry her. Then the ways of my sister and myself parted, and she went on a golden road, while I"—Madame Coralie glanced round the room again with great scorn—"while I made for this goal."

"Did you not see my mother occasionally?"

"Not for many years, my dear. I got married to a gamekeeper—the gamekeeper of Squire Shawe, of Bleakleigh. He was killed by poachers within a year of marriage, and left me with a few hundred pounds in hand. There was no child, and there was nothing to keep me in Bleakleigh, since my parents were dead, so I came to London. Then—" Madame Coralie shivered.

"What happened then?" asked Audrey, sympathetically.

"Trouble. I was born to trouble, my dear. Everything that could go wrong with me went wrong. I tried the stage, and failed. I became a lecturer, and lost my voice—you hear how hoarse it is still. I went to America as a lady's-maid, and was stranded there in San Francisco. I worked as a typist; I laboured in a laundry; I took to reporting; I edited a woman's paper, and did all I could to keep myself above water. As a reporter I was sent to Paris in the interests of the paper. It failed, and I went in for massaging people. Then—well, to make a long story short, I learnt from a friend of mine in Paris all kinds of secrets about the art of making women beautiful. It struck me that I might start in London. I came back and wrote to Dora. There was no difficulty in finding her, as she was by this time Lady Branwin, the wife of a millionaire. I am bound to say that Dora behaved very well. She said nothing to her brute of a husband, but managed in some way to get enough to start me in this business. Then—" Madame Coralie stopped abruptly, with a gesture. "That's all, my dear."

"And does the business pay?" asked Audrey, mindful of what Ralph had said regarding the difficulties of the woman before her.

"Yes. That is, it would pay if I could only get in the money. But all my clients, being women of fashion, are such bad payers—they ask for years of credit. Then there's Eddy, who is extravagant. I was a fool to marry him; but I did so for companionship. I bought him, so to speak, so we understand one another perfectly. Of course, poor Dora's death has done a lot of harm to me; but now that I have money to fall back on, I hope to pull round. It is weary work, though," said Madame Coralie, looking very old—"weary work."

"I am glad that you have saved money," said Audrey, who could not but acknowledge that her aunt was marvellously candid.

"Saved money! My dear, have you not been listening to what I have been saying? How could I save money with Eddy's extravagance and these customers who never will pay their bills. It was Dora who came to my rescue. She gave me her diamonds, poor dear."

Audrey jumped up amazed. "Gave you her diamonds?" she echoed. "But you said at the inquest—"

"I know perfectly well what I said at the inquest and what I am saying to you," interrupted Madame Coralie, sharply. "I denied that I knew anything of the diamonds. For obvious reasons I did so. If I had admitted possession of the diamonds, I would have been suspected as the person who strangled your mother. No one knew that Dora and I were sisters."

"You could have explained at—"

"No," said Madame Coralie, positively, "I could not have explained, for my story would have appeared to be merely a made-up one to account for the possession of the jewels. Of course, the resemblance—for Dora and I were wonderfully alike, save for this birthmark—would have hinted that I was speaking the truth. But in that case I should have had to remove my yashmak, and then all the world would have known of this disfigurement. It would have ruined my business, my dear."

Audrey looked bewildered. "But if my mother was not strangled for the sake of the diamonds, why was she killed?"

Her aunt shrugged her shoulders. "I have asked that again and again; and yet I think that I can see a way. Dora brought me the diamonds, pretending that she wished them to be reset. When we were in the bedroom together she took them out of the bag and gave them to me. Then she placed the empty bag under her pillow. I came upstairs, after tucking her in for the night, in order to put away the jewels. All I can think of is that someone got into the court by means of that skeleton key, and, thinking that the jewels were still in the bag, strangled poor Dora, and then escaped. If you remember, the label was found near the court door."

All this explanation was very frank, and from the mere fact that Madame Coralie admitted having the jewels Audrey was certain that she was not the guilty person, nor had she employed anyone else to commit the crime. Besides, as the two women were twin sisters—and the likeness proved this beyond all doubt—the idea of one murdering the other was out of the question. "I suppose," said Audrey, after a pause, "that you know some people suspect you?"

"Oh, yes," said her aunt, indifferently; "and if they knew about the diamonds they would be certain of my guilt. However, I got Eddy to unset the stones and sell them separately. He has been over to Antwerp selling them, so I am quite safe; that is"—she looked at Audrey—"unless you tell the police what I have told you."

"I should not think of doing so," said the girl, anxiously, for she really believed her aunt to be innocent, "and, more than that, I will try and disabuse Ralph of your guilt."

"Ralph? Oh, yes. Squire Shawe's younger son. Poor Dora told me he was engaged to you. Well, is there anything else you want to know?"

"No; but you must help me to find out who murdered my mother."

"Certainly. I shall do that for my own sake. Come and see me again, and I may be able to give you a clue. Between us we may trace the assassin."

"Oh! aunt, will you do this?" cried Audrey, with shining eyes.

Madame Coralie kissed her. "Yes, even if I ruin myself. You love your poor mother's memory—I would do anything for Dora's daughter."

CHAPTER XII.

THE UNKNOWN CUSTOMER

Before leaving her newly-discovered aunt Audrey extracted permission from her to reveal what she had been told to Ralph. At first Madame Coralie had made some objection, but on being assured that Shawe could and would keep his own counsel she consented that he should be told about the diamonds. "If he's hunting for the assassin, and thinking that I am the one," said Madame Coralie, "he will learn beforehand that I have the jewels, and will not be ready to credit me with disposing of stolen gems. Eddy is sometimes so careless that I fear lest the police should know."

"I think it would be best to tell the police," said Audrey, wisely.

"No; the interest in the case has died away," said her aunt, "and not even Joseph's reward of one thousand pounds can revive it. Tell Mr. Shawe, by all means, but warn him to keep his own counsel!"

Audrey left Madame Coralie with the strange feeling—so close was the resemblance between the sisters, dead and alive—that she had been conversing with her mother. She returned home in a dream, and then thought disconsolately that she was no nearer learning what she wished to know than she had been before. But it was necessary to disabuse Perry Toat of the idea that the proprietress of the Pink Shop was guilty, and Audrey determined to call at the appointed hour the next day. Afterwards she could see Ralph and detail what she had learnt. But to interview both her lover and the detective was not an easy task, owing to the watch that was kept on her every action.

However, Providence stood her friend unexpectedly. Sir Joseph wished to drive some people down to Richmond for afternoon tea at the Star and Garter. He invited Mrs. Mellop to join the party, but to punish Audrey for the way in which she had behaved to Lord Anvers he ordered her to remain at home. His daughter disguised her satisfaction with difficulty, and sent a wire to Ralph asking him to meet her at Perry Toat's at half-past three o'clock. By that hour she would have put the detective off the scent, and then could take Ralph aside and tell him all that she did not wish Miss Toat to learn. Having arranged this, she accompanied Mrs. Mellop to the door, where Sir Joseph, in a magnificent motor-car, was waiting.

Mrs. Mellop was rather doleful, as she now knew that the millionaire had made up his mind, on the authority of Audrey, to marry Rosy Pearl. But the widow did not intend to lose the prize without a struggle, as it was much too valuable. Besides, having seen Miss Pearl on the music-hall stage, she did not think her a particularly formidable rival. She determined, on this day, to be as fascinating as possible in order to carry off Sir Joseph from under the very nose of Rosy Pearl. And, as Mrs. Mellop had a very good opinion of herself, she thought that she would succeed. So happy was she in the hope of success that she kissed Audrey in the hall.

"You poor dear, I wish you were coming," she said affectionately.

"Oh, don't trouble yourself about me," said Audrey, who quite understood what the kiss meant. "Give all your attention to capturing my father."

"Wouldn't you like me for a stepmother?" asked Mrs. Mellop, coaxingly.

"I would like you better than Rosy Pearl," said Audrey, drily. "You will have my undying gratitude if you can save him from that woman."

"Darling!" Mrs. Mellop pecked again at Audrey's cheek with great delight at having enlisted her sympathy so far. "I shall do my best."

When the car glided away Audrey laughed. She felt sure that Mrs. Mellop would do her best. She was also very certain that she would fail, as Sir Joseph never changed his mind. He had declared, with indecent haste, that he

76

intended to marry the music-hall artist, and he would do so, whatever obstacles were placed in the way. Moreover, Rosy Pearl was just the kind of fine woman whom the millionaire admired. Mrs. Mellop was a mere shrimp beside Miss Pearl's massive proportions, and Sir Joseph did not care for diaphanous creatures of the widow's type. However, Mrs. Mellop had intense faith in her own cleverness and in man's stupidity, and went forth to conquer. No wonder that Audrey—knowing her father's adamantine nature—laughed as the would-be Lady Branwin fluttered out, all smiles and chiffons. "If she's going out for wool, she will come home shorn," thought Audrey, and went away to put on her quietest frock.

When she arrived at Buckingham Street, Strand, Miss Toat was duly waiting to hear what she had learnt. Audrey had already arranged in her own mind what to say, and sat down feeling quite cool and composed. So calm did she seem that Miss Toat laughed in a vexed way.

"So you have been unsuccessful—you have learnt nothing," she said promptly.

"How do you know?" asked Audrey, quickly.

"You would be more excited if you had found a clue. Well, Miss Branwin"—she leant her elbows on the table—"perhaps I am wrong. If you have learnt anything likely to be of value, let me hear it."

"I have learnt nothing," said Audrey, cautiously; "nothing of any value."

"You got Madame Coralie to remove her yashmak?"

"Accident did that for me. It was ripped off by a tack as she rose."

"Well?" asked Perry Toat, eagerly.

"Well," replied Miss Branwin, coolly, "that's all."

"But you had some conversation with her?"

"Yes. But she could tell me nothing. She merely repeated what she had said at the inquest—that she left my mother in bed and came up the stairs to the still-room."

"Did you mention anything about the discrepancy in time?"

"Oh!"—Audrey was really dismayed—"I quite forgot to."

"Ah, my dear young lady"—Perry Toat looked vexed again—"that is the most important question of the lot. Although, I daresay," she added consolingly, "you would not have had a true reply. I must look into the matter myself."

"There is nothing to be learnt, Miss Toat. I am quite sure that Madame

Coralie is innocent."

"What makes you think so?"

"I observed her face, and she did not change colour. She told me all that I have told you with the greatest frankness."

"Naturally," said Miss Toat, doubtfully, "she would be on her guard with you."

"I don't think she was," replied Audrey, with studied simplicity; "besides, she has promised to help me to find the criminal. She is most anxious to do so, because of her business."

"I don't see how discovering the real criminal will improve the business."

"Well"—Audrey looked pensive—"Madame Coralie is rather revengeful."

"And very cunning. What is to be done now? You have failed."

"I have not looked into everything yet, Miss Toat. I intend to call again on Madame Coralie."

"I shall do so also," said Perry Toat, with determination; for she recollected the large reward, and felt anxious to obtain it.

Her visitor did not wish to forbid her calling again at the Pink Shop, as such a request might have awakened Miss Toat's suspicions. So she said nothing, feeling certain that Madame Coralie was perfectly well able to look after herself. Meanwhile, Miss Toat, having gathered all she wished to learn, and feeling a faint suspicion that Audrey had not told her everything, made up her mind to look into things for herself. Then she turned the conversation, so that Miss Branwin should not gather her intentions.

"You made a conquest the other day," said Miss Toat, while Audrey rose to take her leave and smoothed her gloves.

"Really!" The girl blushed. "What do you mean?"

"Colonel Ilse fell in love with you."

Audrey blushed again. "That nice military man who came as I went yesterday, you mean, don't you? He is really charming—such a nice smile. If I wasn't engaged to Mr. Shawe I might follow up my conquest."

Miss Toat shook her head. "You would be disappointed. Colonel Ilse has buried his heart in the grave of the wife who died over twenty years ago. If he can only find the daughter who was stolen from him he will be quite content."

"Then I must be the same with Ralph," said Audrey, laughing. "Do you know, Miss Toat, Colonel Ilse put me in mind of someone. I can't think who."

The detective nodded. "Curious you should say that. I had an idea that I had seen someone like him. But then, these military men are all cut to one pattern. See one and you see the lot. Ah! Come in!" She raised her voice as a knock came to the door.

Ralph entered, looking smart and lover-like. "Here I am, Audrey," he said.

"Oh!" laughed Perry Toat, rebukingly, "do you think that this is Cupid's Bureau? What an unromantic place to meet in."

"We have to meet in all manner of places," said Audrey, with a smile. "My father doesn't approve of our marriage, and will not let Mr. Shawe come to the house. Good-day, Miss Toat. We must be off."

When she went out, looking up into her lover's face, Perry Toat sighed. The little office seemed more dingy than ever now that rosy love had flown away. The detective returned to her papers rather discontentedly. She also wished to walk out with a lover; but there was no chance of that unless she gained this one thousand pounds which Sir Joseph Branwin offered for the detection of his wife's assassin. The episode of Ralph meeting Audrey at the office, and the sight of their love, made the little woman more determined than ever to win the reward. "They are the butterflies," said Miss Toat, shuffling her papers, "and I am only the grub as yet."

So while the poor grub worked in the dull room the butterflies fluttered in the sunshine. To be precise, they drove in a taxi-cab to their favourite meeting-place near the Round Pond. Here Audrey related how she had seen Madame Coralie, and what had taken place. Shawe was not easily astonished, but on this occasion he confessed that he was. It was surprising to learn that Madame Coralie was the sister of Lady Branwin, and more surprising still to hear that she so easily confessed to having possession of the long-lost diamonds.

"Oh, she must be innocent," said the barrister, after an astonished pause. "I can't conceive she would admit so much if she were guilty. The very possession of the jewels would make the police certain of her guilt."

"But the police must never know," said Audrey, anxiously. "Remember, I tell you all this under seal of secrecy."

"Oh, I shall say nothing," Ralph assured her seriously—"especially as your aunt has been so candid as to dispel any suspicions that I may have entertained regarding her complicity in the crime."

"Then you don't believe in Perry Toat's theory?"

"No, I certainly do not. I have my own views."

"What are they?"

Shawe hesitated. "I shall tell you what they are when I am more certain of my suspicions."

"Then you do suspect someone?" asked the girl, swiftly.

"Yes and no; that is, I have found a mare's nest."

Audrey looked at him carefully. It struck her that his face was thin and pale, and that his eyes looked remarkably dull. "You are worrying, dear."

"Yes, over this case. I really think"—Shawe passed his hand across his forehead—"that it would be best to leave it alone. Audrey"—he took her hands and looked entreatingly into her face—"why not let sleeping dogs lie?"

She shook her head. "I must learn who killed my mother. Aunt Flora—that is, Madame Coralie—will help me. Why do you wish things to be left alone?"

"Because the wording of that anonymous letter haunts me," said Shawe, irritably. "If you search into this matter you will experience some very great grief. Is it worth risking that?"

"For the sake of my mother's memory it is," said the girl, firmly.

"My darling, I assure you that your mother will rest no more quietly in her grave because her assassin is hanged. Why not abandon the whole business and marry me at once? I have not much money, it is true, but what I have is enough for both of us to live quietly."

"No, no, no!" said Audrey, insistently. "We discussed this matter before, and I told you that I would not drag you down and hinder your career by saddling you with a poor wife; and if I marry against my father's wishes I am bound to be poor. Besides, I have sworn to myself never to rest until the murderer of my poor mother is brought to justice. If you won't help me—and you certainly do not seem anxious to do so—I must work alone."

"Of course I shall help you," snapped the barrister, sharply. "I want to get at the truth as speedily as possible, so that we may be married. And to aid you in your search I now make a suggestion."

Audrey looked at him with interest. "What is it?"

"You say that your father admired Madame Coralie when she was Flora Arkwright of Bleakleigh. Very good! Flora Arkwright may have admired your father, and may have grudged him marrying your mother. Now, why not go to Madame Coralie straight away and rouse her jealousy?"

"Rouse her jealousy?"

"Yes. The Deceased Wife's Sister Bill is law now, and there is no bar against Madame Coralie marrying Sir Joseph."

"Yes, there is. You forget Eddy Vail."

"Oh, the deuce!" cried the barrister, in dismay, "so I do. Never mind, it is as well to try the experiment. Tell Madame Coralie that Sir Joseph is to marry Rosy Pearl, and see what she will say. For your dead mother's sake, if not for her own, she may resent the marriage."

"Of course, the idea is absurd," said Audrey, pettishly. "My aunt has not a shadow of excuse to object to my father marrying anyone. What ever feelings she may have entertained for him once, they have been parted too long for such feelings to exist now."

"Well, the experiment is worth trying," insisted Ralph, anxiously.

Audrey thought for a moment, then rose and walked across the grass. "To set your mind at rest I shall see my aunt at once and tell her."

"Good! I shall wait at the door of the Pink Shop and hear your report."

With this understanding the two strolled across the Gardens to Walpole Lane, and while Ralph lingered on the pavement Audrey passed into the Turkish shop. She had chosen rather an awkward hour for an interview, as Madame Coralie's clients were rolling up in carriage and motor-brougham. But the proprietress of the shop was upstairs in the still-room, and sent down word that she would see Miss Branwin at once. The girl soon found herself in the presence of her aunt, while Badoura, who had introduced her, returned to look after the customers, who were being served by the other three girls. "I can only give you five minutes, my dear," said Madame Coralie, who was again wearing her yashmak. "Is there anything wrong?"

"Nothing particularly; but I thought that it was just as well you should know that my father has made up his mind to marry again."

"What!" Madame Coralie gave a roar like that of a wounded lioness. "Who is the woman?"

"Miss Rosy Pearl, of the—"

"That music-hall creature—impossible!" Madame Coralie clenched her hands, and her black eyes looked extremely angry. "Why, it was Rosy Pearl who was my other customer who slept in this house on the night of the crime!"

"Oh!" Audrey grew pale. In a flash she saw what Madame Coralie meant.

CHAPTER XIII.

A BLIND CLUE

After that significant hint, Madame Coralie refused to speak any more, alleging that she was extremely busy and could not afford the time. However, she told her niece to call and see her again, when she would be more explicit. Meanwhile, the girl was obliged to return to her lover with what meagre information she had gleaned, Passing through the perfumed shop, now crowded with fashionable women, she rejoined Ralph on the pavement. Together they strolled up Walpole Lane in the direction of Kensington Palace.

"I told my aunt, as you suggested, about my father's intention to marry Miss Pearl," said Audrey, abruptly. "And you are right. She is jealous. Strange, is it not, after all these years? Besides"—Audrey shrugged her shoulders in a contemptuous way—"fancy any woman remaining faithful to my father."

"Women have odd tastes," said Shawe, quietly, "and your father is so masterful a man that he is certain to be successful with the fair sex. Humph! She is jealous, is she? Well, and what did she say?"

"Very little. It was her manner of speaking more than what she said. When I told her, you should have seen her eyes flash above the yashmak."

"Oh, never mind her eyes flashing, Audrey," said Shawe, impatiently. "What were her words?"

"All she said was that Rosy Pearl was the customer who slept at the Pink Shop on the night of the crime."

"What!" Ralph stopped suddenly, and stared. "The lady who refused to allow her name to be given—who slept in the upstairs bedroom?"

"Yes. And I think that my aunt means to hint—"

"Oh, I see what she means," interrupted Ralph, quickly. "Her jealousy gives the hint very plainly. Rosy Pearl was in the house; Rosy Pearl wants to become the second Lady Branwin, so Rosy Pearl gets rid of—"

"No, no!" interrupted Audrey in her turn, and looking pale. "I can't think that she strangled my mother."

"She had every reason to," said Ralph, grimly. "And as Madame Coralie admits that she has the diamonds, robbery cannot now be given as the motive for the committal of the crime."

"Do you believe that Rosy Pearl really did murder my mother so that the way might be opened to her to be my father's second wife?"

"I can't say for certain, until I examine into the matter more closely," said Shawe, anxiously, "but it certainly looks like it. Sir Joseph is a millionaire, and from the sudden way in which he announced his intention of making her his wife it is evident that the two discussed the matter while your mother was still alive." He paused, and thought for a few minutes. "I tell you what, Audrey, I shall go at once to Perry Toat and tell her this."

"Can I come also?" asked Audrey, again feeling the detective fever.

"No. It is just as wise not to arouse your father's suspicions."

"Why should they be aroused?" asked Audrey, quickly. "He knows nothing of Rosy Pearl's doings on that night."

"No, I daresay he doesn't," replied Shawe, turning away his face; "but if he thought that you were looking into this case, and that Miss Pearl was suspected, he might make trouble. Go back home, Audrey, my darling, and leave me to deal with the matter."

"Very well; but you must promise to come and tell me all about it. Meet me at the usual place in the Gardens to-morrow afternoon at three."

"Yes." Ralph glanced at his watch. "I must get a taxi and drive as hard as I can to Buckingham Street, or Miss Toat may leave her office. It's after five o'clock as it is."

"What are you going to do exactly, Ralph?" asked Audrey, detaining him.

"Explain matters to Perry Toat, and ask her to look up Miss Pearl," said the young man, hastily, and fairly ran away from the girl.

Audrey returned to her home filled with anxious fears. There was something strange about her lover's unwillingness to discuss matters freely with her. Also, she could not conceive why he wished her to obey the instructions of the anonymous letter and abandon all further search for the assassin. With the instinct of a woman in love, she felt that there was a veil between her and Ralph. But why there should be, she could not conceive. "The only thing to be done is to wait patiently," Audrey thought, as she dressed for dinner. "Sooner or later I shall learn why Ralph is behaving so strangely."

Meanwhile, Shawe, never thinking that Audrey was puzzled by his odd reluctance, had found Perry Toat on the point of leaving her office. When he breathlessly explained his errand she sat down to gather details. The idea that Rosy Pearl had been sleeping in the Pink Shop on the night when Lady Branwin had been murdered revealed matters in a new light. Had she known about the diamonds being in Madame Coralie's possession, she might have been still more certain; but since Ralph had solemnly promised Audrey to keep silent on this particular point, he could not impart all his suspicions to the detective. However, she learnt enough to suggest the building up of another and more feasible theory.

"Of course, Rosy Pearl's desire to become Lady Branwin the second provides a strong motive for the commission of the crime."

"But we don't know that Miss Pearl is anxious to marry Sir Joseph. He is anxious to marry her, but that is quite a different thing."

"Miss Pearl, to my knowledge, is a woman who has always had an eye to the main chance," said Perry Toat, drily. "She has kept herself highly respectable, so that she might make a good match. Branwin is wealthy, and can give her rank and position. She would do much to become his wife."

"Would she commit a murder?" asked Shawe, doubtfully.

"She might, and she might not. I can say nothing more until I learn precisely what she was doing on that night."

"How can you learn?"

"I shall question Parizade."

"The blind girl? What can she tell?"

"I don't know, but I shall be able to get all information from her, whatever she may know."

"But, being blind, she can see nothing."

"She may have *heard* something," said Perry Toat, with emphasis. "Having lost her eyesight her hearing has become very keen, and also she has a very powerful sense of smell."

"What," Ralph joked, "do you expect her to nose the trail like a dog?"

"I don't know what I expect; but the fact is, Mr. Shawe, I have made friends with all the four girls in the shop. Madame Coralie for her own sake will say nothing, but if those girls know anything I may induce them to speak. Badoura"—Miss Toat ticked off the names on her fingers—"can be worked by appealing to her jealousy, as she loves Eddy Vail. Zobeide, who is deaf, is anxious to get money and retire with her mother, whom she dearly loves, to the seaside. Peri Banou is an extravagant little minx, who is always in want of cash; while Parizade has a lover."

"Really!" Ralph expressed his astonishment. "But she is blind."

"She is pretty, and the man who loves her is an artist. Now, if I offer to share the reward of one thousand pounds with any one of these girls I may learn much; in fact, I am going to the shop to see Parizade to-night."

"I thought you had learnt all you wished to learn from her," said Shawe, uneasily. He had been told on a previous occasion what the blind girl knew, and the information had not pleased him.

"I wish to check her statements," said Miss Toat, quickly. "However, to-morrow something may be learnt worth your hearing from Badoura. She is one of the witnesses for the alibi, and I intend to ask her at what time Madame Coralie left the still-room to see Miss Branwin at the door of the shop."

"But I don't quite see—"

"How can you, Mr. Shawe? You are not a detective. Everyone to his trade."

"Her trade," corrected the barrister, quietly, as a return for the snub. "However, I shall see you to-morrow, and I trust that you will have something to tell me."

"I shall do my best. I can't do more," replied Perry Toat, with a shrug. And with this mild assurance the young man was obliged to be content.

Perry Toat had already arranged her plans. She had learnt on the previous day from Badoura, with whom she was in communication, that Madame Coralie was going to the theatre with her husband that evening. Therefore, when she arrived in Walpole Lane, she was not surprised to find the forewoman in a bad temper. This was natural, seeing that she loved Eddy Vail to such an extent that she resented his going out with his lawful wife. This was illogical; but Badoura, having been tricked into caring for the handsome scamp, was far past reason.

"I wish I hadn't fallen in love with him," she wailed to Miss Toat, when that businesslike lady arrived at the shop. "He treats me so badly."

"What can you expect, my dear? As a married man he should remain true to his wife. The mere fact that he pretended to love you when he should not, shows the kind of profligate he is."

"But Madame Coralie is so old," said Badoura, with a flush, which made her look very pretty. "She won't live for ever, and then—"

"Then you hope to marry Eddy Vail. My dear girl, I wouldn't count too much on that if I were you. Mr. Vail will do what suits him best."

"I shall make him marry me," said Badoura, fiercely.

"Can you?" asked Perry Toat, sceptically. "Yes. I know something."

"What is it?"

"I shan't tell you. Eddy Vail has no hold over me, as I have always kept myself to myself, so far as he is concerned. It is only because I am in love that I make such a fool of myself. But I know!" And she nodded.

"Come, tell me," coaxed Perry Toat, seeing in a flash how she could bring the girl to betray whatever she knew about Mr. Vail.

"I shan't. You are a detective, and I'm afraid of you. If I did right I should tell

Madame Coralie how you come here as a spy."

"If you do you will lose any chance of sharing the reward with me," Miss Toat assured her, coolly. "Besides, the mischief is done, and I know a lot."

"But you say that you will share the reward with the other girls."

"Of course. I shall share it with anyone who can put me on the right scent to trace the murderer. If you know anything"—she looked very straightly at Badoura—"remember you risk five hundred pounds by not telling me."

"I shall tell nothing," said Badoura, resolutely, "unless Eddy proves false to me." And she cut short the conversation by going out for a walk.

Perry Toat immediately resolved in some way to prove to the girl that Eddy Vail was falseness itself. "But I wonder what she knows?" the detective asked herself as she went in search of Parizade.

The blind girl was in her bedroom lying down, as the heat of the day and the hard work in the shop had tried her delicate constitution somewhat severely. The moment she heard Miss Toat's step she called her by name.

"How did you know it was me?" asked the newcomer, taking a seat beside the bed.

Parizade laughed. "Oh, I can tell your footsteps," she admitted; "that is one way, and the other is by that scent you use."

Miss Toat sniffed her handkerchief. "Peruvian Fragrance," she said with a laugh; "yes, it is an uncommon scent. George brings it to me; he's a purser on a steamer, you know."

Parizade, in her darkness, groped for the detective's hand. "Yes, dear, I know, and it is because you are in love, as I am, that I like you so much. I don't mind your being a detective at all, but I do hope you'll marry soon and give up the horrid business."

"There's no chance of my marrying George until I get this thousand pounds' reward which Sir Joseph Branwin offers."

"And I am to get half of it, if I can help you, remember," said the blind girl. "Like yourself, I can't marry Walter until we have money. Then we can live in the country in a tiny cottage, and he can paint his pictures while I look after the household."

"But can you do that, Parizade, seeing you are blind?"

"Oh, I have eyes at the end of my fingers," said the other, caressingly. "Why, I know every bit of this large house, so it will not be difficult to learn all about a small cottage. But fancy Walter loving a blind girl like me."

"You are so pretty, Parizade."

"I am glad of that, and it's all really genuine. Oh"—Parizade fell back on her pillows with a sigh—"how glad I shall be to take my own name and leave this horrid Pink Shop. Has what I told you given you any help? I do so want my share of the reward."

"I have got no help from it so far," said Miss Toat, shaking her head. "Tell me again exactly what happened."

"Oh, I have told you over and over again," said Parizade, petulantly. "There was another person in the house on that night."

"I know; Rosy Pearl," said the detective, swiftly.

"Yes; she was the customer who slept in the upstairs bedroom, and who did not wish her name to be known. Inspector Lanton was told by Madame, but as Miss Pearl knew nothing she was not called as a witness at her own request. But how did you learn the name, Miss Toat? Madame warned the girls not to tell it to anyone."

"I learnt it indirectly from Madame herself," said Miss Toat, evasively. "I suppose she was the person you heard breathing in the passage?"

"No," said Parizade, decisively. "I am sure that person was a man."

"Why do you think so?"

"Because the breathing was so heavy, and there was that smell of Harris tweed—you can't mistake that smell—and only men wear Harris tweed."

"Yes and no. Ladies sometimes have dresses made of it. But describe exactly how you came to hear and smell this person."

"Oh"—Parizade yawned—"I have told you so often."

"Tell me again. Every time you tell me I get a fresh idea."

"Well," said the blind girl, lying back passively, "on the night of the murder—of course, we none of us knew anything about it until next morning—Madame and the girls went to bed just after nine o'clock, as we were all so tired. Madame, after she saw Miss Branwin at the door to say that her mother would remain for treatment, sent away her husband and retired. It was just after nine when I remembered that I left a present from Walter to me in the shop. I didn't want the other girls to see it, so I went down about half-past nine."

"In the darkness, of course?" said the listening detective.

"Yes. Darkness and light are the same to me. I know the house so well that I never stumble or miss my way. Well, I found the present—a pair of gloves—just where Peri Banou had been lying in the alcove—I believe she must have seen them. Then, in returning along the lower passage, I heard the sound of heavy breathing at the end near the door which leads into the court."

"That was locked."

"It always is; but it might have been open for all I know on that night. I knew someone was there, and guessed that it was a man, as I smelt the peculiar scent of Harris tweed so strongly. I fancied that Eddy Vail had not gone away, but had come back."

"You mean that he had remained in the house?" corrected Perry Toat.

"Oh, yes. At all events, I fancied it was Eddy; so, not wishing to get myself into trouble with Madame, as she might have asked him to stay, I went upstairs and said nothing. Next day I learnt about the murder, and both Madame and Eddy said that he had really left the house. Then I became certain that there had been a stranger in the passage."

"Rosy Pearl, perhaps?"

"No. She was sleeping upstairs. But you may guess that I said nothing to anyone about what I had heard and smelt."

"Why did you not? It might have given Inspector Lanton a clue."

Parizade shuddered. "Oh, I didn't want to be mixed up with the police. It was best, I thought, to hold my tongue. I never told anyone until you came and said you were a detective."

"Well, and why did you tell me? You were frightened when I told you my profession, if I remember rightly."

"Yes. But, somehow, your being a woman made it seem better. I don't mind a lady detective. Then when you told about the reward I thought I might help you and get half, so that I might marry Walter."

"You shall get it, if I am successful," said Miss Toat, emphatically. "But do you really think that there was a man in the passage on that night?"

"Yes, I do—near the house door that leads into the court. He escaped in that way, and I believe he murdered Lady Branwin. I could swear to it."

"It will be hard to trace the criminal, male or female, by the smell of Harris tweed alone," commented Perry Toat, doubtfully. "It's a blind clue."

CHAPTER XIV.

AN AMAZING DISCOVERY

Mrs. Mellop returned from the Richmond journey in a very bad temper, as she had wholly failed to get her own way with the wary millionaire. Indeed, she was so persistent in her attentions that Branwin put an end to them by hinting very plainly that he was engaged to be married. He also gave the widow to understand that it was time she brought her visit to a close, as he wished to send Audrey abroad for a time. Mrs. Mellop offered to accompany the girl, but learnt that arrangements had been made for the young lady to stay in Paris with a French family. No wonder the widow returned almost in tears, as she saw very well that the vintage was ended, and she had gathered but few grapes. Pleading a headache, she did not appear at dinner, and it was not until the next morning that Audrey learnt about her father's new plans. They did not please her.

"I shan't go abroad," she said bluntly, when Mrs. Mellop had explained matters. "Papa wishes to separate me from Ralph."

"And wishes you to marry Lord Anvers," finished Mrs. Mellop, maliciously.

Audrey laughed contemptuously. "I have refused Lord Anvers."

"He won't take a refusal, neither will your father."

"What does that matter to me?" cried the girl, passionately. "Do you think that I am going to place my happiness in Lord Anvers' hands? A man I detest with all my heart. I shall marry Ralph, and no one else."

"Then you will lose your money," said Mrs. Mellop, with a gesture of despair.

"I don't mind losing it, so long as I have love."

"Love!" The widow made a face. "Oh! love is all very well, but it isn't money, and money is a necessity."

"To you perhaps, Mrs. Mellop, not to me. Ralph would marry me to-morrow if I chose. But I don't choose, as such a marriage would hinder his career. We must wait for better times."

"Well, I'm sure I hope you'll get your own way. But you can have no idea how hard your father is," wailed Mrs. Mellop. "He throws me over as coolly as though I were an old shoe, and I shall have to go to-morrow. Oh! the man's mad," she added, in a petty rage, "to think of marrying that horrid woman."

"Well, you have had your chance," Audrey said, with a shrug; "and, as I told you, my father has taken his own way. I would rather you had married him."

"Then you love me, darling?" cried the effusive widow, caressingly.

"No, I don't," rejoined the girl, removing a pair of fond arms which had been thrown round her neck; "but of two evils I choose the least.

"You would make a better Lady Branwin than Miss Pearl."

"I'm sure I should," assented Mrs. Mellop, with vigour, although she was rather daunted by the refusal of Audrey to accept her advances. "Oh! with all that money I would enjoy myself. And if I married your father, Audrey, I should get him to let you marry Mr. Shawe."

"You have no influence with papa, Mrs. Mellop. However, you are no worse off than you were when you came here."

"Oh! but I am," cried Mrs. Mellop, quite forgetting the jewellery and clothes that she had bought on the credit of her host's name. "Think of what people will say. My name has been coupled with Sir Joseph's, and it is a shame that he should behave so cruelly. But I shan't submit quietly to seeing him carried off by that woman," raged the widow, walking up and down biting her handkerchief. "I shall tell what I know."

"What do you know?"

"I know that Sir Joseph goes out night after night prowling about the streets. Ugh! the horrid old man."

"How dare you!" cried Audrey, flaming up. "Papa goes to help the poor."

Mrs. Mellop laughed contemptuously. "Sir Joseph never helped a single poor person in his life," she said sneeringly. "He goes out for no good purpose, you may be sure. Why, he was out on the night his wife was murdered," hinted Mrs. Mellop, malignantly. "I believe he had something to do with the matter."

Audrey had no reason to be fond of her father, who had always treated her selfishly. But this unfounded accusation was too much for her. She sprang at the little widow and shook her. "How dare you talk in that way?" she said in a cold, hard voice. "You can't connect my father with—"

"Oh, can't I?" interrupted Mrs. Mellop, extricating herself from the girl's grasp with a shriek. "Why, when I was waiting in Walpole Lane on that night I saw your father on the other side of the road."

"You are a fool!" said Miss Branwin, trying to conceal her agitation. "Even if you saw papa, that proves nothing. And you had better hold your tongue, or you will get into trouble."

Mrs. Mellop ran to the door of the room, so as to avoid another shaking. "I shall get Sir Joseph into trouble," she said spitefully. "He shan't play fast and loose with poor little me. I shall go back home to-day."

"Had you not better see papa?" asked Audrey, ironically, "and say what you intend to do?"

"I know what I intend to do," retorted the widow, tossing her head, "and it won't be pleasant for Sir Joseph when he knows. You're a horrid girl, Audrey, and worthy of your common father, who is only the son of a labourer, when all is said and done. I decline to associate with such riff-raff, so good-day to both of you." And Mrs. Mellop, bursting with spite, swept out of the room in what she conceived was a grand way.

Audrey shrugged her shoulders when the little woman disappeared, as she regarded the hinted accusation as merely due to spite; and without doubt it was, as Mrs. Mellop could not possibly prove Branwin's complicity in the crime. Sir Joseph certainly might have been in Walpole Lane, although Audrey did not think that this was probable. Yet, even if he had been, his presence, as the girl had already observed, proved absolutely nothing.

When Mrs. Mellop took her departure, bag and baggage—which she did in the afternoon—Audrey wended her way to Kensington Gardens to keep the three o'clock appointment with Ralph Shawe; but although she waited for over an hour he did not make his appearance. This omission made Audrey confident that there was something wrong, as it was not like Ralph to evade a meeting. Lately she had noted his unwillingness to answer questions connected with the search for Lady Branwin's murderer; and now that he so pointedly avoided her company—for what could be more pointed than a failure to keep his engagement?—she decided to see Miss Toat and ask questions. The detective certainly knew all that Ralph knew, and in what Ralph refused to speak about might be found his reason for behaving so strangely. With this idea the girl left the Gardens and took a cab to Buckingham Street.

For once Miss Perry was not in her office, but the grimy little boy—technically termed a clerk—told her that the detective would return in a few minutes. Meanwhile she was shown into the inner room to wait, and found there no less a person than Colonel Ilse. He rose politely when she entered, and looked at her so hard that Audrey blushed.

"I also am waiting for Miss Toat, Miss Branwin," said the Colonel, offering a chair. "Will you not be seated? I understand she will not be long."

"Thank you. How did you know my name, Colonel Ilse?"

"I must answer like a Yankee by asking another question, Miss Branwin. How did you know mine?"

"Miss Toat told me."

"And Miss Toat told *me*," repeated the Colonel, smiling. "The fact is—I hope you will not mind my saying this, as I am old enough to be your father, young lady—you remind me of someone who was very dear to me. Curiosity made me ask your name."

"And curiosity made me ask what yours was also," said Audrey, quickly. "Your face—your eyes, to be particular—remind me of someone."

Ilse looked at her rather oddly. "Of whom, may I ask?" he said eagerly.

The girl shook her head. "I can't say; but I almost feel as if I had known you before. I daresay it is fancy."

"Perhaps it is, and perhaps it isn't," said the Colonel, quietly.

"What do you mean?"

"Nothing, Miss Branwin; only we may have met by chance."

The excuse did not satisfy Audrey, but she could not very well go on asking questions. She liked the looks of Colonel Ilse. He had a handsome but rather sad face, and his blue eyes were strangely kind and pathetic. "You are searching for your little girl?" she said impulsively. "Miss Toat told me."

"Upon my word," said the Colonel, humorously, "Miss Toat seems to have told you a great deal. Yes, Miss Branwin, I am looking for my daughter who was stolen from me some twenty and more years ago. A hospital nurse took her away, and I have never been able to find her."

"Why did the nurse take her away?"

Colonel Ilse actually blushed through his tan. "It was in a fit of jealousy that she did so," he explained hurriedly. "That is, she—well, it is too long a story to tell you. But I have placed the matter in the hands of Miss Toat, and lately she has told me that she thinks she will be successful in finding my daughter."

Audrey shook her pretty head gravely. "It is a long time after the loss to think of finding her."

"I have been in India for many years," said the Colonel, who seemed to be singularly frank in his conversation, "and a military man has scanty time to attend to his own affairs. But lately I have retired, and as I have come in for a fortune, owing to the death of my uncle, I greatly wish to find my child, so that she may be my heiress."

"I hope you will be successful," said Audrey, sympathetically.

"I hope so too, and I think if we can trace this hospital nurse that the truth will become known. The nurse has— Oh!"—Colonel Ilse stopped explaining as the door opened to reveal Perry Toat—"here is the lady. Miss Branwin, I shall leave you to discharge your business first. My interview can come later." And the Colonel bowed himself into the outer room.

Perry Toat took off her gloves and sat at her desk. By this time the effect of Madame Coralie's improvements had worn off more or less, and the detective was rapidly becoming the drab, unlovely personage she actually was. But Audrey liked her better without the mask of fictitious loveliness, as she had an honest if ugly face. The girl felt that she could absolutely trust her. And she wanted someone to trust, now that Ralph had failed her.

"Do you like Colonel Ilse?" asked Miss Toat when the door closed.

"Very much," said Audrey, frankly. "He seems to be a very nice man, but sad."

"Ah! it is my task to turn his sadness into joy," said the detective, looking keenly at her client.

"By finding his daughter?"

"Yes, by finding his daughter," assented Perry Toat, who looked a sharp little rat of a woman as she sat at the table. "And now, let us come to your business, Miss Branwin. I can't give you much time, so please state what you wish to see me about as speedily as possible."

"I speak in confidence, of course," hesitated Audrey, rather embarrassed.

"Of course, in strictest confidence. What is it?"

"It is about Mr. Shawe. I can't understand him."

"But you are engaged to marry him."

"Yes." Audrey flushed. "And I love him very dearly. I don't mind telling you this, as you are a woman and can understand. But lately there is something queer about him. I wish him to learn who murdered my mother, and he has been trying. But over a week ago he asked me to give up the search."

"Oh"—Perry Toat sat up alertly—"he asked you to give up the search. Why?"

Miss Branwin felt in her pocket and brought out the anonymous letter. "For this reason," she said, passing it to Perry Toat. "This letter warns me that if I persist in searching into the case I shall experience the greatest grief of my life."

"Oh!" said Perry Toat again, and ran her sharp eyes over the ill-written lines. "And Mr. Shawe agrees with this letter?"

"Yes. He is most anxious to get me to give up searching, and always avoids answering my questions as much as he can. To-day I had an appointment to see him in Kensington Gardens, but he did not appear. This is the first time he has ever behaved in this way, so I came at once to ask you if you can tell me the reason for his change of mind."

Perry Toat looked hard at the anonymous letter, and did not answer. After a time she went to a tin box and brought out some papers, with which she compared the missive addressed to Audrey. "Let me look at the envelope, please," she said after a long pause. "Oh, here it is." She picked it up from the table and examined the postmark.

"What do you make of it?" asked Audrey, impatiently.

"Of this letter? Oh, it is written by someone who wants the case stopped."

"By the assassin?"

"Why do you think it might be the assassin?"

"Because only the assassin would like an end put to the case."

"Humph!" said Miss Toat, anxiously. "That is one view; but there is another, Miss Branwin. A certain person may be anxious to prevent your learning the truth in case it should cause you great pain."

"So the letter says," said Audrey, quickly. "But I don't understand, unless—" Suddenly she stopped, with her mouth open. "Oh!" she gasped faintly, for it had just occurred to her what Mrs. Mellop had hinted, "you don't think that my father wrote it?"

"No." Perry Toat looked astonished. "Why should you think your father—"

"It was merely an idea," interrupted Audrey, feverishly. "The fact is, a certain spiteful woman hinted that my father was glad of my mother's death, so that he could marry Miss Pearl."

"In fact, this person said plainly that Sir Joseph was guilty," said the other, bluntly.

"Not exactly. But"—Audrey rose quickly and looked indignant—"it is quite ridiculous to think of such things."

"And yet"—Perry Toat tapped the anonymous letter—"the person who wrote this may have written it because he suspected your father."

"He? Then a man wrote it. What man? Can you guess?"

"I can do more than guess," said the detective, drily. "I know by comparison of handwritings. This anonymous letter was written by Ralph Shawe."

"Oh!" Audrey turned pale. "So that explains his conduct."

CHAPTER XV.

RALPH'S SUSPICION

It took Audrey some time to recover from the announcement so unexpectedly made by Miss Toat. In fact, she felt so faint that the detective made her drink a glass of water. When better she asked a question which had been in her mind all the time.

"You don't accuse Mr. Shawe of—"

"No, no, no!" said Miss Toat, hastily. "How can you think of such a thing? Mr. Shawe is perfectly innocent. He wrote the letter because he suspected another person."

"Who is the other person?"

Perry Toat hesitated. "I think it will be best for you to ask Mr. Shawe to give you an explanation," she said a trifle stiffly. "I can't say for certain whom he suspects. But it must be someone known to you, or he would not have worded his letter in the way he has done."

Audrey leant her elbow on the table, and her now aching head on her hand. "I don't see how you can make out that Mr. Shawe wrote the letter," she said.

For answer Perry Toat placed before her the letters which she had taken out of the tin box. These were from Ralph, giving various instructions to the detective. Beside these she placed the anonymous epistle.

"You can see," said Miss Toat, quietly, "that although the handwriting of the anonymous letter is disguised, there is a great similarity to that of Mr. Shawe's. Here and here"—she pointed out several letters; and then, to clinch the matter, she said positively: "The paper is some which Mr. Shawe's office-boy keeps to make notes on. I have noticed that. Also the postmark is

London."

"But all this is not strong enough to prove that Mr. Shawe wrote the letter."

"I think it is, Miss Branwin. However, it will be easy for him to deny the authorship if you ask him. I must say," added Miss Toat, determined to be perfectly frank, "that the evidence is slight, and I go mostly by the similarity of the writing. Also I told Mr. Shawe something which Parizade told me, which seemed to alarm him. Ever since then he has tried to stop me looking into the matter. Therefore I judge that to enlist you on his side he wrote this," and Miss Toat laid her lean hand on the anonymous epistle.

"But why couldn't he speak plainly to me? I see no reason why he should trick me in this manner," argued Audrey, distressed to find that Ralph had behaved in so underhanded a way.

"I can't answer that question; and, in spite of my belief, I may be wrong in suspecting Mr. Shawe. However, it is easy to learn the truth. Take any letter which Mr. Shawe has written to you and place it before him, along with this anonymous one. Then see what he says, and report to me his reply."

Audrey agreed to do this, and went away, much puzzled. The mystery of the case was affecting her nerves; and, now that Ralph seemed to be on the side of the enemy, she did not know which way to turn for advice. Perry Toat's intentions were good, but she seemed to be more clever at theorising than in finding real evidence likely to be of service for the elucidation of the problem. So far, what discoveries she had made—and these were but trifling—had resulted in nothing. Poor Audrey went home lamenting inwardly that the truth would never become known.

However, there was only one thing to be done, and she did it. That is, she wrote a short note to Ralph asking him to call at the Camden Hill house. As Mrs. Mellop was now absent, and Sir Joseph would probably go out in the evening according to his usual custom, the coast would be clear for Ralph's visit. Besides, Audrey was weary of playing a secret game, and wished her lover to come forward boldly, and claim her even at the risk of Sir Joseph's displeasure. This would fall on her sooner or later, so it was just as well to get it over at once. She sent the letter by special messenger, and then went to lie down, as her head was aching. It was not to be wondered at, seeing what a shock she had sustained.

Sir Joseph came home to express his satisfaction that Mrs. Mellop was out of the house, and ascribed his daughter's weary looks when she met him to regret for the loss of her friend. Audrey hastened to undeceive him.

"I told you that I did not like Mrs. Mellop, papa, and I have not changed my opinion," she said very distinctly.

"Well, my dear, you were right for once," replied Branwin, more amiably than usual. "She talked too much, and I began to feel that she was a nuisance. However, she has gone, and you needn't see her again." He paused, then abruptly made his announcement. "I intend to take you abroad."

"I don't care to go, papa."

"It doesn't matter what you care, you will do as you are told. A change of scene will do you good, as you look pale enough. I wish you to stop with Madame Lemain. She is a charming woman, and her husband is a very good friend of mine. You shall stay in Paris until you agree to obey me and marry Lord Anvers. Not a word. I have made up my mind."

"And I have made up mine," cried the girl, greatly angered. "I refuse to marry Lord Anvers, and I have told him so."

"Oh, that doesn't matter," Branwin assured her, coolly. "Anvers intends to propose again."

"He will receive the same answer."

"I think not, Audrey. A few weeks in Paris may cause you to change your mind, since you will not be seeing that rascal Shawe every day, as I have reason to believe you are doing."

"I see Ralph whenever I can," Audrey confessed, candidly and defiantly, "and if you do not consent to my marriage with him I shall run away."

"By all means, if you choose to risk the loss of your dowry," said Sir Joseph, grimly. "I hold the purse, remember, and if you disobey me not one shilling of my money will you get. I don't intend to talk of this matter any more to you. Either you do what I want or I shall disown you as a daughter. In Paris you may perhaps make up your mind," and without another glance at the pale-faced girl Branwin left the room.

But Audrey was still unconquered. Her father took the wrong tone with her when he hoped to bully her into compliance. Had he spoken affectionately and been more amiable she might have overlooked his previous neglect, and have striven to please him. "But whatever he said or did," muttered the girl to herself, "I should never consent to marry Lord Anvers." So it seemed that Sir Joseph's design of sending her abroad for reflection was likely to prove useless.

The time Audrey had appointed for her lover to call was eight o'clock; but he did not make his appearance. Sir Joseph had not gone out, as the girl had expected him to, and was writing letters in his library. Alone in her late mother's sitting-room Audrey paced to and fro, with her eyes on the timepiece. At half-past eight she grew quite sick with apprehension, as she began to believe that something must have happened to Ralph, or else that he was afraid to face her. Perhaps, after all, Ralph, since he had written the letter, had something to do with the crime, as he so pointedly avoided a meeting. Audrey felt that she could not pass the night without knowing the truth, and at a quarter to nine o'clock made up her mind that as her lover would not come to her she would go to him. He had chambers in the Temple, as she well knew; for when Lady Branwin was alive they had gone there to have afternoon tea with the young barrister. It was impossible to remain in a state of suspense any longer, so Audrey ran up to her room, changed from her dinner dress into a quiet walking frock, and stole out of the house as unobstrusively as she could. Fortunately she had a couple of pounds in her purse, so did not hesitate to call a cab. In a very short time she was speeding along in a taxi on her rash errand.

And it was rash. Here she was, a young girl, going by night to call on a young bachelor. Even though she was engaged to him, this daring was enough to make every matron in Society shriek with horror. While driving through the lighted streets, Audrey could not help thinking of what Mrs. Mellop would say did she know of this escapade; for the little widow herself was terribly afraid of Mrs. Grundy, and, although lively enough under the rose, would never have dared to act in this way. But the girl did not care. Mrs. Mellop was not likely to hear about the matter, and, even if she did, Audrey was too anxious and worried to take notice of spiteful remarks. Her whole life's happiness was at stake, and she felt that it was impossible to wait any longer for an explanation. Ralph apparently knew something, and in some way was connected with what took place on that fatal night. What that something might be Audrey dreaded to think. All the same, she was determined to know what it was. She could bear anything save suspense.

On arriving in Fleet Street the girl dismissed her cab, and walked into the Gardens, wherein rose the tall pile of buildings containing Shawe's chambers. A shilling and a word to a friendly hall-porter soon procured her admission into the building, and she went up in the lift to the third floor. Knowing Ralph's number, she rang the bell, wondering if he was at home, or if her journey had been in vain. In a few minutes the door was opened, and the barrister himself appeared. For the moment, as Audrey wore a veil, he did not recognise her in the dim light of the passage.

"May I inquire what you want?" he asked politely.

"Ralph!" said the girl, faintly, and leant against the wall, as the strength which had kept her up was now failing her.

"Good heavens, Audrey!" cried Shawe, dismay. "What are you doing here?"

"Mahomet would not come to the mountain, so the mountain has to come to Mahomet," replied Audrey, with an anxious smile.

"But, my dear girl, it isn't right, and you—"

"Oh! never mind appearances," she interrupted feverishly. "No one knows me as I wear this thick veil. Let me in, Ralph, I have much to say to you."

Shawe immediately conducted her into his sitting-room. There was nothing else to be done, as he knew that Audrey could be obstinate when she chose, and would refuse to depart without an explanation. Moreover—and this almost banished the enormity of her visit from his mind—he dreaded lest she should have learnt something which he particularly did not wish her to know. The young man felt sure that she really might have gained the forbidden knowledge, since she had dared to take such a bold step.

"Sit down here, dear," he said, wheeling forward a comfortable armchair. "You look pale; let me give you a glass of wine."

"No, I don't want any wine. I feel all right."

"But, Audrey," said Ralph, who could scarcely conceal his dismay, "how did you escape Mrs. Mellop and your father?"

"Mrs. Mellop has gone home," explained the girl, with a faint smile, as she thought of the little widow's discomfiture, "and my father was busy in his library. I slipped out quietly."

"But you should not have come here, darling. Think of what the world will say. It is so rash."

"I don't care what the world says," retorted Audrey, crossly. "The world is doing nothing for me that I should consider it. You blame me for coming to see you, when you have broken two appointments with me."

"I broke the first I admit, my dear; but I made no second appointment."

"You had my note asking you to come to me this evening?"

"Yes, but I did not come."

"You had no intention of coming?"

"No," said Shawe, without hesitation. "I had no intention of coming."

"Ralph"—Audrey caught his hand—"do you think that you are treating me in a straightforward way?"

"Yes and no. Perhaps I should be more open with you, and yet if I was you

100

would be afraid and angry."

"I am angry in any case, seeing that you will not trust me; but afraid"—she looked at him very straightly—"why should I be afraid?"

Shawe dropped into an opposite chair with an air of lassitude. "If I explained that, Audrey, I should have to be more frank than I care to be."

"Why? For what reason?"

"There are things which I do not wish you to know."

"In connection with my mother's death?"

"Yes," said Ralph, after a second's pause, "in connection with your mother's death. Audrey"—he knelt at her feet and looked anxiously into her face —"why not leave this matter alone and marry me?"

"How can I when you refuse to trust me?" she said sternly.

"I do trust you. I trust you entirely."

"Then tell me what you know."

"I can't. It is too difficult."

"Is that why you chose to write me an anonymous letter?" she asked quickly.

The barrister rose and flushed a deep red, while he looked at her with startled eyes. "What do you mean?" he stammered.

"I mean what I say. Perry Toat examined that letter, and by comparing your handwriting with that of my unknown correspondent, by looking at the postmark, and by recognising the common paper as some used by your office-boy to keep notes, she is certain that you wrote the letter."

There was a long pause. Shawe, driven into a corner, said nothing, and did not even meet her reproachful eyes. Standing on the hearth-rug he stared at the floor, opening and shutting his hands.

"Well," said Audrey, after a pause, and very impatiently, "what do you say?"

"I wrote the letter, and for a very good reason," admitted the young man, nervously.

"What is the reason?" she demanded, looking at him searchingly.

"I can't tell you, Audrey; don't ask me."

"But I do ask you, and you must tell me. Why did you write that letter?"

"If you will have the truth," burst out Shawe, "I wished to spare you pain."

"So you said in the letter," Audrey assured him, coolly; "but what pain is it that you wish to spare me?"

"Never mind; never mind." Ralph impatiently waved his hand. "You should not be here, Audrey. Let me take you back home."

The girl laughed bitterly. "Is that all you have to say? I don't leave this room until you tell me the truth. I want to know why you wrote an anonymous letter instead of speaking to me openly."

"Had I spoken openly you would have asked questions which I could not answer."

"You must answer them now. Did you murder my mother yourself?"

"Good heavens! no. How can you ask such a thing?" cried Shawe, furiously. "Is this the opinion you have of me?"

"Very well," said Audrey, coolly; "you are innocent yourself, so we will let that pass. Miss Toat said that you have never been the same since she told you something that Parizade had said. What is it?"

Shawe reflected for a few moments. "I see that I shall have to tell you all, my dear," he said sadly, "although I have done my best to spare you the knowledge. Parizade, while wandering about the Pink Shop on the night of the crime, smelt a strong scent of Harris tweed. Listen," and Ralph told the girl in detail the same story as the blind woman had told Perry Toat.

"Well," said Audrey, much puzzled, "it seems that someone who wore Harris tweed was in the passage hiding. But what has this to do with your desire that I should know nothing?"

"Who is it that constantly wears Harris tweed—almost constantly, that is?" asked Shawe.

"Plenty of people wear Harris tweed—both men and women. Why, my father —"

"Yes," said Ralph, interrupting pointedly, "your father."

Audrey grew red and white by turns. "My father—you suspect my father?"

"I believe that he is guilty," said Ralph, solemnly, and nodded.

CHAPTER XVI.

The moment Audrey became certain of the name of the person accused by her lover, she recalled what Mrs. Mellop had said about Sir Joseph. As the thought came into her mind she turned very white, and leaning back in the chair closed her eyes, feeling deadly sick. It really seemed as though Ralph had spoken the truth, and that her father, of all people, was guilty. No wonder the diamonds had not been stolen. Sir Joseph had not crept into the Pink Shop to steal jewels, but to rid himself of an undesirable wife. A nervous shiver shook the girl from head to foot, and she almost lost consciousness. But the touch of a cold glass rim on her lips made her open her eyes, and she saw that Shawe was offering her some wine.

"Drink this, darling, and you will feel better," he said anxiously.

This time Audrey did not refuse, as she felt that she needed to be sustained at the moment. Without a word she drank half the wine, and then motioned Ralph to remove the glass. In a minute or so the colour came back to her face, and she sat up with renewed strength.

"I am all right now," she declared firmly. "Ralph, sit down and explain."

"What is there to explain?" said Shawe, replacing the wine-glass on the table and resuming his former seat. "You know that I suspect Sir Joseph, and why I suspect him."

"And for this reason you wrote the anonymous letter?"

"Yes," said the barrister, frankly. "After Perry Toat told me what Parizade had said, and after what you mentioned about your father going out at night— ostensibly to help the poor—I suspected him. You mentioned your father's prowling before our Kensington Gardens conversation. I knew if I told you face to face that you would either be indignant with me or you would go straight to your father and make trouble. It was my desire to keep my suspicions quiet, since they are difficult to verify. For this reason I wrote you anonymously, and advised you to stop the search. I knew what grief it would cause you."

Audrey leant back and looked at her lover. "I have no reason to love my father, as you know," she said dully. "He has always been unkind to me, and he was unkind to my poor mother; but I can't think that he killed her."

"The evidence is slight, I admit," replied Ralph, gravely; "and perhaps it is evidence that would not stand in a court of law. All the same, to my mind, it certainly lays Sir Joseph open to suspicion."

"Parizade might have mistaken the smell?"

"No. Being blind, she has particularly keen olfactory nerves—her sense of smell is almost as highly developed as that of a dog. And the perfume of Harris tweed—if it can be called a perfume—that peaty smell, I mean—is so strong and so characteristic that even an ordinary person could guess that,—"

"Other people besides my father wear Harris tweed suits," interrupted Audrey, trying to find excuses.

"Quite so. Ladies wear tailor-made dresses of it and men wear suits. But as a rule that particular kind of cloth is mostly worn by those who shoot, and is worn as a rule in the country. It is rarely that one sees it in London—at all events amongst people of your father's class."

"Yes," admitted Audrey, "father is always particular about his dress. He goes to the City in a frock-coat and a silk hat, and invariably dresses for dinner. In fact, he does what most people in Society do in the way of dress. But remember that I told you how he went on the prowl."

"Which people in Society do not do, as a rule," said Ralph. "Quite so, my dear. But why I suspect your father is that he has quite a craze for Harris tweed, and once or twice told me that for ordinary suits he wears no other cloth. Besides, he certainly wants to marry Miss Pearl, and—"

"Yes, yes, yes! I quite understand, and I admit that he might have been lurking in the passage on that night. Certainly he was in Walpole Lane during the evening."

"How do you know?" demanded Shawe, rather startled.

"Mrs. Mellop saw him. He was on the hither side of the lane when I came to ask if my mother intended to remain for the night."

"Could Mrs. Mellop have been mistaken?"

"I don't think so, unfortunately," said Audrey, with a mournful look. "She knew him so well, and also she saw him in his tweed suit early in the evening when she came to take me to the theatre."

"I thought you told me that he was not at dinner, and went out very early?"

"So he did," said the girl, quickly; "but Mrs. Mellop came early also, and she passed him in the hall when he was going out. He did not stay to dinner. It was six o'clock when he went out—about the time Mrs. Mellop arrived. She mentioned the fact to me."

"And when did she say that she saw Sir Joseph in the lane?"

"To-day. That was one reason why I wished to see you. Mrs. Mellop has been trying hard to get my father to marry her. Yesterday she learnt from his own lips that he intended to marry Rosy Pearl, and lost her temper. My father asked her to leave, and she returned to her own home this afternoon. At our last interview she hinted that she believed my father had something to do with the death of my mother, and stated that she had seen him in the lane."

"Has she any other grounds upon which to base such a statement?"

"I don't think so. And I don't believe she believes what she says. It is simply the petty spite of a woman who has been disappointed. She can do no harm to my father in any way."

"Singly, I don't think she can," assented the barrister, thoughtfully; "but if Parizade's evidence became public property there would be trouble if it were taken in conjunction with what Mrs. Mellop saw."

"I don't think that Perry Toat suspects my father," said Audrey, after a lengthy pause; "at least, she did not say that she did. She told me to ask you for an explanation, as she declared that you seemed disturbed by Parizade's evidence."

"And with good reason," said the barrister. "No one but you and I know how important that evidence is, seeing that we are aware of your father's liking for Harris tweed."

"I can't think that he is guilty, all the same," said Audrey, tearfully.

Shawe walked up and down the room thoughtfully. "Well," he said finally, "I have kept my suspicions from you as long as I could; but now that you know, Audrey, I think you should question your father."

"Oh!"—she shrank back in her chair—"I dare not."

"If you don't Perry Toat may get to know what we have discovered, and as she is anxious to gain the reward she will certainly go to Sir Joseph herself."

Audrey shivered. "Oh, how angry he would be!"

"If he is innocent he certainly would show Miss Toat no mercy; on the other hand, if he is guilty, he would make terms."

"I can't think that he is guilty," cried the girl, in despair. "With all his faults, he surely would not strangle his own wife." She rose to her feet.

"It seems incredible, but—look at the evidence. Audrey, you must speak to your father or let me speak. But tell me one thing"—he took her in his arms —"have you forgiven me for my strange conduct, for I know that it seemed strange in your dear eyes?"

"Yes. I know why you acted as you did. It was to save me from grief. And if my father is guilty," said the girl, shivering, "it certainly will be the greatest grief of my life, as you said in the letter. How can I marry you should my father turn out to be a murderer?"

"My darling"—Ralph held her to his heart—"I don't visit the sins of the father on the child. If he murdered a dozen women I should still make you my wife; and I wish you would leave the whole of this horrible affair alone and marry me at once."

"Unless my father can exonerate himself I shall have to leave it alone. I dare not go on with a matter which involves his honour."

"And more than that. It involves his liberty and life, and—hush!"

He stopped short to listen, and Audrey listened also. It seemed for the moment, so still were they, that they had been changed into stone. "It's a ring at the front door," said Ralph, anxiously.

"Don't bring anyone in," pleaded Audrey, hastily letting down her veil.

"Trust me," replied Ralph, and left the room. He had only been gone two minutes and Audrey heard him open the door, when there came the sound of a loud and domineering voice. The girl recognised it at once.

"Oh"—she clasped her hands and shrank against the wall—"my father!"

It was indeed Sir Joseph who burst into the room, looking as furious as a mad bull. Ralph was trying to detain him, but in vain. "I'll break your head if you try to stop me," bellowed Sir Joseph, who was beside himself with rage. "Oh, there you are, you shameless girl. It is no use your hiding your face with that veil. I know you. I have followed you here."

"And what if you have?" demanded Audrey, throwing up the veil and looking at the intruder with flashing eyes.

"What if I have—what if I have," roared her father, clenching his big hands. "You jade, do you ask me that when I find you here in this scoundrel's rooms at ten o'clock in the evening?"

Ralph closed the door with a crash and faced the millionaire. "I am not a scoundrel."

"You are. Because I declined to allow you to see Audrey at my house you have decoyed her here."

"I came here of my own free will," said Audrey, who was deadly pale but quite firm.

"Then you go away at my free will," said her father, advancing. "I have a cab below. Come away at once. Oh, you minx! You little thought that I told

Ranger to watch you." (Ranger was one of Sir Joseph's footmen.) "Yes, he did watch you, and by my orders. He saw you leave the house, and followed you to hear you tell the cabman to drive to the Temple. When he informed me I guessed that you had come to see this—this—" Branwin could not think of a name bad enough to call this barrister, so contented himself by shaking his fist furiously.

"You set one of your servants to spy on your daughter?" said Audrey, with a look of profound scorn.

"Yes, I did, and it is lucky for you that I took such care of your reputation, you hussy! I can silence the man, but if anyone else came to know of your presence here, think what the world would say."

"I don't care what the world says," said Audrey, contemptuously.

"I care. It is my good name you are dragging through the mud."

"What of your own good name which your own wicked actions are dragging in the mud?" cried Ralph, suddenly, and faced the millionaire defiantly.

"What the deuce do you mean?"

"I shall tell you what I mean. I would not do so but that you are treating Audrey so vilely. You were in the Pink Shop on the night your wife was murdered. Deny it if you can."

Branwin staggered against the wall, and glared at the speaker. "Deny it if I can!" he echoed wrathfully. "Of course I can deny it. You fool, what do you mean by saying such a thing?"

"You were in the Pink Shop on that night," said Ralph, doggedly.

"I was not."

"At all events, you were in the lane," said Audrey, suddenly.

"You also! You also!" Sir Joseph raised his big arm, and would have struck his daughter, but that Audrey swerved and Ralph caught him by the wrist. "Let me go! Let me go, hang, you!" cried Sir Joseph, only he used a much worse oath.

Ralph was the slighter man, but by a clever trick he succeeded in taking the millionaire off his guard and sent him spinning across the room.

"If you dare to lay a finger on Audrey I'll throw you out of the window!" said the barrister, and flung his arm round the weeping girl.

Branwin glared, and wiped his heated forehead. "She and you accuse me of—of murder?" he gasped, trembling with rage.

"No. We simply say that you were in Walpole Lane and in the Pink Shop on the night of the murder. Perhaps you can explain?"

"I was not there, confound you! In the lane—yes, I was in the lane, but I did not enter the shop. By what right do you accuse me of the crime?"

"I say again, as I said before, that I do not accuse you of the crime," replied Ralph, firmly. "But you wore a suit of Harris tweed on that night?"

"I did. I always wear Harris tweed. It is my favourite cloth. Well?"

"One of the girls in the Pink Shop—a blind girl who has a very keen sense of smell—told the detective that I am employing to learn the truth how on the night of the murder she smelt the peaty scent of Harris tweed."

"What has that got to do with me? Plenty of people wear Harris tweed suits."

"Plenty of people don't wish to get rid of their wives," snapped Shawe.

"Ah! so you do accuse me?" said Sir Joseph, who was now calming down. "And my motive for wishing to get rid of my wife?"

"Miss Rosy Pearl can best answer that question."

"What do you know of Miss Pearl? Speak of her with respect, as she is to be my wife."

"So I said," answered Ralph, calmly; "and she was stopping in the Pink Shop also on that night."

Branwin winced and became very calm. It was wonderful to see how rapidly he cooled down from his hot anger. "Miss Pearl was in the shop as a client of Madame Coralie's," he said with an attempt at dignity. "You can have no grounds for saying that she had anything to do with the matter."

"I never said so," rejoined Ralph, drily, "and I only suspect you because of your wearing Harris tweed. Someone clothed in such a cloth certainly lurked in the passage on that night. Was that person you?"

"No," said Sir Joseph, coolly; "and I defy you to prove it."

"Oh! papa, we don't wish to prove it," said Audrey, quickly. "Your word denying your presence there is sufficient."

Branwin turned on his daughter with a great show of courtesy. "Pardon me, but I have not the honour of your acquaintance," he said politely. "You are a stranger to me."

"Papa, what do you mean?"

"I mean that you have left my house to see your lover against my wishes. I now cast you off, and you can stay here. You shall never re-enter the home you have disgraced."

Audrey sank into a chair with a cry of dismay, and Ralph advanced furiously on the millionaire.

"Sir Joseph, you can't mean this?"

"I do mean it. Audrey has disobeyed me, and, moreover, in conjunction with you, she has accused me of committing a murder."

"I did not—I did not!" cried Audrey, wringing her hands.

"Pardon me, but you did," said Branwin, still ironically polite. "You can take your own way henceforth, and I should advise you to change your name as speedily as possible. You can't possibly care to keep my name, when I am in danger of arrest as the murderer of my own wife. Mr. Shawe"—he bowed to the barrister—"I congratulate you on your approaching marriage."

"But, Sir Joseph—"

"Not a word more. My doors are closed on that woman"—he pointed insultingly to Audrey. "Good-night—both of you!" and with a final bow he walked heavily out of the room. A moment later, and they heard the door bang.

CHAPTER XVII.

WHAT AUDREY OVERHEARD

The two young people remained alone, looking at one another, and feeling quite aghast at the position in which they now found themselves. They had not expected Sir Joseph's appearance, much less that he would behave in so brutal a manner. Moreover, he had repelled the hinted accusation so calmly, and had admitted so freely that he had been in Walpole Lane, that both Audrey and Ralph felt certain he was completely innocent. Certainly, they had not directly accused him of committing the crime—the girl especially would have been horrified at the mere idea—but Sir Joseph had taken what they said to mean that they suspected him, and so had revenged himself in the cruel way he had done.

The bang of the door startled both from the momentary state of stupor into which the unexpected behaviour of Branwin had plunged them. Audrey, with a white face and startled eyes, looked at her lover. "What is to be done now?" she asked in a low voice.

"You must drive back home at once," said Ralph, determinedly.

She shook her head. "It is useless. My father will go straight home and give orders that I am not to be admitted."

"Oh, that is impossible. Think of the scandal."

"Papa does not mind the scandal. Already he has shown how far he is prepared to go by having me watched by Ranger. Oh"—she clenched her hand—"think of the disgrace of it all!"

"Then you must stay the night at some hotel."

"I cannot—I have no baggage. What hotel would take me in with no baggage? I have very little money too, and only the clothes I stand up in."

"Oh, the money doesn't matter, my darling. I can provide you with what you require," said Ralph, hastily; then muttered through his teeth: "But it is a confoundedly awkward situation in any case. Your father is a brute."

"He is what he has always been," said Audrey, with a tired sigh, for the late conversation had quite broken her up—"a man who has always had his own way. There is only one thing to be done"—and she rose.

"What is that?" asked Shawe, hopefully.

"I must go to the Pink Shop and throw myself on the mercy of my aunt."

Ralph brightened. "You clever darling to think of that," he said, looking at his watch. "It's half-past ten o'clock. I wonder if she will be still up?"

"I daresay; if not, we can rouse her. Come, Ralph"—she pulled down her veil to hide a very white face—"let us go at once. Oh, I do hope that my father will say nothing of my being here to anyone. I now see how rash I have been. It's terrible."

"Darling, I really don't think your father will say anything; for very shame he cannot. He will account for your absence by saying that you refused to obey him with regard to this marriage with Anvers, and that he turned you out. Everyone who knows what an animal he is will believe this version. I am quite sure that your visit here will never be known."

Thus comforted, and seeing the commonsense view taken by Shawe, Audrey went down the stairs with her lover, and they passed out of the great block of buildings and through the Gardens. The porter was not visible, and as Audrey wore such a thick veil, it was not likely that he would be able to recognise her on any future occasion. In Fleet Street the barrister procured a cab, and they drove westward in silence. The whole thing seemed like a nightmare, and Audrey shivered like a leaf. It was terrible to think that she had no home. If Madame Coralie refused to take her in, Heaven only knew what she could do; but she had every hope that her aunt would stand by her at this crisis, particularly as she seemed to hate Sir Joseph.

"Audrey darling, I think we must get married," said Ralph, after a long silence; "things can't go on in this way."

"But your career?" said Audrey, faintly.

"Never mind my career. Your father has deserted you, so you must become my wife, in order that I may have the right to protect you. Madame Coralie can keep you with her until we can arrange matters."

"But if Mrs. Mellop comes to hear of—"

"When you are my wife no one will dare to say a word," said Ralph, decidedly. "If anyone does, he or she will have to reckon with me. Besides, as I told you before, your father, brutal as he is, will not be such a fool as to soil the name of his own daughter. Popularity is the breath of his nostrils, and people would cry out on him if he talked of your visit to me."

"Yes." Audrey felt cheered when Ralph talked in this way. "I think you are right. But I do hope my aunt will take me in."

"From what you told me of the interview I think she will, dear. She seems to hate Sir Joseph in a very healthy manner. Audrey, I really don't know how you came to have such a father. I don't believe that you are his daughter. There must be some mistake."

"I wish I were anyone else's daughter indeed," said the girl, sighing.

"You will soon be my wife, so that will settle everything," said Ralph, as the cab turned into Walpole Lane. "Here we are, dearest. There is a light in the upstairs window, so Madame Coralie has not yet retired."

Having dismissed the cab, Shawe rang the bell, and shortly Badoura appeared to open the door, and to look with astonishment at the pair. "Will you tell Madame Coralie that Miss Branwin wishes to see her," said Shawe. "She is just returning from the theatre, and we called in here on our way to Camden Hill."

As Audrey wore a long cloak over her dress Badoura could not see that she was in walking costume, and quite believed the story. Of course, she knew who Shawe was, since that young gentleman had accompanied Miss Branwin on the morning when the death of the poor woman had been discovered. She, therefore, readily accepted the false explanation as a true one, and invited the two into the shop while she went upstairs to Madame Coralie, who was, it appeared, working late in the still-room at some newly-invented lotion. In the perfumed and dimly-lighted shop the lovers waited.

"That girl does not suspect the truth, you see," whispered Ralph, hurriedly.

"Thanks to your clever explanation," replied Audrey, in the same low voice. "But what am I to say when I stay here all night?"

"Your aunt will invent an explanation. Don't trouble. Here she is."

Even as Shawe spoke the heavy footfall of the woman was heard, and she came into the shop hurriedly. Her eyes, which were visible above the black silk of the yashmak, looked startled and anxious, although the rest of her face could not be seen. Evidently, and with very good reason, she was alarmed by this late and unexpected visit.

"Aunt Flora," began Audrey, and had only uttered the name, when Madame Coralie pointed to Shawe with an alarmed gesture. "Oh, that is all right!" went on the girl, rapidly. "He knows all about it. I told you that I would tell him; don't you remember?"

"Yes," said Madame Coralie, in her harsh voice, and peering at the young man anxiously, "I gave you permission to tell him. But mind you hold your tongue, Mr. Shawe." Then, without waiting for a reply, she turned to Audrey: "What is the matter that you come here at this hour?"

"My father has turned me out of the house, Aunt Flora, and I come to you for shelter," said Audrey, rapidly. "I have nowhere to go."

Madame Coralie clutched her yashmak and stamped her foot. When she spoke her voice was almost inarticulate with rage. "Do you mean to say that Joseph has dared to turn you from your home at this hour?"

"Yes." And Audrey, assisted by Shawe, rapidly related all that had taken place, although they both suppressed, for obvious reasons, any account of the suspicions they entertained on the evidence of Parizade's keen sense of smell. "So you see," ended the girl, with a sob, "that unless you take me in I have no place to shelter my head."

"My dear!" Madame Coralie made as though to catch her niece in her arms, but checked herself abruptly. "Of course you shall stay here as long as you like. But Badoura told me you had come from the theatre."

"My excuse for this midnight visit," said Ralph, quickly; "and now, Madame, you must invent some reason for Audrey stopping here for the night."

"Oh, that is easy enough"—she stepped back and looked at the slender figure of the girl, scarcely visible in the dim light—"you are too thin, Miss Branwin, and you wish me to treat you."

"Will Badoura accept that excuse?" asked Audrey, timidly.

"Yes," said Madame, bluntly; "she will accept any excuse that I like to give her. If she doesn't she loses her situation. Don't trouble, Miss—"

"Why don't you call me Audrey, Aunt Flora?"

"Because I don't want the relationship known," said the woman, promptly; "it is just as well, therefore, that I should call you Miss Branwin. But we can't stay talking here all night. Go away, Mr. Shawe, and don't come here again until I give you permission."

"But I want to see Audrey."

"You can do so when she walks in Kensington Gardens as usual," replied Madame Coralie, sharply; "but if you come here people will talk, and the quieter this business is kept the better it will be for everyone."

"But if papa talks"—began Audrey, only to be cut short.

"Papa won't talk," said Madame Coralie, in a hard, dry voice. "He will have quite enough to occupy his mind in marrying Miss Rosy Pearl—that is, if he ever does marry the creature."

"Madame"—Ralph started forward—"what do you mean?"

"Never mind; go away at once." Madame unlocked the door. "It is too late to chatter, and Miss Branwin looks quite worn out."

Shawe admitted the truth of this speech, and after a farewell embrace, at which Madame Coralie looked benignly, he took his leave. When the door was once more closed, Audrey followed her aunt up the stairs to the still-room, wherein the four assistants were working.

"You can all go to bed now," said Madame Coralie, with a glance at the clock on the mantelpiece. "Zobeide"—she used her fingers at this point—"you can go to bed. Badoura, Miss Branwin is staying here for the night. We spoke, when she saw me the other day, about treating her for the figure, as she is much too thin. She only made up her mind to come to-night. See that the bedroom opposite—No. 10—is made ready, Badoura."

"Yes, Madame," said Badoura; and, whatever she may have thought of the young lady's unexpected decision to remain for the night, she certainly showed no astonishment in her face as she disappeared. The other three girls departed swiftly, evidently glad to get to bed, as they were tired with their work. Audrey and her aunt were left alone, and the girl would have spoken.

"No," said Madame Coralie, quickly, raising her hand, "don't speak, or you will faint. You are highly strung, my dear, and this position is too much for you. Get a night's rest, and we can talk in the morning."

"But I must thank you, Aunt Flora, for your kindness."

"My kindness!" said the other, bitterly, and her harsh voice took on a softer note. "It is a kindness your coming to me, to cheer me in my loneliness. I hope you will stay long."

"But you have your husband, Aunt Flora."

"Eddy—oh, yes; but he does not sleep in this place. I found him such a nuisance that I gave him money to take chambers. I see very little of him, as I found what a mistake I had made in marrying him. He cares nothing for me, but a great deal for what money I have. Don't speak of him."

Before Audrey could say anything more Badoura returned with the information that the bedroom was ready. Madame Coralie, who seemed to be a singularly capable woman who knew her own mind, at once insisted that her visitor should retire. So it was that in a very short space of time Audrey found herself in a comfortable bed. For a few moments she mused on the strange chance that had brought her to sleep in the very house wherein her mother had been murdered; then the great fatigue she felt overcame her and she fell into a profound slumber, which lasted until the morning. So deep it was that she did not even dream.

At ten o'clock next morning she awoke, and found her aunt standing beside her with a cup of tea. Madame Coralie explained how she had looked in once or twice before, but that Audrey had been sleeping so quietly that she had not had the heart to waken her.

"Drink this tea and take another sleep," advised Madame Coralie, wisely; "as the more you sleep after last night's experience the better you will feel."

Audrey, who still felt languid, willingly consented, and Madame went out quietly. She did not, however, through absence of mind, quite close the door, and Audrey was therefore wakened some time later by the sound of two voices conversing softly. At once she remembered that the still-room was opposite to the bedroom she occupied. Evidently its door was open, and, as her own door was not closed, she could hear very plainly. Half awake and half asleep she listened, not meaning to eavesdrop, but simply because she felt too tired to close the door or to give any evidence of her presence.

The voices were those of a man and a woman, and Audrey recognised the latter one as that of Badoura. But who the man was she could not guess.

"You are very cruel," said Badoura, addressing her companion softly. "You are tired of me, I am sure."

"Well, you always worry me so," said the man's voice, gruffly. "I can't be always running after you."

"You would not have said that once, Eddy," replied Badoura, and the name suddenly enlightened Audrey to the fact that the forewoman was conversing with Madame Coralie's scampish husband. Ashamed of listening, even half involuntarily, the girl would have risen to close the bedroom door, when the next sentence of Badoura made her change her mind.

"If you are going to throw me over," cried Badoura, passionately, "I shall tell all I know."

"What do you know?" demanded Eddy, with a sneer. "There's nothing much you can tell my wife, if that is what you mean. She thinks that I am all that is bad, my dear silly girl."

"And so you are," snapped Badoura, sharply. "But does she know that you put back the clock in the still-room half an hour on the night Lady Branwin—"

"It's a confounded lie!" gasped Eddy Vail, interrupting.

"It's true, and you know it," said Badoura, triumphantly. "I was behind the curtain with Parizade working when you came in about five minutes to eight o'clock. Parizade is blind, and saw nothing, but I did. You put back the hand of the clock to 7.30."

"What if I did?" stammered Eddy, evidently trying to bluff the girl.

"What if you did?" cried Badoura, shrilly. "Why, it means that you were downstairs at the time Lady Branwin was murdered. You stayed until the clock hand was again nearly at eight, and then your wife came up, so that you were able to prove an alibi. I said nothing because I loved you, but since you are going to treat me like dirt I shall tell the police."

"You dare, and I'll kill you!" said Vail between his teeth.

"As you killed Lady Branwin," scoffed Badoura, who was in a towering rage.

"I didn't kill her."

"Yes you did, and you stole the diamonds, and—Hush! there's Madame." Then Audrey heard Badoura quickly leave the room, and the sound of Eddy throwing himself into a chair. She gasped with horror. Was he the criminal after all? The question was a terrible one, but the answer seemed certain.

CHAPTER XVIII.

A LEGAL OPINION

It said a great deal for Audrey's presence of mind that she lay quietly where she was, and did not at once leap from her bed to denounce Eddy Vail. But the girl, although she appeared delicate, and was inexperienced, had a commonsense way of looking at things, which helped her greatly in this emergency. She rapidly reviewed the situation, and saw that it would be wiser, for the present, to hold her tongue. When she laid the matter before Ralph, it would be time enough to consider what was the best course to pursue. It was necessary to obtain further proofs of Vail's guilt, as for the moment it rested merely on the statement of Badoura. And if Badoura changed her mind and became reconciled to Eddy, she might deny that she had made any remark about the clock. Finally, seeing that she was indebted to her aunt for a night's lodging, if for nothing else, Audrey did not wish to make trouble in the Pink Shop. Already the murder had given the place a bad name, and if there was any more scandal Madame Coralie's business would be ruined entirely.

But Audrey could rest no more, and when she heard Madame Coralie go into the still-room to talk with her scampish husband she quietly rose and closed the bedroom door. Then she dressed rapidly, and soon came out, looking much her usual self, although she was decidedly pale. Her aunt was still talking to Eddy, and had just handed him a letter. The scampish husband looked more pretty and dandified than ever, and threw a glance of leering admiration at the charming newcomer. When Audrey remembered that Badoura accused him of strangling her mother, she could scarcely address him politely. Yet she was forced to do so for the sake of appearance, as Madame Coralie introduced her to him.

"Miss Branwin, this is my husband, Mr. Edmund Vail."

"I hope you are well, Miss Branwin," said Mr. Vail, politely, and bowed in a most deferential manner. He even held out his hand, but Audrey declined to see it—she could not bring herself to greet him in this way.

"I am quite well, Mr. Vail," she said coldly, "thanks to a good night's rest."

"You are stopping here, Miss Branwin?"

"Mind your own business, Eddy!" snapped Madame Coralie, shortly. "You have nothing to do with my customers. Miss Branwin is stopping here for treatment, so say no more about it. Take that letter to Sir Joseph Branwin at once."

Audrey started, and looked at her aunt. "To my father?"

"Yes," said Madame Coralie, arranging her yashmak. "I have written to Sir Joseph asking him to send your boxes here, as your treatment will take some time."

"But will my father send my boxes?" asked Audrey, nervously.

Madame Coralie gave her a warning glance, as Eddy's cherubic face was alive with curiosity. "Of course he will, Miss Branwin," said the proprietress of the Pink Shop, easily. "He knows that ladies cannot do without at least a dozen frocks. Never fear," she nodded encouragingly, "I shall send you back to Camden Hill as plump as a partridge."

"If I may be permitted a remark," said Eddy, impudently, "Miss Branwin does not require figure treatment. She is—perfection," and he grinned.

"Eddy, you can go," said Madame Coralie, quietly, and pointed imperatively to the door. "Lose no time."

"Au revoir, Miss Branwin," said the rogue, and walked out of the still-room as delicately as Agag before his execution.

"What a horrid man!" said Audrey, involuntarily, then coloured when aware of her remark. "I beg your pardon, Aunt Flora, I forgot he is your husband."

"I never can forget it," said Madame Coralie, calmly; "and you are quite right, my dear. Eddy is a horrid young man, conceited and impudent, whose one idea in life is to hunt women and spend money. That's two ideas, though, isn't it, my dear?" ended Madame Coralie, with a grim look in her eyes. "Oh! what a fool I was to marry him."

"Perhaps he will improve, Aunt Flora, and I am sure he ought to be grateful to you for keeping him the way you do."

"My dear child, gratitude and Eddy Vail are far apart. He's a rogue and I'm a fool, so we are well matched. Don't let us talk any more about him. I have sent a letter to your father saying you are staying with me, and asking him to send on your boxes."

"Did you mention if you knew why I came to you, aunt?"

"Yes, I did, and I signed myself Flora Arkwright."

"Why not Flora Vail?"

"Because Joseph does not know me by that name; but he knows who Flora Arkwright is," said Madame Coralie, still grimly. "And he will certainly send on your boxes, my dear, as he has been waiting for a chance to get rid of you."

Audrey looked pained. "Why should he desire to get rid of me? I am sure I have always tried to be a daughter to him."

"He doesn't want a daughter, but another wife. You were an obstacle in the way of his marrying Rosy Pearl, and, as he could not induce you to marry Lord Anvers, he seized the opportunity of your making that rash visit to Mr.

Shawe to turn you out of house and home. But he shall make you an allowance, Audrey"—Madame Coralie's eyes flashed—"I'll see to that."

"He will not unless he is forced to," rejoined the girl, mournfully.

"Then he shall be forced, my dear. I can manage him."

"In what way, Aunt Flora?"

"Never mind. I know things about Joseph Branwin which he would not like the world to become aware of."

It was on the tip of Audrey's tongue to ask if the things in question had to do with Sir Joseph's presence in the house on the night of the murder; but her aunt gave her no time to speak.

"There's a gentleman waiting in the lane to see you," she said abruptly.

Audrey ran to the window. "Ralph!" she said quickly and joyfully.

"Yes. He has come in spite of my prohibition, silly fellow that he is. I don't want your stay here to be talked about. However, as he will not go away unless he sees you, I think, my dear, you had better go to him and ask if he will take you out to breakfast. There's a very good restaurant in the High Street. I can't give you the meals to which you have been accustomed, my dear girl."

Audrey took her hand, and Madame Coralie quivered at the gentle touch. "You have taken me in when I had no home," said the girl, tenderly, "and I shall never forget it, Aunt Flora. I wish you would remove that horrid yashmak and let me kiss you."

Madame Coralie drew aside the dark veil, and allowed Audrey to press a kiss on her mouth. Then she dropped the yashmak again over the disfiguring birthmark, and turned away in silence to busy herself with some tiny boxes containing ointments. "You had better go, dear," she said at length, in a low voice, "Mr. Shawe is waiting."

Audrey wondered why her aunt should be so moved by a simple caress; but guessing that she did not wish to converse at the moment quietly left the room, and ran down the stairs. As she passed through the shop the quartette of assistants, who were busy in various ways, looked up with bright smiles. One and all, enlightened by Badoura, had seen the lover pacing the lane, and sympathised with Audrey's haste. The girl blushed and laughed as she left the shop, and ran across the narrow roadway holding out her hands.

"My dear—my darling!" said Ralph, tenderly, and Audrey saw how lean and anxious his face looked. "I have been worrying about you all the night."

"You needn't have," said Audrey, as they walked down the lane. "I have been all right, and the sleep has done me a lot of good. But you can worry about me now, Ralph, because I am dreadfully hungry, and want my breakfast."

"What!" Shawe was rather indignant. "Hasn't Madame Coralie given you food?"

Audrey shook her head. "She suggested that I should breakfast with you, since you refused to go away without seeing me. I could have got food in the house had I chosen. But, Ralph"—she put her arm in his confidentially—"I agreed to see you because I have much to say."

"What is it? Any new discovery?"

"Yes, and a very important one. But I can't talk until I have eaten. Remember, dear, I have had nothing in the way of food since dinner last night, and I have undergone a great deal."

"You poor darling!" cried Ralph, with great compunction. "You shan't say another word until you have had breakfast. I shall have mine also, for, to tell you the truth, Audrey, I could eat nothing this morning. Now that I have seen you my appetite is reviving."

He proved this at the sumptuous meal they ordered at the restaurant in High Street. It was an excellent place with an excellent cook, and the two young people chose exactly the dishes they enjoyed most. In the middle of the meal Audrey laughed, as it struck her as strange that people so troubled as they were could eat and drink so freely.

"No one would think that I was a pauper turned out of house and home by a hard-hearted father," said Audrey, smiling.

"I am glad you see the humour of it," said Ralph, drily.

"Oh, don't be angry, dear. I thank Heaven that I have a gift of humour to enable me to see these troubles in their true light. Aunt Flora has sent for my boxes, and has written to tell my father that I am to stop with her for the time being. She hinted that she could force him to allow me an income."

"How can she force him?" asked Shawe, quickly. "Does she know that he was in the Pink Shop on that night?"

"No; she did not say so, nor did I mention the subject. Besides, papa said in your rooms that although he was in the lane he did not enter the shop."

"I don't see what else you could expect him to say," replied Ralph, with a shrug. "If he was in the shop, he certainly would not incriminate himself by admitting it."

"After all, we have only Parizade's evidence regarding that scent of Harris tweed to go upon," said Audrey, thoughtfully.

"Seeing that your father is so fond of wearing that particular cloth, I must say that the evidence is very strong," retorted Ralph.

"Yet you declared that it would not stand in a court of law."

"Perhaps yes, perhaps no; it is a difficult thing to say, Audrey. However, since you now know what I wrote the anonymous letter to keep from you, there will be no further hesitation on my part in searching for the true assassin. If he proves to be your father I shan't be sorry, seeing how brutally he has behaved to you."

Audrey shook her head. "If I thought that papa was guilty I would ask you to stop searching, and to leave him to the punishment of his conscience."

"He hasn't got one, my dear," said Shawe, scoffingly. "And if he isn't guilty, who is, may I ask?"

"Eddy Vail," said Audrey, without a moment's hesitation.

Ralph pushed back his chair and looked at her in astonishment. The restaurant was almost empty, and they had a corner table entirely to themselves, so they could speak very freely, so long as they kept their voices low. "On what grounds do you make that assertion, Audrey?" he asked sharply.

"I overheard a conversation between Badoura and Eddy Vail this morning."

"Oh, and you learnt enough to make you suspect Vail?"

"I learnt plainly that Vail is guilty, if Badoura is to be believed."

Shawe remained silent through sheer astonishment. "Tell me exactly what you did overhear," he remarked at length.

Miss Branwin thereupon lowered her voice still more, so that no whisper could be overheard by other people, and detailed the words which had passed between Badoura and Madame Coralie's husband. "I saw him afterwards with Aunt Flora," finished Audrey, "as she sent him with the letter to my father. He is a nasty impertinent little man, and wished to converse with me. He even offered me his hand"—she shuddered—"as if I could touch it. Well, Ralph, and what do you think of the matter?"

"Badoura's declaration certainly endorses what you said about the time Madame Coralie came down to see you at the door," remarked Shawe, thoughtfully. "If Eddy Vail came up at five minutes to eight and put the clock back to 7.30, that would account for the twenty-five minutes."

"It was certainly nearly half-past eight before I saw Aunt Flora," said Audrey, quickly.

"Then if she came down immediately after entering the still-room, as was stated at the inquest," said Shawe, "the clock must have been wrong. Eddy Vail himself, Madame Coralie, and Badoura all say that it was five minutes after eight when Madame came down to you. Of course, Eddy putting the clock wrong would account for the extra time."

"But why did he put the clock wrong?" asked Audrey, bewildered.

"Badoura supplies the answer to that question, my dear," said Ralph, grimly. "He wished to provide an alibi. Badoura and Madame Coralie could both swear that he was in the still-room at eight o'clock, when it was really five-and-twenty minutes past eight. He had all that time—seeing that, according to the medical evidence, your mother was murdered at or about eight—to commit the crime. Yes, Eddy Vail may be guilty."

"Then my father is innocent, and was not in the Pink Shop."

"Of course. And going by the evidence of the clock, when Mrs. Mellop saw your father in Walpole Lane your mother had already been dead for some twenty minutes, more or less. Of course"—Ralph looked thoughtful—"he may have killed her, and then have slipped round by the court—the key was in the outer door, remember—to Walpole Lane, guessing that you would call there, and thus he could provide himself with a very good alibi. Did he know that you were going to call for your mother?"

"Yes. I told him when I got home. But I really can't think that he is guilty, Ralph, especially as Badoura accuses Eddy Vail."

"But why should Eddy kill yourmother?"

"Because of the diamonds."

"Madame Coralie said that her sister had given those to her. If that is a lie, it makes out Madame Coralie to be an accomplice after the fact. She must have known that her husband had murdered Lady Branwin."

"Oh, dear, it is impossible Aunt Flora can be guilty. She is so good."

Ralph had his own idea of Madame Coralie's goodness; but it was no use communicating the same to the girl, seeing how kind her aunt had been to her. He thought for a few moments, then raised his head.

"In order to learn positively what took place in the house on that night," he said decisively, "we must find another and independent witness."

"Can we?" asked Audrey, faintly, for she was greatly bewildered.

"I think so. Rosy Pearl."

"Oh!" Audrey stared. "But she will know nothing."

"I am not so sure of that. She was sleeping in an upstairs bedroom."

"Probably she *was* asleep."

"And it might be that she was awake," said Shawe, quickly. "At all events, it is strange that the woman whom your father desires to marry should be in the house where the obstacle to that marriage met with her death. And on the selfsame night, too," ended Ralph, with a nod.

"What is to be done?" asked Audrey, astonished at this new development.

"This. Say nothing about Badoura's conversation with Eddy Vail and wait patiently until I see Rosy Pearl. I shall do so this very day."

"I wonder if she is guilty?" queried Audrey. But Shawe could not answer this question, which was scarcely to be wondered at.

CHAPTER XIX.

MATRIMONIAL ARRANGEMENTS

Ralph did not call on Miss Pearl that day, as he intended to do, for the simple reason that more important business demanded his attention. After returning with Audrey to the Pink Shop he walked away, thinking, with some irritation, over the disagreeable position in which the girl was placed by the callous behaviour of her father. Certainly, as Audrey was supposed to be going in for figure treatment, her stay with Madame Coralie was reasonably accounted for, and Ralph guessed that Sir Joseph would offer this excuse to his friends when they asked after his daughter. There was no doubt that when the old man recovered from the furious rage into which he had fallen when accused of the crime he would think twice before admitting that he had turned Audrey out of doors. Sir Joseph, in spite of his domineering ways, was a coward, so far as social reputation was concerned, and would not risk the finger of scorn being pointed at him. It assuredly would be, when people came to hear of his brutal action.

So far everything was right. But Shawe did not care that the girl he intended to make his wife should remain with Madame Coralie. Even though the woman was Audrey's aunt, and apparently intended to be kind to her niece, Ralph knew that her reputation was none of the best. It would do Audrey harm to remain long at the Pink Shop, especially as, since the murder, it had obtained a most unenviable notoriety. And Madame Coralie—as Shawe learnt through Perry Toat—was looked at askance by the police. Nothing could be said against her, and she had assuredly cleared herself of complicity in connection with Lady Branwin's death, thanks mainly, as Ralph now saw, to the false evidence of the still-room clock. But she was watched nevertheless, and was regarded as a person of doubtful character. Perhaps it was hard on the poor creature that she should be so regarded, for she did her best to conduct her business in a proper way. But that very business was of a decidedly dubious character, and demanded secrecy for obvious reasons. Ladies anxious to renew their youth did not care about their visits to the Pink Shop to be talked about, and this very necessary secrecy lent a doubtful air to Madame Coralie's occupation. On the whole, the young barrister thought that it would be just as well to remove Audrey as soon as possible from that tainted atmosphere.

This could only be done by marriage, as, failing her aunt, Audrey had no friend with whom she could stay. Certainly, there were people who liked her, and would be glad of her company, but an application to any of these meant that awkward questions would be asked. If any woman scented a scandal, she would assuredly be extremely pertinacious until she learnt the whole truth. And as the whole truth involved a confession of Audrey's rash visit to the Temple, and an acknowledgment of her father's drastic behaviour, it was not right to risk such things becoming known. Whereas, if Shawe married the girl quickly it would be looked upon as a runaway match, and Sir Joseph's anger would be accounted for in this way. It was well known that he wished his daughter to marry Lord Anvers, and had refused to permit the barrister to pay his addresses. Therefore, an elopement—for that is what the marriage with Shawe would amount to—would appeal to the romantic nature of Audrey's friends, and every woman would be on her side. The more Ralph thought over the matter, the more he felt that a speedy marriage was the only way in which to adjust the situation.

But this required thought to accomplish. Shawe had a small income, and with economy it would be enough for two until he received larger fees. Already he was a well-known man, and every day he made progress; so there could be no doubt that in the near future he would be well able to support a wife. But at the present moment he could not lay his hands on ready money, which was what he wanted to do. In the ordinary way Audrey would have to live in Kensington parish for three weeks, and so would he, in order to get married. As Ralph wished to remove his future wife from the Pink Shop as speedily as possible, this delay was not to be thought of. There only remained to procure a special licence, and this cost a large sum of money. "I shall go and see my godmother," decided Ralph, after he had turned the question of immediate matrimony over in his mind.

Lady Sanby was the young man's godmother, and had always professed herself to be very fond and proud of him. She had often presented him with a cheque when he was at college, and later when he was studying for the Bar. Indeed, but for Lady Sanby's help Ralph would not have been able to wait for briefs, since his father, the Squire of Bleakleigh, was not wealthy. But the godmother had always behaved generously, and Ralph, therefore, went to her house that same afternoon, instead of visiting Miss Pearl. But before going he wrote to the star of the music-halls, asking her to see him the next morning at eleven o'clock, saying that he had something important to say to her. Having thus arranged matters, the young man went to Dorleigh Crescent to interview Lady Sanby.

She was an ancient dowager, with a merry eye and a great liking for young men, especially if they were handsome and rising. Ralph was both, so Lady Sanby always made a great fuss over him when he called. She went everywhere and knew everyone, and was altogether as gay an old dame as could be found in Mayfair. Also, as she was very rich, her son, the present Lord Sanby, and her daughter-in-law, together with their numerous offspring, paid her the greatest attention. Grannie had money to leave; therefore grannie was regarded as the oracle of the family, and behaved always like a benevolent despot. For no one could deny but what she was a charming old lady, if somewhat sharp in her way of speaking.

"My dear boy," said Lady Sanby, welcoming her godson with effusion, and presenting her withered cheek for a kiss, "what have you been doing all this time? I haven't seen your name in the papers either in connection with your profession. Are you not getting any briefs?"

"Not at present, grannie," said Ralph—for Lady Sanby allowed him to call her by this endearing name, as an acknowledgment of the interest she took in him—"but they will come along all right when I am married."

"Oh!" Lady Sanby shook her old head knowingly, as she knew much of Ralph's love-story. "So you still adore the daughter of that wretched woman who was murdered in the Pink Shop?"

"Yes. And you said you liked Audrey, grannie?"

"So I do; she's a dear girl. But I didn't like her vulgar old mother, though I shouldn't say that now, seeing she is dead. Nor do I like her father. He's a wicked, domineering navvy, and will probably be made a Peer. Those sort of rich labourers always do get Peerages. Well, so you are going to marry?"

"I must if I want to succeed in my profession," said Ralph, quickly. "My head is full of love matters, and I can't think of my clients. Yes, I want to get married in three days, and I have come to you for help."

"Oh, I shall do whatever you want, my dear boy. You are so clever that I look on you as one likely to reflect credit on me. Sanby and his family are all idiots. Well, and how can I assist you?"

"I shall explain. In the first place, I wish to tell you a rather surprising story, about which you must promise to keep silence.

"Oh! my dear lad, I am a well—a very well—for keeping secrets. If I said all I knew I could ruin half the men in London, and all the women. Well?"

Shawe wasted no further talk in introducing his subject, but related all that he knew about the case—from the time Lady Branwin had entered the Pink Shop down to the last words Audrey had told him concerning Badoura's accusation of Eddy Vail. "Now, what do you think?" he asked, when he had finished his long story, and felt vexed that the old lady did not display more astonishment.

"It is a wonderful story," Lady Sanby assured him, coolly, "and truth is always stranger than fiction. But I have had so many surprises in my long life that nothing astonishes me. I am glad you told me, and I can well see that it is a thing one must hold one's tongue about. So vexing; one always has to keep silence about the most wonderful things. Do you think that Sir Joseph Branwin—horrid man!—is guilty?"

"I can't say."

"Perhaps you suspect Eddy Vail?"

"I can't be sure of that either."

"Madame Coralie?"

"No," said Ralph, positively. "I can safely say that I do not suspect her, for she is behaving too well over Audrey's matter."

"That doesn't mean to say she wouldn't commit a crime if it suited her," said Lady Sanby, coolly. "She's not a nice woman, my dear, and the sooner you get that poor girl away from the Pink Shop the better it will be."

"I knew you would say that," said Shawe, quickly, "and for that reason I want you to help me, grannie—to help me and Audrey, that is."

"Of course. I like Audrey; she is a girl of spirit, and will make you a good wife. Well, what do you wish me to do? Ask her here to stay for a time?"

"No, no! Although it is kind of you to suggest it," said Shawe, hurriedly. "But people would talk and ask questions. No. I wish you to lend me one hundred pounds so that I can buy a special licence and marry Audrey at once, and have sufficient cash to take a journey."

"To go on your honeymoon, you mean," said Lady Sanby, humorously. "Well, your idea is a very good one. Marry her at once by special licence, and go away to some quiet place so that she can recover from all these troubles. Then bring her here as your wife, and she can stay with me for a week until you can find a house."

"Dear, dear grannie!"

"Silly, silly grannie, I think. I am a romantic old fool to waste money at my time of life in—"

"It won't be wasted. I shall pay you back."

"No. I shall give you five hundred pounds as a wedding-gift."

"Oh, I can't take that, Lady Sanby."

"Grannie, you foolish boy."

"Well, then, I can't take such a large sum, grannie."

"Don't talk nonsense," said Lady Sanby, going to her desk and producing a cheque-book. "Five hundred pounds won't go very far, seeing that Audrey has been accustomed to millions."

"She won't be accustomed to them any more," said the future bridegroom, in a gloomy tone. "Her father has disowned her."

"Never mind. You marry her, and we'll put matters right between us. There is your cheque." She handed him an oblong slip of paper.

"I really can't take so much."

"Then you won't get less, my dear man. Gracious, haven't I dandled you on my knee and slapped you and stuffed you with cakes and—"

"You have been always good, and that is why I don't like to impose on you."

Lady Sanby laughed grimly. "You needn't be afraid of doing that, Ralph. No one, old or young, ever succeeded in imposing upon me. Now, take your wedding-present and marry Audrey. And, by the way," added the old dame, just as if it was an after-thought, "you had better let me know the time and place. I shall come to the wedding. It will look better for Audrey, and that parvenu father of hers won't dare to say a word when I bestow my approval."

"Grannie, you are an angel," and Ralph, very greatly touched by her kindness, kissed her warmly.

Grannie pushed him away. "Keep your kisses and nice words for Audrey, or she will grow jealous. Now run away. I have heaps to do, and I can't afford to waste my time as a briefless barrister does."

"Briefless," laughed Ralph, who was now, and with very good reason, in excellent spirits. "Well, grannie, I only ask that you will retain me as Counsel in the breach of promise case you are sure to have with one of your numerous admirers!"—a joke which pleased the gay old lady immensely.

Shawe departed, and paid the welcome cheque into his bank. He could now afford to marry Audrey at once, and take her away from all the soiled circumstances of her life. He felt duly grateful to Madame Coralie, but he did not wish Audrey, when she was Mrs. Shawe, to see more of her than was consistent with her being a relation. For the moment he felt inclined to go to Walpole Lane and tell Audrey all about Lady Sanby's offer and her kindness in giving him such a welcome wedding-present; but he knew that Audrey would be disappointed if he had nothing to tell about Miss Pearl, so resolved before he again sought the Pink Shop to see the lady in question.

Miss Pearl wrote and said that she would be pleased to see him at the time he mentioned. Therefore, the next morning, Ralph duly walked to the quiet house in the quiet Bloomsbury Square wherein Miss Pearl had her rooms. A demure maidservant admitted him into the house and conducted him up the wide staircase—it was an old Georgian mansion—to the sitting-room of the lady. When she departed to tell Miss Pearl that her visitor had arrived, the young barrister glanced round the room to see if he could gather from its furnishing what the character of the future Lady Branwin was like. It struck him—oddly enough, considering her profession of dancer and singer—that she was something of a Puritan.

The room was spacious and had a lofty ceiling painted with wreaths of flowers and love-knots of blue ribbon. Under this roof, which suggested gay Pompadour fancies, the room looked cold and drab. The furniture was of a dark wood upholstered in dark green. The windows—two French windows which opened on to an iron balcony—were draped with green curtains, and the carpet was also green, without any pattern. In the centre of the apartment was a prim table on which books were placed at regular intervals. One of these books Shawe found to be the *Pilgrim's Progress*, and another was the *Chronicles of the Schonberg-Cotta Family*. He felt rather astonished as this was not the class of literature he expected Miss Pearl to favour. Then the room was altogether so stiff and formal, and so deadly cold, in spite of its being warm in the open air, that the barrister was puzzled. "I must have been shown into the apartment of some missionary by mistake," was his reflection, and he sat down greatly bewildered. "A woman who dances at a music-hall can't possibly like to live in such a room; but I always heard that she was aggressively respectable."

His reflections were cut short by the stately entrance of the lady he was thinking about. And Miss Pearl *was* stately, being a tall and nobly-formed woman, who walked in quite a majestic way. She had large feet, large hands, a large bust, and large limbs—indeed, she was large in every way, and looked more like the Venus of Milo than a modern woman. Her face was pale and grave and clear-cut, and she had a rather severe mouth with compressed lips. To add to her resemblance to the heathen goddess, her hair was smoothed back from her marble forehead and coiled behind in a simple Greek knot. In a calm and graceful way she moved forward, with her large brown unwinking eyes fastened on the bewildered face of the young man. Those eyes almost hypnotised Ralph, for their gaze was so steady, and made him think that after all she was less like Venus than like the ox-eyed Juno.

"You are Mr. Shawe?" she said, in a low, deep contralto voice.

"Yes, Miss Pearl," he stammered; then he observed her well-cut, tailor-made dress, which was simplicity itself, and worn with a linen collar. But it was the material that brought a startled look into his eyes. "You—you wear a—a Harris tweed dress!" he gasped.

Miss Pearl eyed him with grave surprise. "Why should I not?" she asked.

CHAPTER XX.

A MUSIC HALL ARTIST

Miss Pearl's question was awkward to answer on the spur of the moment, as may be easily guessed. Ralph had intended to lead gradually up to the object of his visit; but thrown off his guard by the sight of the dress, he had committed himself in a most untimely manner. While thinking of a possible answer which would delay explanations he stared hard at Miss Pearl, trying to guess what kind of a woman she was. From the furnishing of the room, from her looks and severe mode of dress, he took her to be a religious woman of a Puritanic cast, who had abjured the pomps and vanities of the world. Yet she was a music-hall dancer, and that profession did not suit either her surroundings or her appearance.

"I shall explain why I made that remark shortly," said Shawe, evading a direct reply as well as he was able; "and, truth to tell, my errand is not a very pleasant one."

Miss Pearl looked at the card she held in her large white hand, and pondered thoughtfully. "Mr. Ralph Shawe," she said, in her heavy voice. "Ah! yes, I remember now. Perhaps, Mr. Ralph Shawe, I can guess your errand."

"Perhaps you can," muttered Shawe, wondering what she would say.

"Sir Joseph Branwin," pursued the dancer, "told me about you, as an undesirable suitor for the hand of his daughter. Am I right in assuming that you have called to enlist my sympathies?"

"Enlist your sympathies?" repeated the visitor, staring.

"Yes. You want me," continued Miss Pearl, in a ponderously playful manner, "to ask Sir Joseph to permit you to pay your addresses. I shall do so with pleasure, as I have every sympathy with you and Miss Branwin."

Shawe still stared in a dazed way, as this speech completely puzzled him, and —in vulgar parlance—took the wind out of his sails. Here he had come practically to accuse a lady of being connected with the murder of a woman whom she had wished to supplant, and this very lady was now most generously offering her assistance to forward his private aims. Shawe could not quite understand if this was cunning on Rosy Pearl's part or mere stupidity, or perhaps the liberal offer of a generous nature. He noted the careful way in which she spoke and her method of picking out well-sounding words, and mentally observed that she was doing her best to correct a defective education by thinking well before she spoke.

In the meantime Miss Pearl did not hurry him, as she appeared to be a singularly leisurely person. With her large calm eyes gazing amiably at him, her gracious, rounded figure, and whole placid pose, she reminded Ralph of nothing so much as a sacred white cow. But cows can be furious when aroused, and the barrister wondered if she would rise in her majesty like Bellona, the goddess of war, when she learnt the true meaning of his visit. But she must be stupid, he thought, else she would have persisted in learning straight away the meaning of his first enigmatic remark. Yet she accepted his postponement calmly, and was quite ready to wait for an explanation.

"I am greatly obliged to you for your kindness, Miss Pearl," he said quietly; "but I fear your offer of help is too late. Sir Joseph has had a serious quarrel with his daughter."

"A serious quarrel with his daughter?" repeated the woman, slowly, as if trying to get the idea well into her head; then she added, after a pause; "I should like to hear what the quarrel is about."

Ralph did not intend to tell her, and he was sure Branwin would be too much ashamed of himself to give the information. "Well, you know, Miss Pearl, that Sir Joseph wanted his daughter to marry Lord Anvers. She refused him, so Miss Branwin left the house, as her father was so furious with her."

"Miss Branwin has left the house? And where is she staying now?"

"At the Pink Shop," said Shawe, promptly. He was unwilling to name Audrey's temporary abode, but did so, to see what effect the name had on this calm and undemonstrative woman.

It had an effect, indeed, for Miss Pearl's white skin slowly became a vivid crimson, and for the first time during the interview she displayed emotion. Perhaps she was aware of the meaning in Shawe's gaze when he saw this agitation, for she gave an excuse.

"I don't think that the Pink Shop is a proper place for a young lady to stay at," she remarked frigidly.

"Why not? You were there yourself, Miss Pearl."

"I have frequently been there, Mr. Shawe. As an artist I have to take the greatest care of what looks I possess, and I find Madame Coralie invaluable."

"You slept at the Pink Shop on the night Lady Branwin was—"

Miss Pearl displayed more agitation, and—a rare thing for so slow-thinking a woman—interrupted somewhat sharply:

"I admit that I did, but I do not wish it to be known."

"For what reason, Miss Pearl?" asked Ralph, pressing his advantage mercilessly.

"You can guess the reason, Mr. Shawe," she replied, with heavy indignation. "I know what evil minds people have. Sir Joseph is an admirer of mine— quite in a platonic way, you understand."

"Of course," murmured the barrister. "I have heard of your unblemished reputation, Miss Pearl."

"I should think it was unblemished," said the dancer, speaking faster than usual. "My dear mother, who was a consistent Baptist, always warned me when I left home to keep myself unspotted from the world. Circumstances have made me a music-hall dancer, but I have always conducted myself discreetly, and I always shall do so. Not by way of advertisement, Mr. Shawe, but because the principles, instilled by my dear mother, will not permit me to behave in any other way."

"It does you credit, Miss Pearl," murmured Ralph, feeling called upon to say something polite.

Rosy Pearl looked at him like an offended goddess. "I do not know whether you mean to be sarcastic, Mr. Shawe, but let me tell you that sarcasm is out of place. Are you one of those men who do not believe that a woman can be virtuous in the midst of temptation?"

"Not at all, Miss Pearl. There are good women on the stage, and often bad women in Church circles. It is a question of temperament."

"It is a question of doing what is right, Mr. Shawe," said the goddess, with a disdainful look. "I am a dancer, it is true, but no one can say a word against me."

"I don't think anyone has said a word," Ralph ventured to remark.

"If they did," said Miss Pearl, sharply, "I would bring a libel action against them without delay. My solicitors have instructions to take notice of any flippant remark made about me, and to deal with it as it deserves."

"With such precautions you must be, like Cæsar's wife, above suspicion."

"I do not know Mrs. Cæsar," said Rosy Pearl, coldly, and betrayed her lack of educational knowledge in the remark. "I attend to my own business and to nothing else. I daresay you wonder, Mr. Shawe, why, with these sentiments, I am on the music-hall stage?"

"Well," Ralph admitted, more and more puzzled by this simplicity, but unable to tell if it were real or feigned, "I must say that I do wonder."

"It's because I am stupid."

"Stupid?" Shawe stared. He had never heard a woman admit as much before.

"Yes, I am," said Miss Pearl, in her rich, slow voice, and looking more than ever like a sacred white cow. "My parents live in a small Essex village, and have a large family. My father is a carpenter, and my mother, as I told you, a consistent Baptist. Being poor, we—the children, that is—have to work, and when I was eighteen I got a housemaid's place in London. But I could not do the work."

"It is not difficult work," said Shawe, marvelling at this candour.

"No, it is not difficult work," said Miss Pearl, who seemed to have a habit of repeating words, perhaps to fix them in her memory; "but I am stupid, and I was always making mistakes, through forgetting things. I lost place after place because of what was called my lack of intelligence. I had to work in some way, and yet I could not, being too slow and heavy. Then an old gentleman—he was a scholar—said that I resembled a Greek statue. It gave me an idea, as a friend of mine knew a music-hall manager. I went to this manager, and asked him to let me appear in living pictures."

"And he consented?"

"Not at once. He admired me for my looks," said Miss Pearl, with great simplicity, "and he made love to me. They all do, and it is a great nuisance, as I don't like that sort of thing. But this manager became quite friendly when I boxed his ears."

"He must have been an odd manager," said Ralph, thinking that so strong a white arm could hurt considerably.

"Oh, he was like the rest of them," said Miss Pearl, heavily. "However, he declared that he saw possibilities in me, and sent me to someone to be taught. When I mentioned what the scholar had said about my being like a Greek; this man—he was a professor of dancing—got an idea of reviving some Attic dances. He taught me three chants—"

"Songs, you mean."

"No, I do not mean songs. I mean chants, to which I dance. You have seen my performance, have you not, Mr. Shawe?"

"Yes, and a very beautiful performance it is," said Ralph. He recalled the scene, which represented a Greek temple, before which Miss Pearl, in scanty white robes, danced in a slow and graceful manner, chanting—she was right, the word was chanting—stately words to solemn music. Also she danced the Flower Dance of the Anthesterian Festival, which was of a more lively character. "It is a very beautiful performance," repeated Ralph, emphatically.

"I am glad you think so," said Miss Pearl, with a slow, sweet smile. "Those three dances took me a year to learn. I thought I would never master them; but in the end I did. Then I appeared, and was a success. I don't quite like the Greek dress," added the dancer, confidentially, "as it scarcely covers one; but, so long as I am respectable, what does it matter?"

Ralph laughed in a somewhat embarrassed manner. He was beginning to like Miss Pearl, because she was so childlike and unaffected. "I think you look perfectly respectable," he said with a smile.

"I am glad you think so," said Miss Pearl once more. She did not seem to have many ideas. "I get a good salary, and for three years I have been dancing everywhere, so I have saved money, and I am able to help mother. She was shocked at first, being a consistent Baptist; but now she is reconciled to the idea, as she knows that I have never forgotten my early teaching. But my success won't last for ever. I am clever enough to see that, so I intend to marry Sir Joseph Branwin, and I hope to make him a good wife."

"I am sure you will," said Shawe, heartily, and felt as though he were encouraging a child. "You have known him long?"

"For two years. He has always been a good friend to me, although I have invariably kept him at arm's length. But now that his wife is dead he wants to marry me."

"And you say that you will marry him?"

Miss Pearl looked at Shawe very directly. "I think I shall marry him; but, of course, I may not. I have not yet made up my mind."

"But you said just now—"

"Yes, I know what I said, Mr. Shawe. But one can never be sure of anything in this world of trouble. However, it doesn't much matter if I marry him or not, as I have saved a lot of money, and I am quite content to go back to my village and live with my parents. And now, Mr. Shawe, that I have told you all about myself, perhaps you will explain why you wish to see me."

Time was getting on, and Shawe had learnt nothing definite as yet, so he lost no further time, but plunged into the middle of his reason for calling.

"I wish to know if you saw anything when you stayed at the Pink Shop likely to lead you to suspect who is the assassin of Lady Branwin?"

"There," said Miss Pearl, colouring again, "I knew some day that I would be asked that question again."

"Were you asked it before?"

"Yes. Inspector Lanton asked me. He learnt from Madame Coralie that I slept in the upstairs room, and questioned me. Of course, I knew nothing, as I was asleep all the time, and I told him so. I also asked him to keep my name out of the papers, as such publicity would not have been good for me. And now," added Miss Pearl, emphatically, "it would do me positive harm seeing that Sir Joseph wants to marry me. People would say nasty things."

"For instance, that you wished Lady Branwin to die?"

"I daresay," said Miss Pearl, in quite a savage tone for so serene a goddess. "But let them, that's all. I have always my solicitors to look after my reputation. Do you think that?" she asked suddenly.

"No," said Ralph, frankly. "I might have entertained some such suspicion, but after seeing you I do not suspect you in the least. Still"—he paused—"you may know of something."

"Know what, for instance?" asked Miss Pearl, sharply.

Ralph evaded an answer, and asked another question. "Did you wear a Harris tweed dress when you were at the Pink Shop?"

"No, I did not. Why do you ask?"

"Because one of the assistants of Madame Coralie—the blind girl, whose sense of smell is abnormal—scented the peaty fragrance of Harris tweed in the lower passage about the time Lady Branwin was murdered, or, at least, one hour later."

"Oh, indeed," said Miss Pearl, coolly. "Then you think that I wore this dress and went downstairs to murder Lady Branwin so that I could marry—"

"No, no! I don't mean that. I said that Parizade smelt the perfume an hour afterwards. You say that you did not wear the dress; but Sir Joseph always, when in tweeds, prefers the Harris cloth."

"Was he in the house?" asked Miss Pearl, bewildered.

"That is what I wish you to tell me."

"I can't." She rose like an offended goddess. "And if he was, I certainly should not tell you, Mr. Shawe. If Sir Joseph knew that you dared to accuse him of murder—"

"He knows what I have told you, Miss Pearl, and knows also that I do not accuse him directly of murder. But someone wearing Harris tweed was in the lower passage. You deny wearing this dress, and as Sir Joseph is partial to the cloth I conclude that he was lurking in the house. He was certainly seen in the lane by Mrs. Mellop."

"I think," said Miss Pearl, frigidly, "that you had better tell this story to Sir Joseph himself. I cannot assist you. I was asleep in the upstairs room all the evening, and I know nothing, as I told Inspector Lanton. As he is satisfied, I do not see why you should not be."

"Of course, I take your word, but—"

"There is no 'but' about it," interrupted the dancer, imperiously, and Ralph found himself thinking what a beautiful creature she was. "My mother always taught me never to tell a lie. And if you think that I know anything of the crime, Mr. Shawe, I shall prove my sincerity and ignorance by refusing to marry Sir Joseph Branwin. Good-day," and she walked out of the room, in as stately a manner as she had entered.

"I wonder," murmured Ralph, leaving the house, "if she's a born liar, or if she is really and truly telling the truth?"

CHAPTER XXI.

THE MARRIAGE

It certainly was not an easy task to come to a conclusion about Miss Pearl. Ralph took her for a beautiful, amiable, stupid woman, narrowed by her early training into a perfect specimen of what a wife should be—that is, a wife to an ordinary British Philistine. But Sir Joseph was not a prim, conventional man after the style of a suburban clerk, but a clever individual who knew how to use his brains. He might certainly admire Miss Pearl for her calm maternal beauty, but Shawe was satisfied that he could not possibly tolerate such a milk-and-water character. Miss Pearl was more suitable to be the wife of a Sunday-school teacher than the second Lady Branwin.

And this consideration brought the barrister round to wonder if Miss Pearl had not been playing a very clever game with him. He had been with her for quite an hour, and all the time she had been so taken up with telling him about herself that he had not been able to cross-examine her. In a dexterous manner she had contrived to keep him at arm's length, and he left the quiet Bloomsbury house about as wise as when he entered it.

Considerably puzzled over the present aspect of affairs, the young man sought out Perry Toat, and described his visit to Miss Pearl. He also repeated what Audrey had overheard as passing between Badoura and Eddy Vail.

Miss Toat listened in silence, and her shrewd little eyes twinkled. "It's really a most puzzling case," she said at length. "Of course, this clue of the scent is a very slight one to go by. Sir Joseph is fond of this especial kind of cloth, and probably asked Miss Pearl to favour him by having a dress made of the same material. But Eddy Vail might also have a suit of the cloth, and he might be the person who lurked in the passage."

"I think he must be guilty myself," said Ralph, insistently, "for if he was innocent he certainly would not have altered the clock."

"Quite so. Let us consider the matter. Now, my theory—"

"I beg your pardon, Miss Toat," interrupted Shawe, rather crossly, "but I am a trifle tired of your theories; they lead to nothing."

Miss Toat was not at all put out. "Oh, to theorise is the only way to get at the truth of the matter. One may have a dozen theories, and then can abandon each one in turn as it seems improbable. Let me conduct this business in my own way, Mr. Shawe."

"Well"—Ralph resigned himself to what seemed to him to be a futile discussion—"let us have your latest theory."

"Bearing in mind what Badoura said about the clock being wrong, and Eddy Vail being the husband of Madame Coralie, I think he is the sole person who had any reason to have a skeleton key made for the door in the wall of the court. Probably he wished to enter and leave the house at his convenience without bothering his wife."

"But what would be the use of his entering the court," objected Shawe, "seeing that he could not get into the house? The door was always locked."

"Yes, and the key was usually on a nail in the still-room," said Perry Toat, cleverly. "I found that out when I was staying at the Pink Shop for treatment. Eddy Vail could easily have taken that key when he chose, and have opened the inner door; then he got a key made for the outer door, and thus would be free of the house."

"But this is all imagination, Miss Toat."

"I am only constructing a theory on the evidence. Let us admit that things are as I say. Well, then, on the night Eddy Vail either had both keys in his pocket or only one—that of the outer door. For some reason quite unconnected with Lady Branwin's stay—since he could not have known of it—he entered the court at the time Madame Coralie was in the bedroom with her patient. Looking through the window he would see the diamonds produced, which Madame Coralie—as you declare—says that Lady Branwin gave her. Madame Coralie put Lady Branwin to bed, and the diamonds were replaced in the red bag under the pillow. Then Madame Coralie left the room, say at ten minutes to eight o'clock, whereupon Eddy Vail scrambled in at the window and strangled the woman. He takes the jewels out of the bag and puts them into his pocket; then, to lose no time, he leaves by the bedroom door, and runs up the stairs to the still-room, arriving there at five minutes to the hour, in order to put back the clock to half-past seven. Thirty odd minutes later Madame Coralie, who has been in the shop, comes up, and Eddy draws her attention to the time as five minutes past eight. But, as we now know, it is really close on half-past eight. Madame Coralie goes down at once to see Miss Branwin, to say that her mother will stop for the night, and this will bring the time to that mentioned by Miss Branwin as the hour she arrived at Walpole Lane on her way to the theatre. Afterwards Eddy Vail goes out by the street door, and returns to the court to drop the label and to leave the key in the lock of the court wall door, so as to encourage the idea of burglars. What do you think of that?"

"It's a very feasible theory," said Ralph, after a pause, "but it falls to the ground in the face of Madame Coralie's admission that Lady Branwin gave her the jewels."

"It only makes her an accomplice after the fact," said Perry Toat, cheerfully.

Ralph shook his head. "She would not approve of the murder of her own sister, Miss Toat," he said gently.

"Yes, you hinted something about the two women being sisters. I forget exactly what you said, as I have been so busy with the case of Colonel Ilse and his missing daughter. I am trying to find a photograph of the hospital nurse who stole the child, you know. Tell me exactly the relationship and all about it. I shall listen carefully."

Shawe related all that he knew, and the little woman nodded her head.

"This, of course, complicates matters. Still, it does not exonerate Madame Coralie. She is not a straight woman."

"What do you mean?"

"Never mind. Since you are to marry Miss Branwin, my advice to you is to keep her away from Madame Coralie. I know something about her."

"Something bad?"

"Very bad."

"What is it?" asked Shawe, with considerable curiosity.

"Oh, don't ask me just now," said Perry Toat, impatiently. "I shall tell you when I am more certain. Meanwhile, go and get your special licence and marry Miss Branwin. The sooner she is out of that Pink Shop the better."

"I agree with you," said Ralph, drily, as he stood up to take his leave; "but while I am on my honeymoon, I wish you to examine into the truth of Miss Pearl's statement that she was asleep the whole time. Also, as to the reason why Sir Joseph was in Walpole Lane on that night."

Perry Toat looked at him suddenly. "You have a theory also?" she said sharply.

"Well"—Ralph drew on his gloves slowly—"it seems to me that Sir Joseph, who knew that his wife was staying at the Pink Shop, might have enlisted the services of Eddy Vail, and have borrowed that key you mention. He might have entered the court and have strangled his wife, while sending Eddy Vail upstairs to put the clock wrong. He could easily have strangled his wife and have left again by the court door to come round to Walpole Lane. Thus he would be able to prove an alibi."

"I don't think so," said Miss Toat, thoughtfully; "for, although the clock in the still-room was wrong, Mrs. Mellop, who saw him, knew the correct time. She would know that he was in the lane at half-past eight and not at eight, which was the time Lady Branwin was strangled. I don't think much of your theory, Mr. Shawe. As well say that Miss Pearl, learning that her rival was in the house, might have crept down to kill her, wearing that Harris tweed frock you mentioned."

"She might have done so," said Ralph, bluntly; "but I am certain of one thing, that either she or Sir Joseph were in that passage about nine o'clock when Parizade came down for her lover's present."

"In that case Sir Joseph is innocent, as he had left the house," said Miss Toat, triumphantly. "Well, well, it's all theory, as you say. But one thing is certain, that Eddy Vail knows something or he would not have provided himself with an alibi by putting the clock wrong. I shall see him."

Ralph shook his head. "He won't speak."

"Oh!"—Perry Toat looked wise—"I shall frighten him and Badoura into speaking. Go away on your honeymoon, and don't worry. I shall attend to the matter during your absence."

The young barrister thought that this was a very fair division of labour, and took his departure. There was no difficulty, now that he had ample funds, in procuring a special licence. With this in his pocket he went to the vicar of a Kensington church and arranged for the marriage to take place next day at a certain hour. Having settled this important point he wrote a note to Lady Sanby, and then took his way to the Pink Shop. It was necessary to see Audrey in order to explain what he had done. After some difficulty Madame Coralie agreed that he should speak to Audrey in her presence in the Pink Shop, and sent the four assistants upstairs to the still-room, so that the lovers might converse undisturbed.

The hour was eight o'clock, and the shop was closed. Only a pink-shaded lamp hanging in one of the alcoves shed a rosy light over the anxious faces of Audrey and Ralph, on which—very naturally—recent events had left their marks. Near them stood Madame Coralie, wearing her yashmak. She looked a weird figure in the delicate light, muffled up and swathed in her Turkish dress with many veils. Her eyes watched the pair attentively, and she signified her approval of the barrister's scheme for an immediate marriage.

"It is the very best thing you can do," she said, in her harsh voice; but there was a catch in her voice as she spoke. "It will never do for Audrey to stay with me here, as people are talking about the shop. Not that there is anything wrong," said Madame Coralie, drawing herself up proudly, "for I have always kept it highly respectable. But I think that Audrey should go."

"It's so sudden," faltered the girl.

"We cannot help that," rejoined Ralph, soothing her; "your father has, so to speak, forced our hand. At present you are in a very awkward position, if it were known that you have left your father and taken refuge with Madame Coralie. Even the excuse for figure-treatment will not serve with some women—especially venomous cats like Mrs. Mellop. But as my wife—"

"Your wife!" said Audrey, under her breath. "Oh! Ralph, I should love to be your wife. But I have no clothes."

"Yes you have," said her aunt, suddenly. "Your father sent all your boxes this evening. You see, he is determined that you shall not re-enter your old home, my dear. Better become Mrs. Shawe without further delay."

"Audrey, do say yes," urged the young man, impatiently. "You must see in what a difficult position you are placed."

"Well, then, yes," said the girl, and Ralph kissed her.

So it was arranged, and Ralph took a long farewell of the girl who was to be his wife on the morrow. Madame Coralie accompanied him to the door. "I must ask you to be kind to Audrey, Mr. Shawe," she said softly; "make up to her for all the unhappiness she has undergone."

"Audrey and I will be as happy as the day is long," said Shawe, with a gay laugh, for he felt that a weight was removed from his mind by the girl's reluctant consent to the ceremony.

The next day Ralph arrived at the Kensington church with Lady Sanby, and shortly afterwards Audrey, quietly dressed, made her appearance, to be eagerly welcomed by the fairy godmother. Lady Sanby kissed her fondly, and tears came into the poor girl's eyes, for she valued sympathy and had received very little of it during her short life.

"Child, child, this will never do," said Lady Sanby, wiping away the tears with her own handkerchief. "A bride must not weep; it's unlucky."

"Nothing can be unlucky while I am with Ralph," sobbed Audrey; "but if you knew, Lady Sanby—"

"My dear, I know everything. Ralph has told me all. And now you had better get married at once, as time is passing."

Shawe returned at this moment, and then the vicar made his appearance in his surplice. It was an exceedingly quiet wedding. Lady Sanby gave the bride away, and the verger was one of the witnesses to the ceremony. A few idlers had, as usual, collected in the body of the church, and commented on the good looks of the bride, but the female portion of the idlers admired the handsome bridegroom. When the knot was safely tied Ralph kissed his wife, and this example was followed by Lady Sanby.

"And now, dear, you can call me grannie," said the old dame, which was a wonderful mark of favour to be shown, as Audrey well knew.

But Lady Sanby's kindness did not stop here. She took the young couple to a fashionable restaurant and gave them a wedding-breakfast, and finally drove them in her motor to the railway station, whence they departed for a quiet seaside town on the south coast. When the train started, and the married pair were alone, Audrey threw herself into Ralph's arms.

"Oh, darling, I am happy at last," she said. "Let us forget the past."

But although Ralph kissed her and agreed, he knew that Perry Toat was yet working at the Pink Shop mystery.

CHAPTER XXII.

THE PHOTOGRAPH

Weed-on-the-Sands is a quiet little watering-place on the south coast in the county of Sussex. Round the original fishing-village a flourishing town of villas and shops has grown, and as it is reached only by a branch line from the main trunk railway it is rarely overcrowded. In fact, a select number of invalids and holiday-makers come to Weed-on-the-Sands every year for cure and enjoyment. The general public find the place too quiet, as the tiny town has no bandstand, or esplanade, or entertainments of any kind whatsoever.

There are smooth sands, with seaweed-covered rocks—hence the odd name of the resort—a rude jetty, which stretches out some little distance into deep water, and one or two or three crooked streets, which are united with the wider and straighter thoroughfares of the new town. A prettier or quieter or more agreeable place could scarcely be found in England, and certainly not on the south coast.

To this miniature Eden Mr. and Mrs. Shawe came to pass their honeymoon, and took rooms at an old-fashioned inn, called the Three Fishers. The landlady was a buxom widow belonging to the Dickens era, and having a sympathy with lovers, or, rather, with newly-married couples, she made them extremely comfortable. Audrey and her husband greatly enjoyed the peace after the exciting events in which they had so lately taken part. They wandered on the sands and drove about the surrounding country, and found, more than ever, that they were all in all to one another. After a week of this dwelling in Paradise the doings of the last few months became more dreamlike and endurable. To poor Audrey this atmosphere of peace and sympathy and love was like a forecast of heaven.

"I wish it would last for ever," she said, when they sat one morning on the rocks at the far end of the sandy beach.

"It will last all our lives," murmured the happy husband, who was lying at her feet with his head on her lap.

Mrs. Shawe looked doubtful. "I don't think so," she said seriously. "We must go back to the world, Ralph, and then our troubles will begin again."

"Well, we can bear them, dearest, so long as we have one another. Besides, I don't see why we should have further trouble. We shan't be rich, certainly, but I daresay we'll manage to keep a tiny flat and one servant. Then while I am working you can stay at home and look after the house. Lady Sanby, as the fairy godmother, will take us into what society we need."

"I don't think we'll need any," replied Audrey, gazing at the bright blue sea that sparkled in the sunshine. "I would rather stay at home night after night with you."

"But, my dear, you would weary of such tame domesticity."

"No I wouldn't, Ralph. All my life I have wanted real sympathy and love, and I have never had any, save from my poor dear mother, who was always kind. It will be a joy to feel that I am at peace, safe in the shelter of your arms."

"Dear," said Ralph, kissing the wrist of the arm which lay round his neck, "I shall do all a man can do to make you really happy. Then, I take it," he added, with some hesitation, "that you have given up all idea of searching into the mystery of your mother's death?"

"I think so," rejoined Audrey, slowly. "Because I am afraid."

"Afraid of what?"

"That I may find papa is the criminal. After what you have told me, it seems to me—but I may be quite wrong—that either papa or Rosy Pearl is responsible for the death. Oh!"—she shuddered—"it's too horrible."

"I don't agree with you, Audrey. To my mind Eddy Vail is the assassin. However, Perry Toat has no doubt seen him by this time, and when we return to London she will have some news for us."

Mrs. Shawe frowned and hugged her knees as she stared at the sea-line. "I really think that it would be best to leave the whole thing alone."

"As I said in my anonymous letter?"

"Yes, you were right in saying what you did. If my father is proved to be guilty it will indeed be the greatest grief of my life. I have no reason to love him, but it seems terrible that he should be a—"

"My darling, you have no proof that he committed the deed. I tell you that Eddy Vail, if anyone, is the guilty person. He altered the time of the still-room clock, and that in itself says volumes."

"All the same, I wish the case to be stopped," said Audrey, doggedly; and from this decision Ralph could not move her. Privately he was pleased, as he was weary of the whole sordid business, and did not wish his early married life to be encumbered with criminal cases.

"I shall see Perry Toat when I return to London and tell her not to bother any more about the matter," he said, sitting up.

It was just at this moment, by one of those odd coincidences not uncommon in life, that Miss Perry Toat made her appearance from behind the rocks. She appeared so pat to the moment, and so suddenly upon the mention of her name, that Ralph almost believed she had been listening behind the rocks for the dramatic moment of appearance. But it seemed from her very first speech that this was not the case.

"Good-day, Mr. Shawe—good-morning, Mrs. Shawe," said Perry Toat, looking more like a sharp little rat than ever. "I just came down this morning from London by the early train, and guessing that you would be on the beach, I came in search of you. Your voices attracted me as I was poking about the rocks, so here I am."

"Yes, here you are," said Ralph, rather glumly.

"You don't seem pleased to see me," said Miss Toat, drily.

"Would any man on his honeymoon be pleased to see a detective?" he retorted; then he laughed, and looked at his wife. "What do you say, Audrey?"

The girl flushed. "I say now what I said before, that I wish the whole case to drop," she said, with a frown.

"It is impossible to drop it now, Mrs. Shawe," replied Perry Toat, in a quiet voice. "In your own interests it is necessary that the matter should be gone into. I am sorry to interrupt your honeymoon, but what I have found out left me no alternative but to come down and report progress."

"What have you discovered?" asked Ralph, eagerly. And even Audrey, in spite of her late speech, seemed anxious to hear what the little woman had to say.

But Miss Toat did not seem very ready to satisfy their curiosity. Sitting down on the rocks she tucked her feet under her, and produced a cigarette. When this was lighted she began to smoke and went on talking, as if the barrister had not asked a pertinent question.

"Besides, I am too anxious to earn that thousand pounds to drop the case," she said quietly. "I am in love as well as you are, Mrs. Shawe, and I can only marry if I get this money."

Audrey shuddered. "I should not like a dowry earned in that way," she said.

"Why not? I am on the side of justice, and it is right to hunt down criminals who vex law-abiding citizens. My profession is a glorious one, although it is looked at askance. However, when I marry Edwin—he is a purser on a liner— I shall give up hunting for criminals. The arrest of Lady Branwin's murderer will be my last achievement in this line."

Ralph glanced at Audrey, and she looked down at her husband. The same thought was in the minds of both. It was Shawe who put it into words.

"Can you expect a man to supply a reward for his own capture?" asked the young man.

Perry Toat raised her eyebrows. "What do you mean? Oh, I see," and she laughed softly. "Set your mind at rest, Mrs. Shawe. I do not believe that your father is guilty." She paused for effect, then added, calmly: "I have seen Miss Rosy Pearl."

Ralph threw away his cigarette with an ejaculation. "Oh! and did she tell you the truth?"

"She told me a great deal which I shall impart to you gradually. Her—"

"One moment," interrupted Ralph, hurriedly, "tell me your opinion of her. Is she really a stupid woman, or is that stupidity feigned?"

"You ask me a hard question," said the little woman, gravely. "She is stupid in many ways; but she has a cunning, protective instinct, like that of many animals with small brain power. And this cunning is cleverly masked by her apparent simplicity."

"Ah!" said the barrister, significantly, "then she was really in the passage on that night?"

"Yes, she was; but she wore a long rough cloak of Harris tweed which Sir Joseph had presented to her. She was therefore right when she denied to you, Mr. Shawe, that she had worn the dress."

"A kind of half truth and half lie?"

"Quite so. But I threatened to set Inspector Lanton to question her unless she was frank with me. She is in deadly terror of publicity, lest it should harm the spotless reputation she is so proud of. For this reason, and because I said that I would not make her confidence too public, she told me what she knew."

"Then I understand," said Shawe, quietly, "that she is not guilty? If she were you would not have given such a promise."

"She is certainly not guilty, to my mind," said Perry Toat, after a pause; "although other people might think different. Judge for yourself, Mr. Shawe."

"Tell us what she said, and then we can judge," remarked Audrey, quickly.

Perry Toat nodded. "Rosy Pearl was sleeping in an upstairs bedroom on that night. She was there for treatment, but found it impossible to sleep because the night was so warm. She therefore sat at the open window, which looks out on to the court, and for the sake of keeping the draught away—this is an important point—she concealed herself behind the curtain. The night was luminous, as it was summer, so in the half gloom she saw the outer door set in the wall of the court open and a man come in."

Audrey and Ralph both uttered an exclamation simultaneously. "Who was the man?" asked the barrister, hurriedly.

"Miss Pearl could not tell me, as it was too dark to see the man's face. She saw him steal round the court, apparently coming to the door which gave admission into the house. She naturally did not know of the door; but as the man disappeared from her gaze she thought that he must have entered the house. For the moment she thought it strange; but not knowing that the door of the court was kept locked she concluded that someone connected with the Pink Shop had simply entered the house."

Ralph nodded. "It was natural that she should not suspect anything. A man's entrance in that commonplace way would not look suspicious to a woman who was ignorant of the constantly-locked door. Well—"

"Well," pursued the detective, slowly, "Miss Pearl grew tired of sitting at the window, and went to bed. Here, according to her story, she fell asleep "— Perry Toat looked queerly at the young couple as she said this—"but later she awakened, thinking something was wrong."

"What did she mean by that, exactly?" asked Ralph, bluntly.

"She simply said that she had a feeling that something was wrong. It was about nine o'clock, or shortly after. She could not—so she said—be quite sure of the exact hour. However, she flung on the Harris tweed cloak and went down in the darkness. On hearing Parizade descend—although she did not know it was Parizade—she ran to the farthest end of the passage and crouched on the floor. Parizade, who, being blind, moved easily in the darkness, then went up the stairs again."

"But why should Miss Pearl hesitate to address her?" demanded Audrey.

"And why should she think anything was wrong?" asked Ralph.

Perry Toat hesitated. "I shall answer those questions later," she said, after a reflective pause. "You must let me tell my story in my own way, as it is not an easy one to tell."

Ralph nodded. "Go on. We are at your disposal."

"Miss Pearl," pursued the detective, "thinking the man might have no right to be in the house, went along the passage and looked into every bedroom. She had a box of matches with her, and struck a light in each room. Thus she found Lady Branwin dead, and, assured of this stole up the stairs again."

"Without giving the alarm?" cried Ralph, astonished.

"Ask yourself," said Perry Toat, vehemently, "what you would have done under the circumstances. Sir Joseph admired Miss Pearl, and wished his wife out of the way so that he could marry her. Miss Pearl recognised Lady Branwin at once, as she had often seen her in the Park and other places. She guessed if she gave the alarm, and was called as a witness, how she might be suspected of encompassing the death. Can't you see?"

"I can see," said Audrey, grasping the position quicker than her husband. "I think, considering the circumstances, she acted wisely. What did she do then?"

"Went back to bed, and told Lanton next morning that she had been asleep all the time. So that is her story, in a way. Other portions of it I shall tell you later, but not just now."

"Why not?" asked Shawe, suspiciously.

"That explanation comes later also," said Miss Toat, with an odd little smile. "But to go on. I left Miss Pearl and sought out Eddy Vail."

"Why did you do that?" demanded Audrey, quickly.

"Because I guessed that only he could have had a key manufactured to fit the court door. He was in a terrible state of mind when, I questioned him, and admitted that he had such a key."

"Then he is the criminal!" cried Shawe, triumphantly.

"He denies that he is," replied Perry Toat, quietly. "He told me that he got the key made as he wanted to enter the Pink Shop when he could without his wife knowing that he was under her roof. Badoura admitted him sometimes by the inner door, as she easily got the key from the nail in the still-room."

"But why should there be secrecy?" asked Ralph, puzzled.

"Well," said Perry Toat, after a pause, "if you ask me, I think Mr. Edmund Vail was in the habit of robbing his wife when he could, with the connivance of Badoura. I don't blame the girl over much, as she was crazy, and is crazy, about the scamp. But we can discuss this later. Meanwhile you must understand that Eddy Vail had the skeleton key made for the purpose I told you of. His story is that he entered the court about a quarter to eight o'clock, and as the window of the bedroom wherein Madame Coralie and Lady Branwin were talking was open, he saw the one display the diamonds to the other. Immediately he resolved to steal them, and, as Badoura had left the inner door unlocked, he ran upstairs at five minutes to eight to put the still-room clock back half an hour and prove an alibi. He intended later to steal out again into the court, and climb through the window to take the jewels."

"And he did?" said Ralph, quickly.

"Not immediately. Madame came up, and he secured his alibi. Then she turned him out by the front door. He went round by the back and entered the court. The window was still open. He got in and found Lady Branwin dead —"

"And the diamonds gone?"

"According to his story he was too terrified to wait and see. He scrambled out of the window again, and fairly ran away. In his hurry he left the key in the lock of the court door, after turning it."

"But the inner door was found locked also, and the key was on the nail in the still-room next day," said Shawe, quickly.

"Of course. When Madame turned Eddy out by the front, Badoura locked the inner door and restored the key to its nail. However, Eddy swears that Lady Branwin was dead when he entered, and he does not know who killed her."

"What is to be done now?" asked Audrey, in dismay.

Perry Toat replied promptly. "You and Mr. Shawe must come with me to London by the midday train. I have arranged a meeting with Madame Coralie and Eddy Vail in my office. Then when you, Mrs. Shawe, and you, Mr. Shawe, are face to face with them we may arrive at the truth."

"Why not arrange to have Sir Joseph and Miss Pearl present also?"

"Oh, you will probably see them down here to-morrow," said Perry Toat, drily. "Miss Pearl assured me that she would do her best to induce Sir Joseph to come down and be reconciled. More than that, she intends to come down with Sir Joseph herself. 'Blessed are the peace-makers,'" ended Miss Toat, grinning.

"Never mind this peacemaking," said Ralph, briskly; "let us go to London and get this particular matter threshed out. Come, Audrey."

"One moment," said Perry Toat, bringing a photograph out of her pocket. "Do you remember how I told you that I was hunting for the hospital nurse who stole Colonel Ilse's child?"

"Yes; but what has that case to do with the matter?" asked Ralph, with considerable impatience, as he wished to do one thing at a time.

"Look at the photograph, Mrs. Shawe, and see," said the detective.

Audrey took the photograph and looked at it hard. Then she started back with a cry of amazement. "It is a picture of my mother!" she gasped.

"Oh, no," said Miss Toat, easily; "you are misled by the resemblance and by the absence of the birthmark, which does not show in the photograph."

"I see," said Ralph, examining the picture. "This is Madame Coralie?"

"Exactly—as a hospital nurse and kidnapper!"

CHAPTER XXIII.

Naturally Mr. and Mrs. Shawe did not care about interrupting their honeymoon by a visit to town, especially on an errand connected with criminal matters. But the necessity of taking such a journey was very great, seeing that Perry Toat assured them how the arranged interview with Madame Coralie and her husband would probably clear up matters in a surprising way. Apparently the detective knew much more than she was prepared to admit, for once or twice she looked at the young couple in an odd way. Ralph saw her stealthy glances, but did not ask her in the presence of his wife what they meant. Warned by experience, he hesitated to be too abrupt in his questioning. He did not know what astonishing fact might be told.

But the young man did express surprise when he examined the photograph of Madame Coralie. It was the woman herself without doubt, for her face, although looking much younger, was too strongly marked to be mistaken. She was dressed as a nurse, and looked quite pretty, as her figure was more shapely and the garb became her. Of course, the birthmark was not revealed by the photographic process, or if it had been—Ralph was not sufficiently an expert to know—was eliminated carefully, so that the subject of the portrait might appear at her best.

"Where did you get this?" asked Ralph, when the trio walked back to the Three Fishers to get ready for the midday journey.

"I have been hunting for it for a long time," replied Perry Toat, replacing the photograph in her pocket, "and at length procured it from an old servant of Colonel Ilse, who had been in the house when Madame Coralie acted as nurse to Mrs. Ilse. She called herself Mrs. Askew then."

"Askew, Askew!" muttered Shawe, musingly. "And her true name is Arkwright."

"She used a false name with the same initial letter because of the marks on her linen, no doubt," said Miss Toat. "Of course, this portrait was taken more than twenty years ago, but there is sufficient resemblance for me to recognise it as that of Madame Coralie."

"But as she always wears a yashmak—"

"You forget my midnight exploration of the Pink Shop, when I saw Madame Coralie in bed without the yashmak and by the light of my bull's-eye lantern," said the detective, quickly.

"Then you are sure that she is the nurse who stole the child?"

"Quite sure. It appears she was jealous of Mrs. Ilse, as she was in love with the Colonel at the time, although she had no grounds to go upon. He was not the Colonel then, of course."

"He is pleased at your discovery, I expect?" said Audrey.

Perry Toat cast one of her stealthy glances at the young wife. "Very pleased indeed," she assented cordially, "since the discovery of Madame Coralie as the nurse may give him back his daughter."

At the Three Fishers Audrey found a curt note from her father saying that he was coming down to see her that afternoon, as he had obtained her address from Lady Sanby. Sir Joseph had learnt all about the wedding and how Lady Sanby had acted as the fairy godmother. Perhaps for this reason he was willing to be reconciled to his daughter. But a letter from Miss Rosy Pearl to Ralph, which had arrived by the same post, put a different complexion on the affair. Miss Pearl wrote saying that she had prevailed on Sir Joseph to become friends again with Audrey, and that she would come herself with the millionaire to Weed-on-the-Sands to witness the reconciliation. "Fortunately I am not engaged at any music-hall for two weeks," wrote the dancer, "so I can stay at the Three Fishers for the night and cultivate the society of your wife. I may tell you that if she were not at Weed-on-the-Sands I would not be able to come down with Sir Joseph, as in my profession one can never be too careful."

Ralph laughed at this display of Miss Pearl's uneasy virtue. "I am afraid that she will not find us here," he said to Audrey.

"Not this afternoon," replied the girl, quickly, "but we can return by the late train. I should like to become reconciled with papa."

"I think Lady Sanby has something to do with Sir Joseph's desire to be on speaking terms with us," said Ralph, a trifle drily. "No doubt she gave him a good talking to. However, I shall leave a note saying that we shall return by— When can we return, Miss Toat?"

The detective thought for a moment or so. "We leave here by the half-past twelve train," she said, looking at the watch attached to her wrist, "and get to London at half-past two o'clock. We shall reach my office in Buckingham Street at three, and there I expect to find Madame Coralie and Eddy Vail waiting for us. The interview will likely be a long one—say two or three hours. You can catch the six o'clock train, and there is also one at eight, if you prefer to dine in London."

"We will take the six train back," said Audrey, quickly, "as I don't want to keep my father waiting longer than I can help."

"To say nothing of Miss Pearl," said Ralph, with a shrug. "She would be horrified if we did not arrive at the Three Fishers until eight o'clock, and she found herself alone with her future husband at that disgraceful hour. By the way, Miss Toat," he went on, quickly, for he saw that Audrey was about to rebuke him for his flippant speech, "does Colonel Ilse know that—"

"He knows that this interview is taking place," interrupted the detective, rapidly, "and he will be present at it, so that Madame Coralie may be forced to tell him where his long-lost daughter is to be found. Of course, we have the affair of the murder to deal with also; but it is just as well to get the whole matter finished off at once."

"I, for one, shall be delighted," said Shawe, with emphasis. "I am very, very tired of the whole sordid business."

"I think you must have been when you wrote that anonymous letter," said Miss Toat, with a sly smile.

Ralph laughed. "It was very clever of you to trace the writing of it to me," he remarked coolly. "However, my wife now understands why I wrote it."

Here Audrey intimated her opinion that they would lose the train if they did not start at once for the station. The other agreed, and a brisk walk soon took them on to the platform. Shortly they were on their way to the junction, and there transferred their three selves to the main express. During the journey they talked a great deal about the case, as they had a compartment to themselves. Ralph saw, although Audrey did not, that Miss Toat was keeping back something which she was anxious to tell, and wondered what it could be.

When the train left the junction it steamed through a clear atmosphere, and in the midst of sunshine. But as it drew near to the metropolis the air became dense and smoky, and by the time it arrived at the terminus the three travellers found themselves environed by a thick fog. Not a glimpse of the sun was to be seen, and all round was a cotton-wool atmosphere, disagreeable and dispiriting. Audrey shivered when she stepped out on to the London platform, and was glad that Ralph had insisted on bringing a fur cloak with him for her to wear.

"What an extraordinary climate," she said, with a shudder; "scarcely an hour ago and we were in broad sunshine. Now look at it."

"Look at what?" asked Ralph, laughing. "We can see nothing."

And, indeed, he was right. From Victoria Station to the Strand they were in a kind of cloud-land, through which the taxi-cab crawled at a cautious pace. It took them three quarters of an hour to reach Buckingham Street, and here the fog was denser than ever. Miss Toat, leading the way up the narrow stairs to her office, simply groped amidst familiar surroundings like a miner in a coal mine. However, the two rooms of the office blazed with electric lights, and the warmth and the illumination were quite comfortable after the chilly gloom of the streets. Madame Coralie and her husband were waiting, but Colonel Ilse had not yet put in an appearance.

The proprietress of the Pink Shop had for once discarded her Turkish dress and yashmak. She wore a quiet costume and a loose cloak to hide her shapeless figure, together with a thick black veil, which masked the disfigured face. Eddy appeared over-dressed and more cherubic than ever in a quite unnecessary fur coat—for the day was warm in spite of the fog, and he did not need it. His face, however, was very pale, and he looked decidedly uncomfortable as he grinned uneasily at Mrs. Shawe.

"Dear Aunt Flora, how are you?" said the girl, coming forward.

Madame Coralie kept her at arm's length, and simply shook her hand. "You are Mrs. Shawe now," she said quietly, "and do not belong to me."

"I shall always look upon you as my aunt, and I shall never forget your kindness to me in my hour of need," said Audrey, hurt by this cold behaviour.

"You are a good child," said Madame Coralie, quietly, and in a steady voice, "but I have not done all that I wish to do. I intend to see your father and make him give you an allowance."

"Oh, papa will do that in any case, I think," said Mrs. Shawe, eagerly. "He is going down to-day to Weed-on-the-Sands to the Three Fishers Hotel, where Ralph and I are staying."

"Your father has gone down to see you, and you are not there?"

"We had to come up at the request of Miss Toat to see about this business, Aunt Flora," said Audrey, quickly; "but we shall return by the six or eight o'clock train to see papa and Miss Rosy Pearl."

Madame Coralie started. "What has Miss Pearl got to do with your father going down to see you?" she asked in an angry tone.

"Miss Pearl, so she says," remarked Ralph, "has persuaded Sir Joseph to forgive Audrey."

"Oh!" Madame Coralie shook from head to foot with silent rage, "how dare she! That woman—how dare she! To go down to Weed-on-the-Sands with your father and on such an errand!"

"She means well, aunt."

"I shall see to that later," retorted Madame Coralie, ominously.

"Quite so," said Perry Toat, looking up briskly, as she sat down at her desk. "Meanwhile we must see to the matter in hand."

"That is what I wish to know about," said Madame Coralie, sharply. "Eddy told me that you had been talking to him, and insisted that I should come with him this day. Perhaps you will tell me what it all means. This fool," she added, glaring at Eddy through her veil, "pretends he knows nothing."

Eddy swallowed something and balanced his smart silk hat on his knee. "I only know that Miss Toat seems to think that I killed—er—Lady Branwin."

"That is ridiculous," said Madame Coralie, resolutely. "Are you going to re-open that painful case?" she asked Perry Toat, abruptly.

"I don't think that it was ever closed," said the detective, quietly, "and in view of what Miss Pearl overheard it is necessary to talk about the matter, however painful it may be to you, Madame."

"What did Miss Pearl overhear?"

"You shall know later."

"It is my belief," said Madame Coralie, folding her arms and speaking in a loud tone, "that Miss Pearl is implicated in the matter."

"We shall prove that in a certain way," said Perry Toat, quickly, "as Miss Pearl certainly saw Lady Branwin dead. She stole down into the lower passage and entered the bedroom about nine."

"What was she doing wandering about my house at that hour?" demanded Madame Coralie, fiercely.

"You shall learn soon. Meanwhile, we must wait for the arrival of Colonel Ilse," and she looked directly at Madame Coralie to see what effect the name had on her.

Whatever recollections the name brought to Madame Coralie, she did not reveal that they startled her, but remained silent behind the thick folds of the veil which masked her face. Audrey would have spoken, if only to ask why Perry Toat was badgering her aunt, when the door opened and Colonel Ilse made his appearance. He looked spic and span, and entirely military in his upright carriage.

"I am glad to see you, Colonel Ilse," said Perry Toat. And Audrey, whose hand was on the arm of her aunt, felt the woman quiver, although she did not open her mouth.

The Colonel seemed rather perturbed, and addressed himself to Miss Toat after a hurried glance at Audrey.

"You wrote saying you had found the nurse who stole my daughter Elsie," he said in faltering tones.

"Yes," said Perry Toat, deliberately pointing to Madame Coralie, "there she is, Colonel."

"It is a lie!" breathed Madame Coralie, under her breath.

"It is not a lie," said the detective, coldly, "no more than the fact that your husband killed Lady Branwin is a lie."

Eddy jumped to his feet with a shrill, hysterical laugh. "I did not kill Lady Branwin," he said excitedly. "I can prove that I did not."

"Hold your tongue, you fool!" cried Madame Coralie, savagely.

"Prove your innocence," commanded Perry Toat, who looked puzzled.

"Lady Branwin," said Vail, still shrilly, "is not dead."

"Not dead?" Everyone looked bewildered.

Eddy stretched out his hand and pulled the veil from his wife's face. "This woman is Lady Branwin," he said, with a choking note in his voice.

"My mother—my mother!" cried Audrey, rising to her feet and grasping at Ralph for support.

CHAPTER XXIV.

ANOTHER PART OF THE TRUTH

It was indeed Lady Branwin who sat there, quiet and silent and immovable, gazing at the astonished company. Eddy, with a look of fear on his craven face, had sunk back into his chair the moment he had torn off the veil and had told the wonderful truth. The others could only stare and marvel at the revelation. Audrey, womanlike, was the first to recover the use of her tongue, although Perry Toat—also womanlike—was on the point of breaking into speech.

"Yes, you are my mother!" cried Audrey. "Yet I saw your face before at the Pink Shop. How was it I did not recognise you then?"

154

Lady Branwin, as it will be now convenient to call her, laid her finger on her right cheek. "You see, the birthmark of my sister Flora is not here," she said quietly; "for that reason you know me for certain. Even when the mark was there you thought I was your mother, because of the wonderful likeness, and it was only the mark which made you change your mind."

"You painted the birthmark on your face?" said Miss Toat, who seemed as astonished as anyone at this extraordinary development. She had expected to learn much, but never that the woman supposed to be dead was still in the flesh and masquerading as Madame Coralie.

"Yes, I did," said the other, defiantly, "for reasons which I am now about to tell you. I was nearly discovered by Audrey when my yashmak was torn off in the alcove of the shop, and I half believed and half wished that her instinct would tell her the truth. But her father had mentioned my sister to her, and she was, therefore, prepared to believe that I was her aunt when I told her that I and Flora were twins."

"And were you twins?" demanded Ralph, quickly.

"Yes," said Lady Branwin, coolly. "In face and figure we were exactly alike, though not in mind, as Flora was always the clever one. Perhaps I may have been a trifle prettier, as the birthmark disfigured Flora—Joseph always said that I was. But Flora's mark was not nearly so dark as this"—she touched her cheek. "Oh, I forgot, I have washed it off."

"Why did you do that?" asked Perry Toat, quickly. "Did you come here to declare your real name and explain?"

"Yes and no. I came prepared to put aside my veil and show my real face, according to what took place. Eddy has taken me by surprise. But you can now understand, Audrey"—she addressed herself to her daughter—"how it was that the birthmark and my story deceived you."

"Yes," said Mrs. Shawe, faintly, and sitting down by her husband to cling to him as if for protection. "And I really believed you; your manner was so different from your true one."

"I acted a part, my dear, and, although I say it myself, I acted it very well, as all of you must admit."

"You wouldn't have kept your secret so long had you not worn the yashmak," Ralph ventured to remark.

"Perhaps not. The yashmak was a very good mask. I often wondered why Flora wore it, if not for business purposes; as her birthmark was not so disfiguring as the one which I painted on my face."

"It was very faint," said Colonel Ilse, speaking for the first time, and in his crisp, military voice—"over twenty years ago, that is. But then Mrs. Askew, as she called herself, was a much younger woman."

"And not so fat," supplemented Lady Branwin, calmly. "Yes, I remember Flora then. After she left Bleakleigh as a widow she tried many ways in which to make money. I told you some of them, Audrey, although I don't think that I mentioned she had been an hospital nurse."

"And for an obvious reason," put in Perry Toat, in an acrid voice. The little woman was annoyed that her search for the hospital nurse had ended in this unexpected way. "You were afraid."

"Why should I be afraid?" demanded Lady Branwin, coolly. "It was Flora who kidnapped Colonel Ilse's daughter, not I. She told me all about it, and did so out of jealousy. She was in love with the Colonel."

"I certainly was not in love with her," said the soldier, stiffly, and the flush which Audrey had noticed on a former occasion appeared on his tanned face. "She made my life a burden to me, and finally took away my own child. I was left lonely," added Ilse, pathetically, "as my dear wife died when Elsie was born. Perhaps, Lady Branwin, you can tell me what your sister did with my child."

"I can tell you many things which will astonish you," said the unmasked woman, drily, "and I intend to. Perhaps had this fool"—she shot a glance of scorn and wrath at the unhappy Vail—"not torn off my veil I would not have revealed myself. But you can see from the fact that I have washed off the pretended birthmark that I intended to do so if it were necessary. I now see that it is very necessary."

"I think it is," said Perry Toat, sharply, "as we have yet to learn who murdered Madame Coralie."

"Are you going to accuse me of the crime? Why not accuse Eddy here, who put back the still-room clock?"

Vail became violently emotional. "I put it back because I intended to return and steal the diamonds," he said loudly. "I don't mind owning that, as I have already told the story to Miss Toat. But when I came back after you turned me out of the house and found that my wife was strangled, I—"

"Your wife?" interrupted Ralph, suddenly. "How could you think it was your wife who was dead when she—as you thought, I presume—had just dismissed you from the still-room."

"I did not think that the dead woman was my wife," said Eddy, sullenly. "I

156

knew that there was a resemblance between my wife and Lady Branwin, as Flora had long since told me that they were twins. But I saw the birthmark on my wife's face, comparatively faint as it was."

"Then you knew all the time that Lady Branwin was masquerading as Madame Coralie?" demanded Perry Toat, much mortified, for she saw that this foolish, effeminate little creature had tricked her.

"Yes, because she threatened to say that I had killed Flora."

"And because I gave you my diamonds," retorted Lady Branwin.

"You went half shares," snapped Eddy, crossly. "I didn't make half as much out of the business as I expected. I held my tongue and allowed my wife to be buried as you, because I knew that by putting back the still-room clock I laid myself open to having committed the crime. But I am perfectly innocent, and you know it."

"Permit me to speak," said Lady Branwin, in harsh, hard tones, which recalled more than ever her assumption of her sister's character. "I intend to explain everything and to clear up the mystery."

"Do you wish me to go?" asked Colonel Ilse, rising. "As you are not Mrs. Askew, and cannot tell me where my child is, I don't want to stay."

"I think you had better stay," said Lady Branwin, without wincing. "I told you before that I have much to say. I am tired of myself and tired of my life. I was unhappy as the wife of Sir Joseph, who always treated me in a most brutal fashion, and I am still more unhappy masquerading as my sister. I have to put up with the blackmailing and insolence of this beast." And Lady Branwin pointed an accusing finger at Eddy, who shrank in his chair.

"You had better take care," he threatened, looking white-faced and cowardly, "for although I have told much, I can tell more."

"There is no need for you to tell anything," said Lady Branwin, scornfully, "since I am capable of revealing everything."

"Perhaps," said Perry Toat, looking at her watch, "you had better get on with your story. It is growing late."

"I shall tell my story when it suits me," snarled Lady Branwin, turning on her savagely. "I am no longer the timid fool that I was. I am hard, I tell you; hard and determined in every way. Now don't say a word," she went on, imperiously throwing up her hand; "let me talk. When I finish, you can make your comments. Not that it matters to me what any of you say."

"Mother," said Audrey, imploringly, and strove to take Lady Branwin's hand.

"You are a good child, Audrey," said the elder woman, preventing the action, "but when you know all you may not be so ready to be kind to me."

"I don't care what you have done," cried Mrs. Shawe, impetuously, "you are my mother; nothing can alter the relationship between us."

"Oh, I think so," began Perry Toat. "You left the upper portion of the window open when you were conversing with Madame Coralie," she added, addressing herself to Lady Branwin, who sat looking as still and hard as any statue, "and you conversed rather loudly, so—"

"Ah!" interrupted Ralph, with a start, "is this what you kept back at Weed-on-the Sands, Miss Toat?"

"Yes," she assented calmly. "I made Miss Pearl confess that she was not asleep. When Eddy Vail entered the court and disappeared into the house—"

"I did not disappear into the house," said the scamp, rudely. "I hid in the shadow, and watched the window to see the diamonds."

"Ah! Miss Pearl lost sight of you, as you were in the shadow, no doubt," was Miss Toat's reply; "but perhaps you heard what your wife and Lady Branwin were talking about?"

"I didn't gather much," said Eddy, quickly. "I saw that there were diamonds, and then ran upstairs to the still-room to alter the clock, and get ready to steal them. Badoura, as she frequently did, left the inner door open. After I left on that night she locked it again and restored the key to—"

Miss Perry Toat waved her hand impatiently.

"We know all about that," she said sharply. "But you"—she again addressed herself to Lady Branwin—"talked so loudly that Miss Pearl overheard your secret, and I forced her, by threatening to bring her in as an accomplice after the fact, to tell it to me."

"There is no need for you to call it a secret," said Lady Branwin, quite unmoved. "You have already told Audrey that something can alter the relationship between us. I prefer to explain the matter myself since Audrey is married, and I shall see no more of her."

"Oh, yes, mother, you—"

"I am not your mother. You are no child of mine."

Colonel Ilse leaped to his feet, greatly agitated. "Then she is—"

"Yes, yes, yes!" cried Lady Branwin, impatiently. "She is your daughter!"

"Elsie! Elsie!" cried the Colonel, and striding across the small room he caught the bewildered girl in his arms. "I might have guessed the truth at the first glimpse of you. You are so like your dear mother. I told you that you reminded me of one who was dear to me, and now—"

"Yes, yes," murmured Audrey, feverishly. "And I thought that you reminded me of someone."

"I remind you of the face you see in the glass," said the Colonel, with deep emotion. "You have my eyes, dear. Oh, my child—my darling Elsie."

"Ralph! Ralph!" muttered Mrs. Shawe. "What—what"—she stretched out her hands to her equally bewildered husband—"can it be true?"

"I believe it is true, Audrey—"

"Elsie—Elsie!" interrupted Colonel Ilse, vehemently.

"Well, then, Elsie—for the moment, at any rate," said the young husband. "I mentioned to you how impossible it was that Sir Joseph could be your father. He is not at all like you."

"Neither am I," said Lady Branwin, who had been looking at the embrace of the newly-discovered father with sad and envious eyes. "But you had better restrain your emotion." She rose and crossed the room to lay her hand on Audrey's arm, and in doing so brought herself near the door. "My dear, although I am not your mother you have been very dear to me. Don't forget me entirely, my child."

"No, no!" said Mrs. Shawe, much agitated. "I shall still look on you as my mother, dear Lady Branwin."

The woman winced at the name, and drew back. "I only ask you to think kindly of me," she said in a low voice, "for we may never meet again. When you know everything—"

"Oh, no, no!" cried poor Audrey, anxiously. "I have learnt as much as I can bear just now. I do not wish to hear anything more," and she clung to her husband, while her father tightly clasped her hand as though fearful of losing her again.

"You must know all," said Lady Branwin, calmly, "because you won't see me again. I pass out of your life very, very soon."

"What would you do?" asked Colonel Ilse, sharply.

"I would tell you the whole truth."

"Perhaps I know it," put in Perry Toat, who was on her feet. "You were quarrelling with your sister over the stolen child."

"Ah! Miss Pearl heard that much and told you, did she?" sneered Lady Branwin, taking care to keep near the door. "What more?"

"Nothing more. She said that your voices ceased suddenly."

"Ah," said Lady Branwin, coolly and reflectively, "that must have been while I was strangling Flora."

"Oh!" There was a general cry of dismay and horror. Eddy staggered to his feet and pointed a shaking finger at the woman. "You—you murdered my dear wife?" he stammered.

"Yes," mocked Lady Branwin, sneeringly, "I murdered your dear wife, who for years had been blackmailing me. Colonel Ilse, you will understand that Sir Joseph was angry because I had no children; there was no prospect of my having any. Then Flora told me how she wished to be revenged on you, and offered to bring me your child as soon as it was born. I agreed."

"You wicked woman!" cried the Colonel, glaring.

"Yes, I am very wicked," said Lady Branwin, with a weary air. "And if you had lived my life you would have been wicked also—that is, if you could have endured such a life for so many years as I did. You needn't look so savage. Your child had a good home. I was sorry it was not a boy, but under the circumstances I adopted the baby when Flora brought it as my own, and Audrey cannot say but what I have been a good mother."

"You have been very kind," said the girl, in muffled tones, and hiding her tearful face on her husband's breast.

"You are a wicked woman!" repeated Colonel Ilse again, shrinking from her.

"And a murderess!" said Perry Toat, indignantly. "Why didn't you tell me?" she asked, turning on Eddy.

"I didn't know for certain," stammered the young man.

"No one knew," said Lady Branwin, who was much the calmest of the party. "I managed to keep my secret very well, and you should not have known it now but that I chose to admit the truth. I grew weary of Flora's blackmailing. For years and years she made my life a misery by threatening to tell Sir Joseph the truth. I took my diamonds to her on that night so as to pay a large bribe which she demanded. She said that the amount was not enough. In despair I sprang at her throat when she was threatening to go to Sir Joseph the next day and say to him that Audrey was not his daughter. I knew that Sir Joseph would turn my poor girl into the streets, as he had never loved her. I strangled Flora, and I am glad that I did so."

"But I wish to know," began Perry Toat, springing forward, "what—"

160

"You shall know no more. I go to do justice," and before anyone could move Lady Branwin was out of the room.

Perry Toat, crying out that she must be arrested, ran out of the office in pursuit. She arrived at the street door to see Lady Branwin disappear into the thick fog. All pursuit proved useless. The woman who had slain Madame Coralie vanished into the dense blackness of the fog, like the ghost she had long been supposed to be. Only there rang in Perry Toat's ears her concluding words: "I go to do justice!"

"What does she mean?" cried the detective, helplessly. "What does she mean?"

There was no answer, and the fog came down thicker and darker than ever.

CHAPTER XXV.

REVENGE

Sir Joseph Branwin and Miss Rosy Pearl duly arrived at Weed-on-the-Sands, and proceeded to the Three Fishers. Here the millionaire, who had quite a Bourbon dislike to be kept waiting, found a note from his daughter, which greatly annoyed him. Mrs. Shawe wrote that with her husband she had gone to town on business—she did not mention what the business was—and would return by the six o'clock train, which was timed to arrive at Weed-on-the-Sands at eight. There was nothing for it but to await the return of the newly-married couple or return to London.

"And I have a good mind to do so," fumed Sir Joseph, furiously, tearing up the letter. "How dare Audrey treat me in this way, when I have taken the trouble to come down and see her—the minx!"

"I must say," remarked Miss Pearl, with her most virtuous air, "that your daughter shows little consideration for my feelings."

"For your feelings?"

"Certainly. I came down here only on the understanding that Mrs. Shawe would be present to play the part of my chaperon."

"Pooh! Pooh! Audrey is much younger than you are, Rosy."

Miss Pearl coloured. "She is a married woman, Sir Joseph, and as such is able by her mere presence to protect my character. And I beg that you will not call me by my Christian name in public. I do not know," went on Miss Pearl, in her heavy, rich voice, "whether it would not be better for me to return to London by the next train."

"Nonsense! Nonsense!"

"Pardon me, Sir Joseph, but it is not nonsense. I have accompanied you here to witness a family reconciliation, and to show Mrs. Shawe that I am not an undesirable relative. But I have come down with you alone in the hope that Mrs. Shawe would be present. As she is not, I doubt the propriety of remaining here. In my profession one cannot be too careful. What is to be done?"

"We can wait here until Audrey and her confounded husband return at eight o'clock. Then everything will be all right."

"Mrs. Shawe may miss the train."

"Well, well," said Branwin, impatiently, "there is another at eight o'clock from London, which gets here at ten."

"At that hour it would be too late for me to return," Miss Pearl reflected. "I shall wait for the eight o'clock train, and if Mrs. Shawe does not return I shall go back to London by the nine o'clock."

"Oh! I thought you were going to remain here for the night?"

"If Mrs. Shawe were here I should not do otherwise. What can you be thinking of, Sir Joseph, to suggest such a thing. Even the fact that your portmanteau and my trunk have arrived together, as we have, is a reflection on my character, now that we have learnt the absence of Mrs. Shawe. However, I shall put the matter right. Permit me."

Then Miss Pearl sought out the landlady, and pointed out with many words that she had come to Weed-on-the-Sands as the guest of Mrs. Shawe, along with Mrs. Shawe's father. As Mrs. Shawe was not in the hotel, Miss Pearl expressed her determination to return to London by the nine o'clock train if the young lady did not come back with her husband. "Therefore," ended the dancer, with an excessively virtuous air, "you will be pleased to see that my trunk is taken to the railway station if by eight o'clock my friend does not come."

The landlady quite understood, and promised to comply with the request, so Miss Pearl, having defended her character, graciously consented to partake of dinner: in the company of Sir Joseph at six o'clock. As the pair had arrived somewhat late in the afternoon the meal was served almost immediately, and during its preparation Miss Pearl chatted on select subjects with her companion. When the dinner was over and they had indulged in coffee, Sir Joseph proposed that Miss Pearl should accompany him for a stroll on the smooth sands.

"It is a lovely night," said Branwin, looking out of the window at the full moon, "and quite a change after the fogs in London. You'll enjoy it."

"Not on the sands," said Miss Pearl, majestically. "People would talk if I went with you on the sands at this hour without a chaperon. But I do not mind walking to the pier, which I notice is directly in front of this hotel. There we shall be in evidence, and—"

"I don't want to be in evidence. I wish to have you all to myself.'

"You are getting me all to yourself," said the dancer, coldly; "but it does not do for a professional artist, such as I am, to invite ill-natured criticism. My mother, who is a consistent Baptist, always told me to be careful."

As they strolled across the road to the rude little pier Sir Joseph reflected how handsome she would look when the Branwin diamonds were round her white throat and the Branwin tiara was on her graceful head. She was rather a prude, he considered, but she was also extremely beautiful, so he had little to complain of. Beauty and a passionless nature so rarely go together.

With the gait of a Juno Miss Pearl walked on to the pier. It was now close upon eight o'clock, as they had lingered for some time over their coffee. The pier ran some little distance out into smooth water, and at the end were several seats. But there was no parapet round the verge of the jetty, and Miss Pearl chose to consider this somewhat dangerous.

"Anyone might fall in with ease," she said. "Bring the bench into the very middle, Sir Joseph, and we can then sit in safety."

The obedient millionaire did as he was told, although he would have laughed the former Lady Branwin to scorn had she proposed such a thing. But he was under the impression that his old uncomely wife was dead, and that he was free to marry this lovely and imperial creature, who ordered him about so freely. In fact, having always had his own way, he found a certain amount of delight in obeying her slightest whim. So the two took their seat on the bench, which was placed at the end of the pier, in the very centre, and well away from the dangerous water on either side.

The night was extremely lovely, being very still. The round moon floated like a golden bubble in a starry sky, and the Channel waters were spread out for miles like a carpet of silver tissues gleaming with tiny points of glittering light. The sands stretched for a long distance towards a bold headland, which jutted into the gleaming sea, and along the front of the shore gleamed the many lights of the town. People were moving up and down to enjoy the beauty of the night, and there was the murmur of many voices and the sound of laughter. After the fogs and chill of the great city, the scene was ideal. Miss Pearl so far forgot her uneasy virtue in the presence of this calm beauty that she actually leant her head on Sir Joseph's shoulder and permitted him to slip a fond arm round her substantial waist. And this, with many people walking and talking only a stone's-throw away, although it must be admitted that they had the entire pier to themselves.

"Did you do what I asked you to do, Joseph?" demanded Miss Pearl, gently.

Her use of his Christian name informed the millionaire that he was entitled to the same privilege. "Yes, Rosy, my dearest," he whispered softly—that is, as softly as such a domineering bully could whisper. "You mean the allowance to Audrey?"

"Of course. She is your daughter, and, however badly she may have behaved, she should be looked after. If you cut her off with a shilling, as you said you would do, people would blame me, and I do not care about beginning my married life with the reputation of being cruel to my step-daughter. One can never be too particular, as my mother, who is a consistent—"

"Yes, yes," interrupted Branwin, who was rather weary of Miss Pearl's constant reference to her mother; "I quite understand. I have told my lawyer to write to Audrey informing her that she shall have two thousand a year during my life, and I have to-day made a codicil to my will leaving her the same amount should I die. Had she obeyed me in the matter of marrying Lord Anvers she would have had more; but I altered my will and reduced what I intended to leave her to that amount."

"It is quite enough," said Miss Pearl, after a pause, and rather nervously. "I hope everything is arranged legally?"

"Yes, I have signed the codicil, and the letter will be sent to Audrey at the Three Fishers to-morrow. Why do you ask if I have arranged things legally?"

"Because," said Rosy Pearl, still nervously, and leaning her head more fondly on her elderly lover's shoulder, "I have a confession to make to you. On the night poor Lady Branwin was murdered I was sleeping at the Pink Shop."

"I know, I know," said Sir Joseph, impatiently. "I heard from Audrey that my wife intended to stay there also, and for that reason I came round to Walpole Lane. I thought that you might meet, and that there would be a row, for Dora was always jealous of you. How she found out that I loved you I don't know, but she did." Sir Joseph drew a deep breath. "I was glad when in Walpole Lane I saw that everything was quiet. Mrs. Mellop saw me, however, when she and Audrey called at the shop at half-past eight, and because she did hinted that I was concerned in the murder."

"I said just now," continued Miss Pearl, slowly, "that Mrs. Shawe was your daughter. She is not."

Sir Joseph violently pushed away the woman and sprang to his feet. "What is that you say?" he demanded, in an angry voice.

"You heard me, didn't you?" said Miss Pearl, doggedly. "Mrs. Shawe is not your daughter," and then she related what she had overheard about the kidnapping of Colonel Ilse's daughter, and the fraud that had been perpetrated on the millionaire by his wife.

"You knew this when you asked me to allow Audrey—"

"Yes, I did," said Miss Pearl, with mulish obstinacy, "and you must let the codicil remain, also the allowance."

"I'm hanged if I will!" said Branwin, savagely. "Why should I give my hard-earned money to another man's brat?"

"What is two thousand a year to you?" demanded Rosy Pearl, scornfully. "Look what a reputation you will buy with it when the truth becomes known. It is worth the money. Besides, whatever your wife and Madame Coralie may have done—and I don't deny that they have acted very badly—Mrs. Shawe is at least innocent. She should not be punished."

"She shan't have the two thousand a year."

"Yes she shall. If you change your codicil, I change my mind."

Sir Joseph scowled at her. "You mean that you won't marry me?"

"Yes, I do. After all, I can make a better match if I so choose. Why, Lord Anvers asked me to marry him."

"What—when he was making love to my daughter—I mean to Audrey?'

"Yes. I thought that I could reform him, but he is a man of such a notoriously bad character that I decided to refuse him. But I have many offers, and I accept yours for certain reasons which I have no need to explain; but if you don't allow Mrs. Shawe this money I shall marry someone else. I assure you, Sir Joseph," said Miss Pearl, standing up in the full splendour of her beauty, "that I can marry anyone I like."

"I quite believe it," said Branwin, grudgingly, for her beauty was undeniable and he wanted to possess it badly. "I shall take a few days to decide what is best to be done, as your revelation has taken me by surprise. I never cared much for Audrey, but I really believed that she was my own child. The scheming women!"—and he clenched his huge fist fiercely. "Tell me, Rosy, have you any idea who murdered my wife?"

Miss Pearl shook her head. "The voices stopped suddenly, and when I went down the stairs later with the idea of seeing Lady Branwin and telling her what I knew, I found her dead. I believe," added Miss Pearl, cautiously, "that Madame Coralie murdered your wife."

"I quite believe it. Just what that infernal Flora would do," said Sir Joseph, grimly. "If she did—but there, as Dora is dead I shall let the matter rest, although I should dearly like to bring Flora to the gallows. The re-opening of the case would do me no good."

"Nor me," said Rosy Pearl, decisively, "for I should have to confess to the police what I have confessed to you, and then I would be blamed for having kept it quiet so long. I only hope that Miss Perry Toat will leave the matter alone."

"Who is she?"

"A detective who is looking into the case on behalf of your—of Mrs. Shawe, and who called on me after she had heard that Mr. Shawe had seen me. I was forced to tell her all I knew, so she may—"

"She will," interrupted Sir Joseph, in an angry tone. "I daresay Audrey and her husband have gone to town about the business, and—"

"Hush!" Miss Pearl stopped him with a gesture. "Someone is coming. Do not speak of these very private matters so loudly."

Sir Joseph turned, and down the pier came a short, dark figure very rapidly, panting for breath. The figure was that of a woman, and advanced straight up to the millionaire. Branwin pushed the newcomer back, and was about to speak, when she flung aside her veil. The millionaire staggered against Miss Pearl, and turned quite green with terror.

"What is it? Oh! what is it?" cried the dancer, infected with his terror.

"Who is it, you mean," said the woman, with a taunting laugh. "It is Lady Branwin, Miss Rosy Pearl. You won't be able to marry my husband after all."

Miss Pearl, for once, was shaken out of her calmness, and but for her fashionable hat her hair would have risen on end. "Lady Branwin is dead!" she gasped, shrinking from the shapeless figure.

"Lady Branwin is very much alive," jeered the other woman, pointing at Sir

Joseph. "Look at that beast—that beast!" She glared.

Sir Joseph, astonished at this speech from his hitherto meek wife, recovered himself with a violent effort. "You aren't Dora. She would never had dared to speak to me like that. You are Flora, who—"

"I am Dora, who has been hammered into hardness by your cruelty. Flora is dead, and I masqueraded as her with the yashmak, and—"

"Then—then," stammered Miss Pearl, with genuine horror, "you killed her?"

"Yes," said Lady Branwin, simply, and looked triumphantly at her husband. "I killed her because she threatened to tell Joseph that Audrey was not his daughter."

"You—you fiend!" stuttered Branwin, with a look of positive terror in his eyes. He could not understand how his formerly meek wife had changed into this hard, desperate woman, any more than he could exactly grasp how she had arisen from the dead in this startling fashion.

"I am what you have made me," said Lady Branwin, fiercely. "I was a good woman until you turned me into a fiend. But I have seen Audrey, and I have told her all the truth. Then I came down here to do justice."

"How—how did you know that I was here?" demanded Sir Joseph, who did not like the sinister looks of his wife.

"Audrey told me that you and that woman were coming down to see her. I ran away into the fog when Perry Toat would have arrested me, and caught the six o'clock train. On arriving here I went to the hotel, and they told me that you were on the pier. And now"—she turned violently on Miss Pearl—"don't you dare to marry my husband."

Miss Pearl drew herself up. "I certainly shall not do so. My reputation—"

"Is of the worst, you slut!" sneered Lady Branwin, beside herself with rage.

"It is wholly false," gasped the dancer, on her dignity at once. "I have an unspotted reputation, and my mother—"

"You are here alone with my husband. That is enough for me. How dare—"

"Don't cry out so, Dora; you will draw a crowd," said Sir Joseph, noticing that several people were turning their heads towards the pier.

"Yes, I will draw a crowd." She came towards Branwin, looking so fierce that he backed away from her. "You have ruined my life. I have lost Audrey through you. There is nothing left for me to live for, and if I do live I shall be arrested for Flora's death. You brute—you beast—you—you—" She backed him right to the end of the pier, and then, springing forward, threw her arms round him. "We will die together," she screamed wildly.

The next moment the two fell over into the deep water, and Miss Pearl ran wildly up the pier shrieking for help. It came too late. Both man and wife were dead.

CHAPTER XXVI.

FINAL EXPLANATIONS

One month after the death of Sir Joseph and his wife at Weed-on-the-Sands, Ralph was talking to his fairy godmother in her boudoir. He was dressed for a journey, and Lady Sanby was saying a few last words to him. Audrey was yet in her bedroom, making final preparations for departure. Since the occurrence of the tragedy she had been staying with Lady Sanby along with her husband, and the young couple had only waited for all things to be settled to start on a voyage to Australia. Lady Sanby was expressing now, as she had expressed before, her approval of the trip.

"I think you are very wise, my dear boy," she said, leaning back in her comfortable chair. "A journey round the world will do Audrey endless good."

"Audrey?" said Shawe, with a smile. "Colonel Ilse will call her Elsie."

"Well, that is natural, since it was her mother's name. The Colonel seems to be devoted to the memory of his wife. Had she lived, he would not have worshipped her so much."

"Grannie, that is cynical. Some men can remain lovers always. I am sure that I shall always worship Audrey."

"Well," said Lady Sanby, with a charming smile, "in your case there is much excuse. You and Audrey—Elsie—oh, dear me, how puzzling it is for her to have two names!—but you have come through so much trouble in company that you understand one another better than most married people, and anxiety has drawn you together. Natural—very, very natural."

"Poor Audrey! She has had a very unhappy time lately," said the young man, gravely; "and, indeed, all her life she has had trouble, more or less. Sir Joseph never cared for her, you know."

"Oh, that man never cared for anyone save himself," said Lady Sanby, tartly. "He was a bear—a clever bear, I admit, but still a bear. I suppose that one should not speak evil of the dead. All the same—well, I shall say no more."

"Let us speak of Sir Joseph as kindly as we can," observed Shawe, quietly, "for, after all, he has left Audrey two thousand a year."

"Out of an estate worth a million or two. It isn't much."

"It is enough for us both until I make an actual success as a barrister."

"Ah!" Lady Sanby wagged her old head, "that is the only thing I have to say against this very sensible journey. Is it wise, Ralph, to interrupt your career?"

"Yes, on the assumption that absence makes the heart grow fonder. But even if it were not wise, grannie, I should still undertake the journey for the sake of Audrey. So much of the case has been published in the papers that if Audrey and I remained in London we should constantly be bothered by silly people asking questions. If we travel for a year—as we intend to do—the affair will be forgotten."

"Lady Branwin went down with the deliberate intention of killing her husband, did she not, Ralph?"

"I really can't say. She certainly said in the office that she would never see Audrey again, and was going away to do justice. Perry Toat would have had her arrested, but she slipped away in the fog. Having learnt from Audrey that Sir Joseph and Miss Pearl were at the Three Fishers Hotel at Weed-on-the-Sands, she caught the six o'clock train and arrived at eight. Then she asked at the hotel where her husband was to be found. In this way she came on to the pier, and, having made a scene which attracted the attention of those on the promenade, she suddenly jumped at Branwin and flung both herself and him into the deep water. When the bodies were discovered they could scarcely be parted, so tight was Lady Branwin's embrace."

"Well, I expect the miserable woman had some idea of punishing the brute to whom she had been bound for so many unhappy years," said Lady Sanby, after a pause; "but I also think that she took sudden advantage of his being on the pier to drown both him and herself. Miss Pearl made a fine lot of trouble over the matter."

Shawe could not help smiling. "Miss Pearl was very much concerned about her reputation, and caused it to be generally known that she, like Sir Joseph, had really and truly believed Lady Branwin to be dead. Miss Pearl also made public the fact that she had induced Sir Joseph to make the codicil to his will giving Audrey, as my wife, the two thousand a year. Finally, she wrote a letter to the papers, and stated at the inquest that she had accompanied Sir Joseph to Weed-on-the-Sands with the sole idea of reconciling him to his daughter. In fact, she made herself out to be a conventional martyr, and everyone believed her."

"Oh, I don't think the woman was really ill-natured," said the old lady, with a shrug. "She certainly behaved very well over Audrey's money; but I expect she did so in order not to appear the unjust stepmother."

"Grannie, grannie, will you never credit anyone with good intentions?"

"Oh, I credit Miss Rosy Pearl with all the virtues. She says she has them, so we must believe her. All the same, she has thought it necessary to accept an American engagement for three years."

"I expect she will return as the wife of an American millionaire."

"Not at all," said Lady Sanby, coolly. "She is going to marry Lord Anvers, with the intention of reforming him. He has followed her to the States for that purpose."

"Poor Miss Pearl!" said Ralph, in a sympathetic tone.

Lady Sanby laughed. "Poor Anvers, I think," she said seriously. "But what about the Pink Shop?"

"It has been shut up, and the assistants have dispersed to the four winds, resuming, I believe, their real names. Zobeide has gone with her mother to Devonshire to live, Parizade has married her artist, and Peri Banou is Audrey's maid, as you know."

"Fancy having a dumb maid, and yet it has its advantages. Peri Banou—I do hope your wife will give her a less heathen name—will keep Audrey's secrets thoroughly."

"Audrey has no secrets," said Ralph, somewhat stiffly, "and Peri Banou is devoted to her."

"She has every reason to be. Few women would take a maid from that Pink Shop. It was too notorious."

"Oh! my dear grannie, it was conducted in a most respectable way, both by Madame Coralie and by Lady Branwin when she masqueraded as her sister."

"Humph! I certainly heard nothing against it," said Lady Sanby. "But how did Lady Branwin manage to conduct a business about which she knew nothing?"

"Well, Eddy Vail learnt the truth, as he found his wife dead. Also, in order to carry on the business and keep up her disguise, Lady Branwin had to tell Badoura who she really was."

"Then Vail and Badoura were accomplices after the fact?"

"Yes, they were. How learned you are, grannie," said Ralph, with a smile. "For that reason they bolted before the police could get hold of them. Inspector Lanton was very anxious to bring them forward as witnesses."

"It is just as well that he did not, else many more details would have been in the papers. As it is, the romance of those two sisters and the substituted child, and Dora strangling Flora, or Flora, Dora—I'm sure I don't know which—has startled everyone."

"That is why I am taking Audrey away, so that people may forget the affair, grannie. And it was Dora Lady Branwin who strangled Flora Madame Coralie. She did it, I believe, on the impulse of the moment when Flora threatened to tell the truth to Sir Joseph."

"Do you think that the man would have turned Audrey out of doors had he found she was not his daughter?"

"He turned her out of doors when he thought that she was," said Shawe, grimly. "And but for your help, dear Lady Sanby, Audrey would have been in a terrible position."

"I think you should rather thank Lady Branwin, who took the poor child in when Sir Joseph behaved so brutally."

"Yes. She loved Audrey, and it was for Audrey's sake that she strangled her wicked sister, even if she drowned Sir Joseph for her own sake. It is very strange," added Ralph, musingly, "that Audrey never suspected the false Madame Coralie was her mother."

"Oh, the very resemblance and the knowledge that Flora and Dora were twins put Audrey off the scent," explained Lady Sanby, easily. "I see no difficulty about the matter. Then the birthmark was misleading, and Lady Branwin changed her voice by some drink, from being soft into a harsh note. Finally, she nearly always wore that yashmak."

"Lady Branwin did more than change her voice, grannie. She changed the whole of her nature; and from being a meek, timid little woman she became as hard and cruel as Madame Coralie had been."

"The twin natures got mixed up, I suppose," said grannie, flippantly. "Well, both the sisters are dead, and so is the man who played with them as a child, so let us say no more about them. What has become of Sir Joseph's money?"

"Beyond the two thousand a year to Audrey, which was left to her as my wife, and various legacies, the rest goes to his next-of-kin."

"Miss Pearl must have been angry that she did not get any money?"

"She was. Sir Joseph intended to make a new will after he married her, as it was useless to make one before. But Lady Branwin, rising from the grave, upset everything. Poor woman!" sighed the barrister. "She is dead, so all we can say is 'Rest her soul.'"

Lady Sanby nodded solemnly. "By the way, where have Vail and Badoura gone to, and who is going to carry on the Pink Shop business?"

"I don't know where they have gone. Bolted to America, I understand. At all events, Lanton can't find them, and I don't expect they will turn up in England again seeing what a record they have left behind. As to the Pink Shop, it is closed for ever. I told you so."

"One last question," said Lady Sanby. "Who dropped the label near the door of the court to make the police think robbery was the cause of the crime?"

"Lady Branwin, masquerading as Madame Coralie, and Eddy Vail managed the whole wicked business. He also got the diamonds, or the most part of them, and it is with that money that he has bolted to America with Badoura. Do you wish to hear any more? For I am anxious to stop talking about this business."

"Tell me," said Lady Sanby, quite forgetting that she had asked what she had called a last question, "What of Perry Toat?"

"Oh, she has got the reward, as, really and truly, it was through her that the truth came to light. Sir Joseph's lawyers paid her the money last week, and she told me that she intends to retire from business and marry her purser. Any more questions?"

Lady Sanby thought, and was about to ask another, when the door of the boudoir opened and Colonel Ilse, looking years younger, appeared on the threshold.

"Pardon me for entering unannounced, Lady Sanby," he said, in his most polite manner, "but I have brought my motor to the street door."

"You couldn't have very well brought it to this door, Colonel," said the old dame, drily. "So you are going with the young couple?"

"Not immediately," said the newcomer. "I must allow Ralph and Elsie to resume their interrupted honeymoon. I shall join them when they reach New York, after their trip through Australia and New Zealand. Perhaps it is selfish of me, but I have been without my daughter for so long that I want to have her to myself."

"What do you say to that, Ralph?" asked Lady Sanby, with twinkling eyes.

"Oh, it is natural, and the Colonel and I get on splendidly together," said the young man, laughing. "When we return the Colonel is going to live with us— or, rather, Audrey and I are going to live with the Colonel."

"What is mine is yours," said Colonel Ilse, readily. "I have a country house and plenty of money, to which Elsie is heiress, so when I go you will have no troubles in a pecuniary sense. I really wish," added the Colonel, somewhat anxiously, "that Miss Pearl had not induced Sir Joseph to leave Audrey any money.

"Oh, that is only fair, considering how he behaved to her and to her mother—I mean to Lady Branwin—when he was alive. And the more money Ralph and Audrey have the sooner will he reach the Woolsack and get a title."

"That is a long way off yet, grannie."

"Well, I don't know. Audrey is ambitious and will make you work, my dear boy, after you have had this long holiday. But there is one point to be settled straight away."

"What is that?" asked the Colonel and Ralph simultaneously, for the old dame looked wonderfully serious.

"Is the girl to be called Audrey or Elsie?"

"I shall call her Elsie," said Ilse, promptly, "after her mother, my dear wife, and I am sure Ralph will not object."

"No," said Ralph, after a pause, "I don't think I shall. In fact, when I get used to the change of name I shall prefer it, as I should like all memory of Audrey's connection with the Branwins to be forgotten."

"Well, call her Elsie," said Lady Sanby, "and the sole memory of a very disagreeable time will be the two thousand a year."

"Which ought to be given to charity," said Ilse, abruptly.

"Give it to Miss Pearl," suggested Lady Sanby.

"No, no," said Ralph, with great common sense, "we shall keep it. Sir Joseph owes Audrey something for the way in which he treated her."

Lady Sanby arose. "You said that before," she remarked. "My dear boy, you are beginning to repeat yourself, so it is time you went."

Colonel Ilse looked at his watch. "If Elsie is ready we must go, if we want to catch the Fenchurch Street train for Tilbury Docks."

As if in answer to his question Mrs. Shawe entered ready for the journey, smiling and happy, although she looked rather thin. This was not to be wondered at, after all she had gone through. Her father embraced her tenderly, as he always did when she came into his presence. It seemed as though he never could love her enough. Then came fond farewells on the part of Lady Sanby, who insisted on descending to see the party off.

"And I hope you will be happy, Elsie," she said, kissing her at the street door.

"Do you call me Elsie, as father does?" asked Mrs. Shawe, smiling.

"Yes, and I shall call you Elsie also," said her husband, assisting her into the motor-car. "From this moment we leave Audrey Branwin and her miserable past behind. Now begins the happy existence of Elsie Shawe."

"Thank Heaven," said the girl, piously, and her father and husband echoed the wish as the motor-car hummed away towards the new life of peace and

174

pleasure which waited for them all.

"Thank Heaven also," said Lady Sanby, waving her hand. "That is the last of the Pink Shop and all its misery."

THE END

Lightning Source UK Ltd.
Milton Keynes UK
UKHW010702070820
367857UK00003B/722